CHICAGO AFTER DARK

A CITY ALL-STAR STUDENT ANTHOLOGY

EDITED BY TAYLOR CARLILE, JASMIN DELACERDA,
TRAVIS FORTNEY, JACOB HALL, ROBERT O'CONNOR,
JASON PETTUS AND KELSEY SOHNS

WITH AN INTRODUCTION BY
DON DE GRAZIA

COLUMBIA COLLEGE DEPARTMENT OF CREATIVE WRITING,
LEAD INSTITUTION

CHICAGO CENTER FOR LITERATURE AND PHOTOGRAPHY
2014

Printed and distributed by the Chicago Center
for Literature and Photography. *First paperback
edition, first printing: September 2014.*

ISBN: 978-1-939987-23-5

This collection is also available in a variety of
electronic formats, including EPUB for mobile
devices, MOBI for Kindles, and PDFs for both
American and European laserprinters, as well
as a special deluxe handmade hardback edition.
Find them all, plus a plethora of supplemental
information such as interviews, videos and
reviews, at:

cclapcenter.com/chicagoafterdark

CONTENTS

The editors of this anthology would like to immensely thank Jotham Burrello and Julia Borcherts at Columbia College Chicago for their advice and assistance in putting this book together.

INTRODUCTION
DON DE GRAZIA

Some day that burning white fire would know me too. I'd move around it with confidence, taking cabs, tipping bartenders who knew me by name, hanging out with Royko, who'd see me as his protégé, the real thing, a true Chicago kid.

Why live there, people would ask me. Why not Paris? Why not New York?

Why, it is my city, I would reply. It contains everything one could ever desire.

—George Saunders

One night, in 1986, I was wandering around the halls of a community college in northern Illinois. I stepped into a big, white, brightly-lit room, and saw a man at a podium with some papers in his hand. Thirty or so people sat on folding chairs, waiting in silence. I was a teenager, and this scene looked so unbearably boring that I turned around to leave, but as the man started to read stories filled with indelible images of Chicago, the city where I was born—a young couple kissing on an El train, a boy who goes missing in right field during a pickup baseball game—I stopped, and sat down, and it is not hyperbolic to say that the experience changed my life profoundly. I'd had fantasies about going back to Chicago and becoming a writer, but now I was absolutely determined to make it happen.

The author was Chicago legend, Stuart Dybek, and, a quarter century later, when he read at a literary series that a buddy and I put together at The Underground Wonderbar called *Come Home Chicago*, I told him the story. To my surprise, he remembered the community college reading quite clearly. And what came back to him most vividly was his own impatient hunger to get back to Chicago—famed Polish trumpeter Tomasz Stanko was playing at the old HotHouse on Milwaukee Avenue that night, and Dybek was so eager to catch the show that he sped down a dark stretch of highway for twenty minutes before realizing he was headed in the wrong direction. I imagine him leaning over the steering wheel, lost in anticipatory reveries of sipping a cocktail by a dark and smoky jazz stage, enveloped in warm, avant-garde notes, until he is finally snapped out of it by a big sign welcoming him to Wisconsin.

As soon as I started thumbing though *Chicago After Dark*, I encountered kindred feelings about this city—its energy and opportunities and mythos. In Virginia Baker's "Because of Daniel," another jazz-mad guy drags a young woman to yet another fabled club (The Green Mill) and as she reflects on her life it becomes clear that the main character in the story is Chicago: "I came because I wanted a second chance. I wanted to start again in a city that revived itself, that rose from the ashes after it had been burned to the ground. It sounded limitless, like it couldn't be defeated."

It's fun to read through these stories and try to predict which of these student-authors will go on to write and publish their own books—because some of them surely will. A young writer's singular determination to get a book in print has actually never been *less* of a pipe dream than it is today, thanks to the advent of passionate independent outfits like the one responsible for *Chicago After Dark*. I'll admit to being particularly fond of Jason Pettus' Chicago Center for Literature and Photography, for many reasons, not the least of which being the fact that they published the well-received story collection, *Sad Robot Stories*, written by my former student at Columbia College, Mason Johnson. I was asked to read at the release party CCLaP threw for *Sad Robot*, at Cole's Bar in Logan Square, not far from where Mason was born. While introducing me, Mason recalled a day back when he was attending high school somewhere in the suburbs, sitting in a brightly-lit room, and listening to an author read from a story set in Chicago. He went on to say how the experience inspired him to return to the city and become a writer. I found the story kind of poignant (probably because I was the author who had visited Mason's school) but it was also a startling reminder that my own experience in 1986 was not unique. Every day, some young reader is discovering some Chicago author and making the same vows, and acting on them, for better or for worse. As everyone knows, a big city can be cold and ugly and unforgiving (a fact that is dramatized in many of the stories in this collection) but young writers who are truly serious about pursuing their dream will also find a one-of-a-kind generosity of spirit here. If you're looking for proof of that, *Chicago After Dark* is a good place to start.

SHIKAAKWA
CAM ENOS
UNIVERSITY OF ILLINOIS-CHICAGO

I want to claim this city, fold it into my marrow
and grow it all over again, its artificial stars
heaving raw electricity like Tesla hungover,
nurture its naked precipices snapping at the night;
I will render it precious, the White City, immortal as sin.

Adoptive mother, tucking in a million beds:
all its junkies as my horse-sick children,
its poodle-pampered yuppies preening in bars,
its suitably suited businessmen slicking back their hair,
the little jazzmen who bleed soul in the subways.

Here forever, never evicted, sleeping in every stone and stoplight;
I will leave my fingertips in places they can't kill them.
Prairie Paris, Lover by the Lake, my lady, my sweetness—
in the city, a garden. Here I will.

GRAFFITI EVANGELISM
ALICIA HAUGE
COLUMBIA COLLEGE

KATHY WAS TAKING A SHIT at The Ugly Mug when she received her calling from God. She had started visiting her gritty neighborhood coffee shop only because she didn't have to take the "L" to get to it, and she needed some place to do her pathophysiology homework. Gritty wasn't really her type. Her ironed Banana Republic trousers didn't sit well on the grease- and coffee-stained chairs. The bathroom stalls, though, were the most unpleasant place to sit in the entire shop. They looked as if they had just been through three days at Lollapalooza and turned over to some thug's can of spray paint. She always glossed over the graffiti sprawled across the door, side panels, toilet paper cover, trash can, and even the toilet itself. It was merely obnoxious. Too bright, like an animated rainbow had broken into jagged pieces all around her. Kathy preferred a serene color palette while she was doing her business; but today nature called her to sit for a while, and as she did, her eyes combed carefully over all the pieces of the disharmonious puzzle. The tags crawled like roaches over each other, each screaming to be heard the loudest. In the midst of all the

2

drawn pictures of penises and hearts, band stickers, and "Fuck You's," there were written statements—manifestos, world-views, people's actual beliefs. Kathy looked at them closely, blocking out the noise around them, and saw them for what they were. They were cries for help from people searching for the Truth—more like chains than words. And then, Kathy had that moment she had been waiting for. Other Christians at church would say "God's said to me," or "God called me;" especially her small group leader Carol, who said it so casually, like God was a friend. When Kathy asked her "How?" Carol said "You just know." And at that moment, Kathy knew.

"Kathy, they need to know the Truth," God said to her. It was like an inaudible Skype conversation—distant but close. "Give the Truth just as you've been given the Truth."

"Oh, Lord! Yes, Lord!" She wished she could have said something more profound. The moment came and vanished so quickly. It was like the scene with Simba and his father in the sky, except without the form-shaped clouds. And they were in a bathroom, not an African savannah.

The line of graffiti that first took her attention was written in thick, black ink:

It's okay with me if you tell the people you hate to fuck off.

In obedience to God, she wiped, flushed, went back to her café table, and promptly returned with a whiteout pen—her sword—in hand. Just beneath the statement, in white, overpowering ooze, she wrote:

Love Your Enemies.

Then she added:

Turn the Other Cheek.

3

The sound of snapping the cap back on the pen punctuated her satisfaction. She could already see people sitting there where she'd just sat, reading this new message of love, thinking of the world in new ways. No longer would this stall be saturated in the stench of shit, of people's shit. Instead, the sweet fragrance of the Lord would inhabit this space.

KATHY HAD MET THE LORD SIX MONTHS AGO when she was in the midst of a rebellious lifestyle, using booze for comfort and using her body for attention. She was on a Panama City Beach spring break vacation when a group of Christians walked by her. Their matching clover green T-shirts popped against the white sand, catching her attention. As the gaggle came into focus, she saw that the words on their shirts declared: *3 Nails. 3 Days. 1 Way 2 God.* Her friends were a long stretch down the beach, preoccupied with their fifth game of volleyball while she continued to lay out. She felt free to be curious.

"What does that mean?" Kathy asked, pointing at their shirts as they passed. The green shirts stopped in a huddle around her, the guys forcefully averting their eyes from the tanned curves of her bikini-clad body, as if her cleavage was Medusa. She didn't remember every word of that conversation, but one phrase stuck out like a neon Chinese restaurant sign: *Like a sheep with no shepherd.* At the same moment the phrase became obvious, a hot pink frisbee whacked her on the head. She took it as a sign from God. While she nursed the swollen, red mark above her eyebrow, she felt her soul healing on the inside.

Kathy had felt like a sheep for quite some time, but Brian was hardly a shepherd. She had met him senior year of high school during the homecoming game. He was sitting in the opposing team's stand, watching her on the sidelines shaking her pom-poms and bouncing in a uniform so tight it looked like it was stick-on. When he approached her afterwards, he seemed like he was all a part of the goodness—the celebration, the cool air against their warm bodies. It stayed that way through high school. Then he followed her to Chicago where he sacked groceries while she went to classes. After five months, he made his first "mistake," as he called it. The imprints on Kathy's skin stayed a few weeks and disappeared as if they had never been there. Then, they would be refreshed and disappear again— on her back, her arms, and occasionally her face. Kathy marveled at them sometimes, like they were watercolors painted on her skin. She hid them, of course, behind veils of cloth and makeup until he could return to his normal self. He just needed time to adjust to the change, she thought. But three years later, he was still derailed.

Brian had to work through spring break, and Kathy knew he wouldn't exactly receive her conversion like he would a hit of ecstasy, so she hid it from him. Her life was a constant tug-of-war, hiding either bruises or Jesus, afraid of what the church or Brian might do or say. It was Carol, her small group leader who always smelled like chamomile, who noticed an uncovered bruise and gave her the courage to leave Brian. Carol even let Kathy have refuge on one of her overstuffed beige couches until she found her own place.

"God is your protector now," Carol said frequently to Kathy— especially when she caught her shivering with terror. The buffet of a beige couch, cups and cups of tea, constant prayer and scripture strengthened her soul. And then she started to see people's souls, as if they were dotted outlines of their bodies that needed to traced over and filled in. She knew only Jesus could restore them just like He restored hers. She became desperate to see the dotted outlines restored.

GRAFFITI EVANGELISM AT THE UGLY MUG became more addicting than the caffeine she was drinking. The statements she found written in the stall hung like loose strings desperately needing to be tied. She began visiting The Ugly Mug more regularly, consuming mass amounts of liquids to push the frequency of her bathroom urgencies. She didn't want to evangelize under false pretenses.

There were several more statements to respond to:

Love Yourself, with a large purple heart around it.

-God loves you more than you love yourself

NEVER SAY DIE, written large with a red paint marker.

-Everyone dies. Where are you going?

May the bunny rabbits protect you, etched with a key.

-Bunny rabbits can't protect you like Jesus can

On the third day, Kathy had to make an extra trip to the office supply store and bought a brand new six pack of whiteout pens. She conducted "Operation Graffiti Evangelism" with the same precision each time:

- Step One: Wear pants with pockets.
- Step Two: Tuck pen firmly in pocket (so it doesn't fall out when doing business).
- Step Three: Do business and wipe, but DO NOT FLUSH YET!
- Step Four: Stand up without moving feet. Graffiti without moving feet. They must always appear as if she was stationary on the toilet in case someone walks in, lest she raise suspicion.
- Step Five: Stay in stall no longer than four minutes, lest she raise suspicion.
- Step Six: Cap pen and tuck firmly back in pocket.
- Step Seven: DON'T FORGET TO FLUSH!

- Step Eight: Wash hands and pray.

The fifth day into her calling, she had just been in the stall and was washing her hands and praying when two girls bursted into the bathroom, babbling loudly. One entered the stall as the other stood outside the door waiting.

"Oh my gosh," said the babbler inside. "Someone wrote in response to my graffiti 'bunny rabbits can't protect you like Jesus can.'"

The blabber outside snickered. "Oh my gosh. How insulting to bunny rabbits." They cackled together. Kathy gushed water out of the sink to shut the sound up. She could see the face of the girl in the mirror above the sink. It was contorted with a devilish grin. If the girl looked into the mirror, she would see Kathy's face begin to sweat and scowl. It felt to Kathy like a million little daggers tearing through her hot skin. This feeling was familiar to Kathy.

The same thing happened whenever Brian started to rev up his antagonism and she could see the scene already unfold before her— the one where she would wind up cowering in a corner while he paced around her like a bull ready to stab its horns—and she felt like this. It was somewhere caught like a bug in a spider web between anger and fear. She could never say anything back, though she always wanted to hit him before he hit her. Kathy wanted to slap that defiant grin off the girl's face that moment, but she quickly wiped her hands and pushed through the heavy bathroom door.

THE COLLEGE GIRLS SAT IN A RING on plush, beige couches at the weekly Wednesday night small group in Carol's home. They had just finished praying and were picking at heaps of various dips with fragmented chips. Kathy picked up plates of mostly eaten strawberry shortcake with Carol and followed her to the kitchen where they soaked the plates in the sink.

"I need to share something with you," Kathy said.

"My ears are always open," Carol said, plunging her arms up to her elbows in strawberry flavored dishwater.

"God called me to something really important."

"Well of course he did! We are all important to our Lord."

"No I mean something specific. But people are mocking me. If God called me to this, why is it so hard?"

"Hmmm." Carol scrubbed at a dish, splashing red drops onto the counter. "That must be difficult, but you know, Jesus himself was mocked all the way to the cross."

"Yes, I know," Kathy said. "But the persecution is so hard. I mean, the way these girls laughed...it was like Satan himself."

"Hold on," Carol said, wiping her hands. She left briefly to retrieve her thick, leather-bound Bible. The frail pages were crinkled at the corners and the gold on the edges was wearing off. Carol flipped through the New Testament chapters and landed on John 15.

"Here," Carol said, pointing at a spot on the page and handing it to Kathy. "See what it says here."

Kathy read diligently, "If the world hates you, you know that it hated Me before it hated you. If you were of the world, the world would love its own. Yet because you are not of the world, but I chose you out of the world, therefore the world hates you. Remember the word that I said to you.... If they persecuted Me, they will also persecute you.... Because they do not know Him who sent Me."

The words were like mint flushing over Kathy's spirit.

"You see," Carol said. "You know that this war is not our own. It belongs to God, and He's fighting it for you. And you can expect persecution. It's all a part of being a child of God. Know that they are rejecting the Lord, not you."

Kathy's eyes glistened and she crossed her fists to her chest as if embracing a long-awaited present.

"Thank you Carol," she said. "That's just what I needed."

THE NEXT TIME KATHY WENT TO THE UGLY MUG, she guzzled a large coffee, anxious to get to the Lord's work. She had been regularly visiting the stall for a full week and could count a total of sixteen "redemptive responses" she had made. She would not stop until she reached seven times seventy. She found her next statement to respond to: *I aim to misbehave* in a drippy, spray-painted blue. She was in the middle of writing *Joy comes from obedience to the Truth* underneath it when something caught her eye. Beside her original response of *Turn the other cheek*, someone had drawn giant, plump butt cheeks with an orange paint marker. Someone else drew with a Sharpie an arrow pointing upwards into the crevice where the asshole would be and wrote *Turn Those Cheeks Out*.

Kathy gasped as if she just saw Christ crucified right there before her eyes. She took the tip of her pen to the butt cheeks.

Do NOT mock the Lord. He will judge you in the end.

Her handwriting came out big and messy, unlike her previous, perfectly formed letters. Then something else snagged the corner of her eye. Next to another one of her responses, someone had drawn a picture of a giant troll with hair like flames and a large cross necklace around its neck. *GO AWAY YOU CHRISTIAN TROLL* it screamed in mean block letters. Kathy's skin felt hot again, and her pen hand began to shake. She wanted to write so many things in response. She thought of *You started it!* and *You go away first!*, but nothing sounded right. She stormed out of the bathroom, repeating God's words under her sweaty breath until they became a steady, soothing mantra: If they persecuted Me, they will also persecute you.

"THEY ARE MAKING WAR AGAINST THE LORD GOD! And I will fight for Him!" Kathy said to Carol at the next small group.

"Kathy, you seem a little disheveled," Carol said. Kathy's eyes swirled, and she had been too preoccupied by her mission to care about ironing or showering regularly. "Do you want to tell me a little bit more about this calling of yours?"

"It's just that.... Well, I heard a very distinct call to use graffiti to share the gospel message. I respond to offensive comments in bathroom stalls by telling them the right way to think."

Carol looked like she had just bitten through a kumquat—tasting the bitter skin at first, then quickly sweetening at the taste of its sugary flesh.

"When we share the Good News, we do expect persecution. That's true. But there's a fine line between receiving persecution and instigating arguments."

"What do you mean?" Kathy felt a bit betrayed. "This is my calling from God."

Carol tapped her chin and pursed her lips.

"I'm not sure if graffiti is the most respectful way to reach out to people," Carol said. Each word came out stressed, like a mother's hand stroking her crying child's back.

"It was already destroyed." Kathy clenched her teeth. "That's not the point."

"You're right," Carol said. "The point is the gospel message is not scribbling words out. Do you know any of the people? It might do good to understand something before you blurt something out."

"I thought you understood me." Kathy crossed her arms.

"I'm just looking out for you." Carol reached out to Kathy, but Kathy moved out of her way.

"You are?" Kathy said. The other girls in the small group stopped munching on their chips to peek glances around the corner at them. "Well, you can't be looking out for me while hindering my work for God! I'm not the problem. The persecutors are the problem!"

"Kathy," Carol's words were now more like a mother's frantic patting to silence her child, as she suddenly noticed eyes turning their way. "If you don't consider what I'm saying, I might have to bring this to the elders. That's just church discipline protocol."

"Good. Maybe they'll get it." Kathy left the group without saying goodbye. Maybe the Bible meant persecution comes from Christians, as well.

THE NEXT DAY, Kathy returned to the coffee shop armed with her whiteout pen. She didn't even wait for the natural urge to use the bathroom before marching into the stall. There was the troll with its big, goofy grin and ridiculously large cross, a few fresh *HAHA*s written to the side of it. When Kathy told Brian she was leaving him, he laughed in her face. It sounded like congealed milk. She kept waiting for that hit in her face or for a shove to the ground, but it never came. She packed her bags and walked out the door to a soundtrack of sarcastic laughter. She fantasized long after about him hitting her one last time. Or her hitting him. One or the other. Kathy whacked the troll with her palm, making the plastic barrier rattle, and began to scribble underneath it. She pressed down so hard on the pen the whiteout was oozing out in globs:

You're the ignorant one! Persecute me all you want, but I'm gonna keep on speaking up. At least it's worth more than the shit that drops in this toilet everyday!

Kathy hadn't used language like that since she became a Christian. But, in that moment, she didn't care. She hunted down other fresh nasty comments to argue back:

What an ignorant bitch
-At least I have a fucking purpose!

Go back to church camp
-Go back to rehab!

The series of stacked responses looked like cascading waterfalls being pulled to the ground. Justice took a seat in a large, sturdy throne inside of her, but anger still buzzed like a maddening bee flying around her head. She looked at the waterfall of words pouring to the ground. She squinted her eyes, and it all blurred into the same looking squiggles. She reached out to touch them. Her whiteout was wet and dripping.

Then the bathroom door opened. Someone was waiting for the stall. Kathy flushed, tucked the pen away and passed the girl quickly to get to the sink to scrub the whiteout off her hands. The girl went inside the stall and after a few moments and a flush, the voice spoke up.

"Hey! You're the Christian Troll, aren't you?"

"What?" Kathy snapped back. The girl came out of the stall. She was wearing a leather vest, and her hair was buzzed on the sides.

"Yeah, you're her. I can tell because the ink is still wet." The girl showed a white smudge on her index finger then pointed to Kathy's smudges, still stubbornly clinging to her knuckles.

"Look, bitch. This is America. Freedom of speech. I have a right to speak over your God-forbidden hedonism. And if you want to go get your friends to write all kinds of nasty things in there, then fine. I can write them too! I have my own words to say!"

"Whoa, chief. Slow down." The girl held out her palms as stop signs then slowly lowered them. "I'm actually fascinated by some of the things you've been writing."

"What?" Kathy said.

"Sorry." She stuck out a hand. "I'm Denise. Nice to meet you. Tell me, how did you become so secure in what you believe?"

"I am a sheep..." Kathy couldn't remember the other part. Her mind was turning to goo. Everything she ever learned about God was blurry and distant.

"You're a sheep? Interesting. I'm gonna trust there's more to that? You know, you wrote on there that God restores souls. Do you think he can restore my soul? I might be beyond hope."

Kathy just stood there. She thought about all the things that she had written on the bathroom wall. Things she couldn't erase.

"I know this is weird. Do you wanna get out of the bathroom and chat about this more over coffee?"

"I'm sorry," Kathy said. "I need to go to the bathroom."

She shut herself inside the stall and heard Denise call out maybe next time before leaving. She sat there, staring at the mess of words around her. She traced over her own painted writing with the tip of her fleshy finger, the stench of shit filling the stall.

SPARROW'S NIGHTCAP
KENDRA HADNOTT
NATIONAL LOUIS UNIVERSITY

"YOU STUPID, STUPID GIRL. *House sparrows only chirp in the daytime. Go to bed. You're feeling ill, I see."* I could hear my father's voice in my mind so clearly that I covered my ears. It had been years since he passed away, but I heard his voice every so often, right before I thought or did something foolish.

But even through my father's gruff, gravelly voice, I could hear *his* song—Francisco's—so clear. The house sparrow standing outside of my patio doors serenading me on top of the nighttime street buzz of Little Italy was real. I turned my TV down and concentrated on listening. There again was the familiar chirpy love song that Francisco had sung to me day after day. My father had been wrong.

I walked over to the blinds, ignoring the melting tub of ice cream sitting on the table. I opened the blinds and pulled them back slowly so as to not scare him away. But he couldn't be frightened easily. He was a bird that had flown over the swells of Taylor Street hipster chatter by day, and the constant swishing of cars on Racine Avenue's smooth, dark pavement by night.

There he stood, boldly, on top of my dusty black BBQ grill, none the wiser that he was perched on top of a makeshift graveyard. He stopped chirping when he saw me, his eyes beady and dark like Dean's. "Hey there, Francisco," I said gently. "You've come to see me at night, huh? Just like Dean used to." I caught my reflection in the patio door: small, red-haired, barely dressed with tiny pajama shorts and a tank top. It was what Dean liked. I slid the patio door open slowly.

Francisco was beautiful even in the nighttime. Traces of black were blotched on his neck as if someone had dabbed it with a sponge and black paint. His underside was a glowing cream color. Streaks of black feathers lined the deep brown ones on his back.

He opened his beak and started to chirp again, looking off into the distance and away from me. I imagined that he was calling out to some long distance lover, his constant chirps as smooth and melodic as Spanish. When he finally stopped, we both looked at each other silently. It was the way Dean used to look at me. Like I was the only thing in the world that mattered.

"You want to come in?" I asked Francisco. "Come on. I won't bite. I promise." He stared at me with his head cocked. "Come on," I urged him gently. "It'll be fine. I promise."

He quickly flew inside of the small slit of the open patio door, a black, white, and brown blur. He flew around the living room table in circles, disappointed that my townhouse hadn't been an extension of outside.

"Hey...hey...it's okay...it's okay," I said as I sat on my couch. The soft microfiber—cooled by air conditioning—was a nice source of comfort from the chaotic scene.

Francisco flew his last circle over the table and plopped into my tub of melted ice cream. I laughed at the sight of him covered in green mint-flavored ice cream and chocolate chips. The wet goo made a few of his feathers stick together.

"Dean used to do stuff like that all the time. Get into the strangest situations." I laughed, which finally seemed to get Francisco's undivided attention. He froze and stared at me again.

"Who is Dean? He's my boyfriend, silly. Well…*was* my boyfriend. I guess you can say ex, but I rarely use that word. It's so final."

Francisco stared at me blankly, so I continued.

"Him and dad didn't get along, but mom loved him. He dumped me last month. Dean, that is." I paused and looked at Francisco curiously. "Francisco, why have you come to visit me at night this time around? Have all of your friends left you, too?"

Francisco started to move his feet in the gooey ice cream.

"Did I tell you how he left? How he did it?" I asked.

Francisco chirped.

"Dean, of course, silly. I never told you how he left."

Silence.

"With a letter. This stupid letter," I said, picking it up and putting it back on the table. "Five years and this is how he breaks up with me. We've been together since we were twenty-one. Did you know that?"

Chirp. Chirp.

"And it doesn't even give a reason. It just says that he needs some time. Isn't that about the dumbest excuse you've ever heard?"

Francisco tried to flap his wings, but the goo seemed to have glued them to him.

I leaned in closer. "You two even have the same eyes."

Chirp. Chirp. Chirp. Chirp. Chirp. He was calling someone. Probably his lover, again.

"Dean's might be a little more brown, though."

Chhhhhiiiiiirrrrpppp. Chhhhhhiiiiiirrrrrpppp.

It sounded like he was crying. I imagined him and his lady bird friend on the ledge of Pompeii— him reaching out a wing as he bid her farewell, and her choosing to remain hidden, flying just below Sweet Maple Café's wide, black awning. Poor Francisco.

"Awww it's gonna be okay, little birdy. We'll be good friends. I'll make sure you're comfortable here."

Chirrrrrrrrrrrrrrrrppp! Chhhhhhiiiiirrrrppppp! He moved his feet desperately in the sticky mess, still stuck inside of the ice cream container.

"Oh! Sorry for being stupid. You're uncomfortable. Let's get you all cleaned up. I'll be right back, Francisco." I ran to the bathroom and wet a brand new face towel with warm water.

When I came back into the living room, Francisco had his head buried deep into the gallon of ice cream. His head popped up like a jack-in-the-box once he saw that I was back in the room. I chuckled.

"Silly bird. I miss you too!"

Chirp. Chirp.

I took the towel and wiped down Francisco's feathers until they felt smooth and velvet-like again. "There! You're handsome again. Now, you must be hungry," I said, going into the kitchen. "I'll get you some bread."

Right then, I heard a tapping; it was almost rhythmic. Francisco must've been panicking again. "One minute, Francisco!" I yelled from the kitchen. I opened the bread bag quickly. The taps grew louder and faster.

Tap. Tap. Tap. Tap. Tap. Tap.

I broke the soft bread up with my fingers and crumbled it onto a paper plate.

Tap. Tap. Tap. Tap. Tap. Tap.

I pulled an old, red cat food dish from the cabinet and filled it with water.

Taptaptaptaptapta—Silence.

"Francisco?" I called. Had he hurt himself? Why had the sound started and stopped so suddenly? I rushed back into the living room. "Francisco?" I ran over to the tub of ice cream. I looked inside and then at the outside of the container. A medium-sized hole was at the side of it. Melted ice cream oozed through.

He was gone. He had left through the open patio door just as readily as he had come in it. And just like Dean, he hadn't even left a reason; just a single brown, wet feather that sat on top of Dean's breakup note.

I guess he needed some time.

INNOCENCE AND EXPERIENCE IN THE CITY AT NIGHT

THOM KUDLA
DEPAUL UNIVERSITY

WE HAD ONLY RECENTLY FLIPPED our golden tassels after high school—and we were new to the city that summer night. At first, it was just my friend Tyler and me. Later that night we met up with one of our mutual friends from high school, Brad, who planned to attend Indiana University like me. We all somehow ended up in Chicago, and that night our naivety would give way to a special brand of experience that you could only gather in a big city.

It was dark, but you couldn't really notice just how dark it was—the city was alive with lights. Storefronts opened their arms to us as we walked down Michigan Avenue. The tops of buildings had peculiar colors beaming into the sky—greens, blues, yellows, oranges, reds. There seemed to be a moving spotlight in the distance, highlighting the moonlit clouds as if on a stage. It very well could have been a stage. I stood under one of the buildings and looked up, feeling the cool air off the lake swirl in my hair. I bent my head far back, my eyes nearly perpendicular to the side of the building. It seemed to reach for

God. Having been accustomed to the quaintness of the suburbs for so many years, I was in awe over this massive edifice.

"You thirsty?" Tyler asked, trying to make sense of my fascination with the imposing structure. His eyes shifted upward, but not his whole head like mine. I turned my head back down, making eye contact with Tyler. "I'm thirsty. Let's get a drink," Tyler said, already walking toward the nearest restaurant, his short legs stepping quickly.

I followed. The restaurant was small, but they had a patio on the third floor overlooking the city. We sat out there for a while. I ordered an energy drink. It was the first time I ever had an energy drink, and it would mark the beginning of a childish love affair with the bitter-strong carbonated substitute for coffee, a near-addiction that still grips me now even as a thirty-something professional. Being younger than the legal age for drinking alcohol, I was actually kind of surprised that such a strong drink like this would be available to consumers of all ages. It rushed down my throat, strong and burning, jolting me awake and alert in anticipation of what the night had in store for me.

After we quenched our thirst, we roamed the streets some more. The city was so different after dark. It was still busy, but in a different way—the pressures and responsibilities of the day faded into the passions and desires of the evening. People were different at night. Some parts of the city were absolutely dead, especially the Loop. Whereas during the day the sidewalk to Union Station featured the impressive music of drumming on canisters or creative messages on signs, during the evening those very same sidewalks cradled scruffy men and unseasonably dressed women in a death-bed repose.

We walked farther and farther, deeper and deeper into the city. By now, we were near Lake Shore Drive not too far from Streeterville. Eventually, we spotted a trendy hotel, with a sign that was somehow both bright and subdued, a sublime purple. The people walking in and out of the entrance looked like movie stars—the women wore tight formal dresses and spiked high heels, measured makeup glorifying their gorgeous faces, while the men were clean-shaven and sharp in the kind of attire I had only recently seen at my prom. Was this a celebrity gathering? Had we come upon some special event? It didn't occur to us that every night in the city had the potential to be that special, a cause to dress up and pretend the red carpet had been rolled out for you. It was common, but we didn't see it that way. No, we imagined something greater.

"This is magical," Tyler said, pointing at the neon sign, his deep brown eyes sparkling like a child opening a Christmas present. "I wonder what's going on in there."

I watched two couples get out of a limo. All that was missing was the paparazzi. Since we weren't old enough to get into the club, we wondered all kinds of things about what was going on in there. I remembered reading about a movie currently being shot in the city. I figured that was the reason for all the glitz and glamour. "I heard Julia Roberts is in town for a shoot," I said.

"Nah, it's more of a mystery than that," Tyler said, edging closer to the curb. He looked at a woman standing outside the entrance, her dress well above her knees and her cleavage in clear view through the low-cut hem. "Look at these people," he said, pointing somewhat inconspicuously at the woman. "I bet it's like *Eyes Wide Shut*—one of those underground sex clubs."

I knew the thought was preposterous, but we liked to imagine things so grandly. Tyler was really only speculating because he had never seen this place before in the city; I was speculating because I hadn't a clue back then about much of anything in the city. But even to this day, we probably still feel as if there was something magical about that place—it had this aura, this mystique, which left us yearning.

As we walked deeper into the city that night, things only became more mysterious. By now, we were nearly lost. We stopped at a shabby hotel at the edge of downtown. A woman in tight neon pants and a see-through nylon blouse walked back and forth in front of the hotel, her high heels making her look about six inches taller than she was. We were both a little naïve, but we still knew what this was. We went to the enclosed glass reception area.

"Any vacancies?" Tyler asked the man behind the counter.

The man looked at Tyler, and then he looked at me, and then he looked back at Tyler. His wiry mustache danced below his large nose as he spoke. "No vacancies—only vacancies for men with female guests," he said.

We knew what that meant. The hotel manager here had confirmed our suspicions about that woman sashaying back and forth in front of the dilapidated hotel. I pointed toward the end of the block—a sizable sign with red neon letters overlooked the woman and us. It read, "JESUS SAVES." We both laughed and continued on our way.

Soon we met up with Brad, who had been at the Cubs game with his parents. After he said bye to them at the end of the game, he apparently ventured out of Wrigleyville and saw some sights of his own before catching the L to meet up with us. Once he found us, he ran over to us, his short and spiked dark brown hair matching his dark-rimmed glasses. "Just saw a man on a leash—I didn't even know that was a thing," Brad said, his smile wide, relishing our subsequent laughter.

"It's been one weird night for us too," I said.

While walking, we passed this couple who really seemed to be enjoying each other's company. The voluptuous woman started laughing as she yelled, "I'm not into all that booty shaking!"

Like this, our laughter continued into the night. We'd enjoy each other's company, and maybe even see some more things that opened our modest and relatively innocent eyes to a very adult city experience after dark. I stayed over at Tyler's place that night. The next morning, I walked to the train station. The city came back to life, but not in the same way it was alive the previous night. People seemed responsible; they were busy doing what they had to do instead of doing what they truly wanted to do. Like I said, it was a different kind of busy.

I walked by the hotel that Tyler had called "magical" the night before. The sign was off. There wasn't anyone nearby, not even a doorman or a bellhop. It seemed like it had just gone out of business. There were no near-famous people dressed up in their fancy garb. It wasn't a place where everybody wanted to be; it was a place to be avoided. By moonlight, it was magical; by daylight, it had disappeared into the periphery of the busy city. Maybe Tyler was right. Maybe it was a secret mystery. Maybe it was something to behold, something special, something unique that we saw here last night. Or maybe it was just Chicago after dark.

VIOLET IN THE NIGHT SKY
MAGGIE McGOVERN

I

GOD RUSHES DOWN THE ALLEYWAYS HERE, pulling stenches off rusting train tracks elevated high above flickering street lamps, funneling gaseous ice up reddening nostrils, sweeping the putrid odor of city over brittle cheeks, seeping the grime of unshowered humanity into pores. And bodies plummet down concrete sidewalks under her reign. Their feet scoot along, giving in to her immense power. Shuffling, feet gliding faster than knees can bend, citizens move forward, the bottoms of coats pressing against knees, clothing suctioning onto skin, sometimes advancing in opposition to her force. They wish to release their tension, to give in, to close their eyes and allow her arms to sweep them backward—to suspend them weightlessly in the air—but citizens move forward here. They plow onward. They squint eyes as ice encrusts in their tear ducts, as she rips open unbuttoned coats, pulling tight at the fabric like a fishing reel.

She spins scarves into nooses here, pelting tiny knives at exposed skin until it is split, until eyes are veined, until water streams, burning hot tracks down tender cheeks. But citizens move forward. Because God does not say no here. When she speaks she simply says try harder and when she speaks she roars—engulfing eardrums, pounding hearts, pumping blood, reopening scars.

Then sometimes she whispers, hums a gentle lullaby, lightly combs baby hairs across foreheads, nudges clouds out of the sun's way and bathes the black and gray city with gold. She lets it sparkle in the water—the multitudes of windows climbing up the skyscrapers and the shine of the river bouncing off each other's reflection. The city glimmers in the light. On these days citizens move slowly. Or don't move at all. Lying in the sparse grass, eating lunch on sidewalk patios. No one goes inside. On these days they don't wear jackets, no matter the temperature. They refuse. And they don't sit still for long. Citizens move forward. They bask in their city's glory momentarily and then they rise. They get on bikes and put on gym shoes, they strap tape on sore muscles and helmets over sweating heads. And they race. Sprinting along the lakefront, feet pounding on the concrete, eyes pretending to watch the blue-green lake as they survey their surroundings, feel the heat of others. Everyone's perspiration evaporates and blends together in the air and they don't care. They love the density it creates. Humidity prods at them—pushes them forward.

Citizens move forward. They do not remove suit jackets nor do they loosen ties. They wear heels until feet go numb, until moisture builds within and skin slips and sticks to leather. And they face onward, never up or down, to the left or right side. Yet they feel everything, each presence surrounding them, each step of each sole of each shoe. They hear each bum's cry and each word of each phone call of each passerby. They march to work—to skyscrapers filled with rooms filled with white. And some wash the glass that scales the outside. Some wear jeans in 100-degree weather, hardhats glued to wet foreheads, sweating profusely—the accumulating oil on their skin a badge of honor, a source of pride. And they build this city. They dig deep, plant the roots and then let the steel and metal rise until it's taller than the last building that was closest to the sky.

People don't trust here. Because a God rules this city who would let it snow in May. Shorts could be worn all weekend then a full winter coat needed by Monday. So citizens move forward. They check their heart rate daily, skeptical of its constant beating. They know it will stop at some point but doubt the organ will let the rest of the body know on that fateful day. So they check as they move forward. They feel the beat followed by beat followed by beat by beat by beat by beat by beat. Beat beat. Beat beat. Beat beat.

And sometimes a woman feels two beats. Beats beats. Beats beats. And a kick and a squirm and then her legs open and there's a cry.

Daniella Rossi cried and pierced the night sky.

II

THEY SAID THE LAKE would never be warm enough to swim in that summer. Said the winter had been so harsh there'd still be ice melting in that filthy blue mass in August. So Marisela figured that'd be a good way to die. Wading out into ice cold water and never coming back. Letting the temperature choke her all up under a purple night sky. She rested her hand on her back, her pregnant belly gorging like a balloon. She was ready to pop. Panting and breathing like they did on TV since she'd never taken a Lamaze class. Heehee-hooo heehee-hooo. Dragging her feet against the sand. Limping towards the water—stretching and retracting across the beach. Heehee-hooo heehee-hooo. Cars were buzzing down Lake Shore Drive behind her when she just collapsed, her legs flailing apart, pushing so hard she thought her head might pop. Marisela's body opening so another could depart.

Daniella Rossi was born that night with her eyes open and no one knew.

Her full head of hair was as dark as dried blood, matted against her viscous skin, still decorated by motherly excrements, and she was screaming. In a tone and at a decibel as piercing as her violet eyes, already heavily lined by thick pillows of lashes. Her mother's lids were closed and her chest was rising more than it was falling. She did not make a sound. She did not look at her daughter. Instead Marisela bled. Red trailing through the sand like snakes slithering to the water.

Daniella Rossi was born with her eyes open and no one knew.

Because her mother's were closed and her mother was sinking further into the sand, her body sighing as her breath slowed. Letting the warmth engulf her trembling flesh. No more heehee's but just hoooooooos. Daniella screaming and shrieking. Marisela making a fist so tight the grasp exploded. Went limp. Like her body. Still warm but turning cold in the sand. The baby crying. The mother lying on the beach feeling nothing at all.

III

MISSY KNEW THE BABY HAD BURNED HER, but she also knew that wasn't possible.

Then again, that baby wasn't possible to begin with. Had apparently spent her first night on earth lying next to her dead mother on North Avenue Beach. Just didn't add up. Found her five hours later, rushed her to the hospital, some civilian who found her was still clenching these dog tags that had been at the baby's feet like it was a clue to her origin. At least something dumb like that. But Missy knew the universe didn't just drop around pieces of the puzzle of existence. Things just didn't get tied up in forty-seven minutes like a *Law & Order* episode. Still, the tag said Daniel Rossiii so they added a *la* to make it feminine. Figured Daniella Rossi had a nice ring to it.

Missy worked the 11 p.m. to 11 a.m. shift at the hospital stationed in the nursery where babies never slept like babies. She was fresh out of UIC and had only been working three weeks—her cheeks sore from forcing smiles and hiding gritted teeth. Missy was rolling in a fresh cart of formula bottles around 3 a.m. when she noticed the little Rossi girl's cradle was empty. A breeze pricked up the goose hairs on her skin and she could hear a distant whirring like someone had left a window open. All the other babies were still, their breathing soothing and almost in sync. The quiet was excruciatingly loud. So Missy spun around, her heart racing fast. Wondering where Daniella could be, if someone could have taken her, if maybe she had fallen ill, if maybe her journey had caught up to her. Slipped away and died. Missy even thought *hey at least she didn't have a family* and *hey at least it'd be one less lonely orphan.* The honest thoughts haunting her before she'd even finished speaking them when the light above her fell dark. A shadow covered the fluorescent light. Missy's armpits instinctively moistened, reactivating her deodorant's fresh scent. She looked up.

Baby Daniella Rossi was in silhouette and spinning in somersaults just below the popcorn ceiling—her raven black hair already long enough to hang when turned upside down then flop back to her scalp when right-side up. She was smiling like she'd just soiled herself and got satisfaction out of making adults wipe her bum.

Missy went to scream but there was no air to sustain her breath.

The nursery was suddenly arid. All the room's oxygen concentrated into the small bubble surrounding the tumbling baby girl—audibly giggling now, enjoying the breeze of her own personal wind tunnel. And Missy was sweating so natural instinct worked faster than the need to comprehend. She reached up on her tiptoes and grabbed for the baby, swatting her hands.

The moment Missy's fingertips broke through Daniella's bubble, a cool burst popped into the room like the *ahh!* on a spearmint gum commercial. But the nursery's previous heat had to go somewhere and heat tends to go up. Up and transferred to Daniella. So the baby was boiling hot like fire and her eyes just got brighter and narrowed like she was real ticked off and then, the baby, she just got even *hotter* and Missy was holding Daniella over her head Simba style, looking right into the baby's daggers and she wasn't sure which was more painful, Daniella's violet lasers or the pure scorching heat of her body temperature, prickling at Missy's palms bubbling with blisters. Then Missy's fingers lost their function. Gave way. Dropping the baby as Missy let out a howl and braced for impact. Throwing her hands over her head and ducking and waiting for a screeching baby-falling-to-death sound. When none came Missy parted her forearms to see Daniella suspended. Flopping round from her stomach to her back like a log and then gracefully, gracefully, the baby rocked and cradled herself down, swaying in the air as if in a mother's arms. Down from the ceiling—rocking back and forth gently, gently to her original bed.

All the babies were crying now. Missy was staring at her red inflating hands. Other nurses were running in, tracing the sound. Almost all the babies shrieking now. Mouths wide open and trembling, baby spit flying, nurses' sneakers squeaking, asking Missy what was wrong. Daniella smiling with her eyes wide and bright, basking in the scene of chaos surrounding her own serenity. Beautiful. Looking like she should be on a billboard. Not making a sound.

IV

ALL OF MRS. P'S KIDS were the worst in their own unique way. Reid Calloway never got why they all looked so different, with varying shades of skin from pink freckled to dark brown. His dad said that's because they're foster kids. So they weren't related. But Reid didn't buy it. They were all too awful not to come from the same place.

"Dad can we move?" Reid had asked one day after The Worst of the crew had punched him in the gut so The Worster could grab his bag of Oreo minis while The Worstest rolled on the ground in agony so the other neighbors would think Reid had kicked him in the shin first.

"You have to face bullies head on. Can't run away from them." His dad had adjusted his glasses and looked long and hard at his son before returning to the book reports he was grading.

Reid figured they could at least runaway up one more floor. Maybe two flights of stairs would prove enough of a no-man's land to keep his sanity. Anything more than the thin laminate that separated his room from the pack of wolves in the apartment below. Always nudging broom handles at their ceiling to shake Reid's bed frame while he attempted sleep.

Reid was ten and average sized at the time. Had this thick auburn hair and a prettyboy face that would later accrue him spoils. At ten it just subjected him to ass kickings. Him looking so angelic and pretty and small just made him seem like a girl. But Reid was strong in mind. Shied away from the barbaric physical violence the other kids on the block founded their hierarchies on. Reid knew this was an immature system of government and therefore decided to follow his father's advice. Marched right down the front steps of their four-story apartment building. Had his Bulls pullover sweatshirt on figuring he'd be making Michael Jordan proud, palms grasping his new shiny basketball.

Mrs. P's clan was shooting hoops in the alleyway next to their building. The red white and blue net fraying at the edges from overuse, the whole backboard trembling every time an L train passed overhead—the monster's growling shaking down dying leaves from all the overgrown sickly city trees. Reid knew there were five boys in the clan but it always seemed like they were multiplying. This time there appeared to be a little girl Reid's age sitting on the sidelines hugging her knees watching the oldest and The Worsterest of the boys conducting the younger ones, all of them with their gym shoes scuffing against the pavement faded to gray.

"Hey! It's the little guy from upstairs!" one yelled.

Reid tried not to look over at the boys. Just kept his steady feet pushing forward, eyes locked on the little girl with the pools of violet for eyes.

"Yeah, yeah, look at that little guy! What? He think he's gonna play with us?"

Reid ignored them and kept moving forward. Shuddered a bit and maybe it was from the wind circulating around that mystifying little girl—flinging her long black hair around in chunks. But the breeze didn't even come near to touching Reid. Only swam around her purple corduroy skirt and flitted about her frame, making her look like she was dancing in that vacuum of wind even though she was sitting on the curb. Head down now, picking at a scab on her knee.

"Hey! Little guy! What do you think you're doing, huh?"

Reid was on the court, the clan surrounding him, still staring straight ahead at the newcomer. She smiled at him and his previous shudder warmed like butter melting in his belly—same as he'd seen on his morning toast.

"I'm here to play basketball," he pronounced pointedly, still not turning to the boys.

"Yeah right you are!" The Worst pushed him.

"This is our court!" The Worster threw in a shove.

"Yeah, maybe you should go back inside and read a book, crapbrain!" The Worstest cackled.

"Ha! Yeah! Read! Like your name! Reid! Ha!" The Just-OK Scrawny One giggled uncontrollably.

The Worsterest stepped forward and slapped the ball out of Reid's hands—a smirk curling on his massive hulk face, two heads taller than Reid.

Reid couldn't even open his mouth. Just stared as the giant lumbered away with his ball, each of his Godzilla steps shaking the earth as he headed to the chain link fence separating the alley from the abandoned grassy lot next door. He paused at a bended stick on the pavement serving as a makeshift three-point line. He started to dribble.

"Hey Samuel," a new fiery voice spoke up from the curb, "why don't you see what he's got?"

The little girl was standing up now and walking towards the cluster of boys all spinning around to her voice. She glided when she walked, that hair still blowing behind her but not gracefully. It was a mess. She was a mess. Cuts and bruises. Dirt on her knees. Tangled hair. Wrinkled skirt. Most beautiful thing Reid had ever seen.

"He's got nothing." Samuel laughed and the boys followed with a chorus of *she don't even know* and *new girl* and *yeah yeah she'll see.*

"How do you know?"

"Look at him!"

"What're you scared? Just 'cause he's younger doesn't mean he can't shoot. Go ahead. Show them." Reid was frozen on Samuel the whole time and didn't even realize the last was directed toward him. "Go on!"

Reid's face was all dumb, mouth open, but the little girl's eyes scared him they were so direct. She pushed him forward. Samuel just shaking his head. The other boys parting like the Red Sea to either side. The girl leaning on the brick wall beside the basket, neck up and eyes fixed on the hoop.

Samuel chucked the ball at Reid and he twitched a little on impact but managed to catch it. Swirled the thing a couple times in his hands as he stepped up to the stick.

"Let's go!" The girl sighed heavily, leaning further into the brick and a couple of the guys laughed in an appreciative *hey she's all right* kind of way.

So Reid sighed, dribbled one two three and swirl and lifted his head up and just as he was about to let the ball leave his hands a gust of wind pushed his back but his body remained still and the ball went sailing, spinning and swoosh right through the basket. Nothing but net. Reid's mouth agape. Samuel scrunching his face in disbelief. The clan all looking around at each other for some explanation. The girl smiling to herself. Wind still blowing around her.

"Looks like the little guy can shoot," she said, and started to walk back towards the apartment building.

Reid ran after her. "Hey…uh. Wait!"

She spun around. "Yeah?" She shoved her neck out like a challenge.

"You're, uh…new?"

"Yeah Mrs. P just acquired me."

Reid thought how his dad would like that word. Acquired.

"Well, yeah. Cool. Well…I'm Reid." He stumbled.

"I'm Daniella." She nodded suspiciously then turned away.

"Daniella!" He ran up to her side to whisper. She kept walking as he spoke. "That uh basket…I uh…I don't usually…I can't usually shoot… it seemed like you…I know it's weird but…did you do something?"

Daniella stopped.

"What? You think I can control the wind or some shit?" Her

wide eyes and tilted head mocked him and her vulgarity made his neck twinge.

"No, I just...it seemed...weird."

Daniella didn't talk for a minute, staring at the sweating, nervous little boy. "You're welcome." She smirked and walked up the front steps.

Reid later told his dad, the History Channel murmuring in the background, but just as he was about to speak his theory of her mystical magical supernatural whatever power thingy she must have, Reid remembered that the History Channel was on and figured maybe he'd just keep his superhero fantasy to himself. Just like he'd later keep the times he saw objects flying in the backyard to himself. Just like he'd never tell anyone about the ballet of various plastic lawn chairs he'd once witnessed or how when he looked down into the lawn, Daniella was there lying on her back with her curls cascading into the grass, hands up conducting the whole thing like an orchestra. Reid assumed he had to be crazy. Especially when he saw her fly. Launch right off the sidewalk zooming higher and higher with that trail of violet light until she dissipated into the clouds. The exhaust she'd leave behind making a negative-degree winter feel as hot and humid as summer next to a bus.

After a couple years of Daniella Rossi, Reid wasn't sure he knew the difference between love and fear. So he mostly shied away from her. Though the breeze always seemed to pull him closer.

V

FOR DANIELLA ROSSI life seemed to pass in flashes. Flashes of foster homes always ending with some mishap or some hospital visit or some chair getting thrown through some wall.

"Now Daniella, do you want to talk about the heat?"

After an incident involving a broken leg Samuel insisted was caused by little Daniella somehow tossing massive Samuel up in the air and letting him drop on concrete, Mrs. P was starting to think it was time Daniella got some counseling. When Daniella said she'd rather move on, since four years at one home was her longest stint anyway, the agency let Daniella know Mrs. P was basically her dead end at the bottom of a long list of foster parents too starched white for kids like Daniella. So at fourteen Daniella finally saw a shrink.

"Daniella? Did you hear the question?"

"Yeah I can hear." Daniella forced a quick closed-mouth smile then went back to cracking her knuckles on the coffee table. She was in her track uniform so her bare legs were sticking to the leather sofa. JustCallMeDave was sitting across from her, leaning forward on his knees. Squinting his eyes at her so his thick-rimmed glasses squished further up his round face. His light blue polo looked too big.

"You said sometimes things happen and you get hot? What makes you hot?"

Daniella almost laughed. *What makes you hot?* Perv.

"When I lose control," Daniella blurted out and didn't intend to answer any more stupid questions.

And she didn't. After a half hour of fluff Daniella ran home and let the wind guide her like always. Daniella could run so fast she'd blur, but she was smart enough to convert her superhuman powers into talents. Ran fast enough to be a prodigy but slow enough to avoid inquiries. She wanted to be in the Olympics not locked up for scientific experimentation. But sometimes when Daniella ran, she let her feet get away from her. Usually only at night and usually only when no one was looking.

On those nights when Daniella ran, she felt control despite her lack of it. She felt her mind latch on to an entity that was not her own and she could close her eyes and still end the race exactly where she needed to be. And when Daniella ran, it was not her feet guiding but her core propelling her through space, her bones and muscles extending and contracting in response to the pull, all rippling as a product of the energy radiating in her center, heat streaming through her veins, power bubbling in her blood and expelling through her pores. And when Daniella ran, matter could not describe her form so much as mass. She existed but could not be seen. She could hear but could not be heard. Like she could hear yoga-pantsed women gabbing in boutiques as they searched through sliding clothes hangers. She could hear the sweat dripping down a chef's neck over the roaring fire and flamboyant profanities spewing in an upscale restaurant. She could hear a whispered lullaby from a studio apartment and the quiet dribbles and coos of a baby drifting to sleep in a mother's arms. She could hear the horns of taxis and the charging L train, she could hear the bass from a car radio, the cry of the newspaper salesman "Streetwise! Streetwise!" And she could hear street performers. She could hear their drums. And when Daniella ran, she could fly. A trail of violet zigzagging behind as she burst through clouds and twirled and twirled and twirled until teetering out of control as if spinning in a field of daisies. And down on the street the people kept their eyes forward, moving forward, not looking around. And then every once in a while one eye would stray a glance to the sky, but the color was so fleeting the image was dismissed after a double take. And when Daniella ran, she grew. She absorbed the stories the city told as if living in fast forward and felt all those surrounding her, felt their hearts beat with her own, accelerating, and she accelerated and accelerated until she felt she might implode and so when Daniella ran, she always had to stop.

"I've seen you fly."

Daniella was catching her breath on the front steps to her building when she noticed Reid Calloway leaning against the door like he'd been waiting. High school had taught him pretty faces meant popularity so his old nervousness was quickly slipping away, now that he was used to girls hanging on his arms. Apparently girls thought he was some Adonis these days. Like some artist had taken a chisel to him. Daniella still thought he looked dumb. Leaning there, wearing a gray cardigan and looking like he thought he was classy like his dad.

Hours had passed since Daniella left JustCallMeDave and it was dark outside. A little nippy out with Chicago September. Streets empty except for flickering streetlamps.

"What?" She asked more like a warning than like she hadn't heard.

"I've seen you…" His glance up to the sky finished his sentence. "Ever since you moved in here. I've seen you…" Reid was smiling then. Excited and eyes gleaming like the stars. "You talk to the wind or something? I see you whispering sometimes. How do you do it? I mean where did you come from? Are you like…I don't know…you a superhero or something?" He was almost out of breath like a little kid talking about Legos.

Daniella felt her palms sweating and she wished she could answer him. Sometimes she'd try to remember where she came from, but when she reached far back all she could remember was the sound of rushing cars and lapping water and someone breathing slow like it was their last.

"Why do you care?" She stepped closer and felt her body heat rising. Reid felt it too and backed into the door with a thud.

"It's just…not…usual? And I don't know, it just seems like you could…well, like the basketball. You know when you made me score."

"What, like four years ago?"

"Yeah. I don't know. Guess I was just thinking and if you can do all that…you could help people?"

37

"With great power comes great responsibility and all that dumb Spiderman crap?"

"Yeah." Reid saying it all easy like it was simple math. "Or Batman. Superman. The X-Men. Whoever."

"No." Daniella laughed.

"But you have to!"

Daniella's heat was escalating now, her eyes darting between Reid's and Reid was pushing harder and harder against the door he was so scared and trying not to look it.

"Don't tell anyone or I'll eat your family." She spat then hissed after for effect before walking through the door.

That night like most nights Daniella sat on the roof. Closed her eyes and felt and heard the entire city beating inside her. Calling to her like drums so she took off. Flew up, up and high. The breeze conquered her eardrums, created a hum, a roar. Her eyes remained closed but the flashes came next. Flashes of life flying past her line of vision. A police officer riding on a horse. A pigeon nibbling on bread. An old woman rattling up the stairs, leaning on the railing for support.

And then she was there. Daniella dropped from the sky right beside the old woman. Gave her back a nudge and let the Wind do the rest, gently propelling the old woman effortlessly up the stairs. When she turned for an explanation Daniella was already gone.

Daniella never allowed herself to be seen. She hid around corners and on balconies. Sometimes threw burglars through glass windows. They'd be pleading and shrieking to an invisible god as they flailed down the street. The storeowners would run out next and search around the corners and up the skyscrapers, looking for an angel.

Such covert adventures were games to Daniella—a way to pass the time when no book or movie could satisfy her, when giggling over boys could not distract her, when her legs could not take her far enough away. But that didn't mean she wanted to make a difference.

Always figured that'd make too much of a mess.

Until the sometimes that Daniella saw death.

Saw an innocent boy take his last breath, his heart pierced by a bullet intended for someone else. Blood painted the pavement. The whites of the young boy's eyes flickered light into the night sky as his lids fluttered and then settled, and the street was quiet except for the feet of the last gang member's escape, a distant patter against the wet asphalt. One last puff of air released from the boy's lips—a small mushroom of water vapor visible in the freezing air. Daniella watched the boy transition into the world of stillness, watched his dark skin dull. Her heart raced as did her brain, the drums pounding through her entire body. One silent word to the wind and she could return air to his lungs, fill them until his chest rose, until it pushed the blood back through his veins. She could open his mouth and his nasal cavity and let the wind move through him, like it moved through her. Daniella could bring him back. Easily. She clenched her fists and closed her eyes and imagined the glow that would result if his eyes flickered open again. But instead she opened her own. She shivered and took off, the wind engulfing her body and transporting her back to the roof. Plopped on the tiling and looked out at her city. Her ears opened to more screams and more ambulances and she saw more senseless blood and even more lingering mushrooms of undeserved last breaths and that was when she cried.

Reid awoke to tapping at his window. Jolted right up. He had slept light ever since the broomstick incidents of his childhood. When he noticed the sound was coming from his window he turned to see Daniella hovering, her hair flapping more than usual. She was crying.

"I let someone die," she said as he sat her on his bed, trying to figure out where your hands were supposed to go when you comforted someone.

"I'm sure you did all you could." Reid placed his hand robotically

39

on her back.

"But I didn't. I let him die. I watched him." She was sniffling hard and looking ugly and thinking how gross and puffy her eyes were gonna be in the morning.

"It's not your fault."

The wind howled outside, high pitched like a bird. Both kids felt goosebumps. Daniella shoved her fists into her eye sockets, trying to dull her tears with pain. Wanted the open wound to hurry up and become a scar so she could move on and grow hard. But Reid's hand felt warm through her t-shirt.

"It is my fault. You were right. I'm not gonna let anyone else die."

Daniella Rossi looked up and her violet eyes pierced the night sky.

DISSERTATION OUTLINE
KENDALL STEINLE
DEPAUL UNIVERSITY

DISSERTATION OUTLINE
A THEMATIC ANALYSIS ON THE
PHENOMENOLOGY OF INEBRIATED
CATASTROPHES:
HOW TO LOOK GOOD ON YOUR DOWNWARD SPIRAL
K. Steinle

I. INTRODUCTION: HOW MAGNIFICENT YOU APPEAR IN A STRICTLY SUPERFICIAL SOCIAL CONTEXT
II. OPERATIONALIZING NORMS OF FAILURE
   a. Discussion of "selective brown-outs" to full-scale black-outs
   b. Evolution of initial aversion to inevitable, full-fledged dependency on poison
   c. Criteria for judgment calls on who "kinda looks almost like your boyfriend"
   d. Impediments to finishing, like, anything while sober
   e. Obligations toward impressing the parental units (also: master the art of "lying")
III. DOCUMENTATION OF PROFOUND DEBT INCURRED
   a. Paradigm dissecting one's misunderstanding of one's dire financial plight

b. Itemized hospital bills
    b.i. Shattering of digitus secundus manus and implementation of four screws, one growth plate, and some pocket change ($25,000), followed by a qualitative analysis of how incredibly joyous of a bike ride that was
    b.ii. Learn the hard way how expensive Chicago Emergency Medical Services are sans insurance and implore drunken self (and possibly God) to hail a cab next time, even if shot in the face (note: aforementioned fracture detailed in "i" was not an isolated incident)

IV. THE MODEL: FIRST SIP TO FINAL AMBULANCE RIDE

V. LIMITATIONS OF STUDY
    a. Unable to remove drunken voicemail from professor's phone
    b. Bringing crowbars to parties is frowned upon
    c. Out of money
    d. Out of tears

VI. CONCLUSION AND SUGGESTIONS FOR FUTURE RESEARCH
    a. Realization that bus ride to closest AA meeting passes an estimated fourteen bars
    b.

INSOMNIA
HAL BAUM
COLUMBIA COLLEGE

JUST GO TO SLEEP. Just fall asleep. Sleep. Come on. Sleep. Just sleep. Sleep goddamn it! Try counting sheep. One. Two. Three. Four. Five. Six. I just wish I was asleep. Why can't I be asleep? I need to wake up at seven in the morning. It's already midnight. I need to be asleep now. Just go to fucking sleep you stupid fucking idiot!

Morgan opened her eyes. She glanced sideways to the bottle of Eszopiclone pills on her bedside table. She took the bottle and opened the childproof cap. The bottle was full of little blue circles, each with a different serial number etched onto it. She poured a handful in her hand, took one between her fingers and put the rest back in the bottle.

So what's it going to be Neo? Red pill or blue pill? Do you want to see how far the rabbit hole goes?

Morgan put the pill on her tongue and swallowed it with just spit. She closed her eyes and lay her head back down on the pillow.

Half an hour later she still wasn't asleep.

Goddamn it. Goddamn it. Goddamn it! Why can't I just fall asleep. Why don't these stupid fucking pills do what they're supposed to!?

Morgan opened her eyes. Her eyelids were heavy. She grabbed her phone off the bedside table, and messaged her boyfriend Lucas. They had met on OKCupid. He had messaged her. "Hey. You like Zelda. Want to talk?" She had looked at his profile picture and thought, "*Whatever. Why not.*" He was the first guy she had ever met on the internet, and also the first guy she ever introduced to her parents. Mostly just because her cousin Sarah was visiting from Texas and he was around. So they had all gone to the zoo. She couldn't tell if her parents liked him or not; she thought maybe they were weirded out because he was black. But Sarah liked him, and that was more important to Morgan anyway.

That was a month ago. Now she was lying in bed, unable to sleep and all she wanted was for him to be there with her, his arms around her body, talking her to sleep.

She texted him: "Hey. You up?"

AND ONE HOUR LATER she heard his car driving down the dirt road in front of the townhouse. She looked out the window to make sure it was him. Yup. That stupid white Prizm, rolling along. It was always so tempting to spray paint something on that car. Like a big dragon or a zigzag pattern or something. All that blankness, just begging to be filled.

She waited for him to knock at the door before she went downstairs, so it wouldn't seem like she was just sitting in bed waiting for him, which she had been, and she walked slowly down the stairs, taking her time.

She opened the door, and he was standing there in his grey hoodie, and the light blue jeans with the hole in the left knee. He was tall and skinny, with a lean face and scared eyes. A slight goatee. He smiled a squinting smile when he saw her and leaned in for a kiss. They kissed a little longer than usual. She was dazed and exhausted, and he was high. They separated, he came inside and she closed the door.

"Hey."

"Hey."

"What's up?"

"Nothing. Just waiting for you."

He laughed. "That's sweet. You're crazy."

She sniffed. "Were you smoking?"

"Yes."

"With who?"

"Your mom."

Morgan rolled her eyes, but she smiled too. "You're the worst person ever."

"You are. Can I have something to drink?"

"Like *drink* drink?"

"Like water."

"Oh, yeah, sure."

She led him into the kitchen and started filling a plastic cup, the blue one with the companion cube on it, from the sink.

"I almost got into a car accident on the way over here."

"Yeah?"

"Yeah. I was driving down 113th, and this guy comes flying out of nowhere." Lucas demonstrated, his hands acting as cars. "Going down Cullom at like 70 miles an hour, I slammed on the brakes. Missed hitting him by like inches."

"Oh my god." Morgan turned off the water.

"Yeah, I almost died tonight because of you."

"Because of me?"

"Yeah, waking me up at ungodly hours of the night to come over here and hang out with you."

Morgan went around the corner and sat on his lap, handing him the cup of water. He took a long gulp, and Morgan put her head on his shoulder.

"I like that I can call you at one in the morning and you'll show up," she mumbled into his hoodie.

"Well," Lucas took another sip. "I love you." He said it matter-of-factly like it was not a big deal at all.

Morgan raised her head. "I love you too." And she kissed him, a long high/sleepy kiss, putting her hand around his head as he put his hand on her ass.

She stopped.

"What?"

"Where were you coming from?"

"What?"

"Where were you coming from to get over here?"

"My house."

"You don't pass Cullom to get from your house to here. That's on the other side of the bridge."

"Yeah. I got lost. I went too far and had to circle back. You know I'm shitty with directions."

She paused. "Okay." She put her head back in his hoodie, but he pushed her back upright.

"What? You don't believe me?"

"I don't want to do this right now. I just want to sleep on you."

"Where do you think I was, Morgan? Where do you think I was? Where could I have possibly been?"

"I don't know. It doesn't matter."

"It does matter, because you don't trust me."

"Lucas. Please. I'm too tired for this. Can we just go to bed?"

"Fine. Whatever."

Morgan got off him and slowly walked upstairs, Lucas following behind her.

"Where are your roommates?"

"Matt's at Rebecca's, Paul's at his parents, and I'm not sure where Jess is. Probably just asleep."

They walked down the carpeted hallway towards Morgan's room. Morgan crawled into bed first, already in her pajamas. Lucas stripped to his boxers and undershirt, putting his phone and wallet on the bedside table and tossing his clothes on the floor, next to other piles of clothes and books, and got in bed after her.

He put his arms around her and suddenly Morgan had a pang of regret. She wished she hadn't called him over. She wished she had just taken another pill and gone to sleep. His arms around her felt wrong, like an intrusion. But she reminded herself, *this is what you wanted.* So she pulled him tight around her like a blanket, and closed her eyes. She could feel him breathing in her ear and the scruff of his beard scraping her neck. He shifted trying to get more comfortable and she wished she was asleep. His hand around her stomach started creeping downwards. She felt her body get warmer. She was tired, sure, but she wasn't sleeping anyway. She turned to face him.

"Hey."

"Hey."

MORGAN WAS SITTING ON THE BED. She had put her pajamas back on and her hair up. Lucas was in the bathroom. She felt horrible, like her skin was paper thin, like a balloon, like if you rubbed her against the sidewalk outside she would pop. Her eyes were throbbing, and her head was killing her. *I shouldn't have invited him over. I should have just taken another pill. I'm so stupid.*

She wanted for him to be gone; to never come back from the

bathroom. To disappear forever. *At the very least, I can try to fall asleep before he comes back.* She grabbed the bottle of pills off the table, and popped a couple in her mouth, swallowing hard without water. Then something caught her eye—Lucas's cell phone on the bedside table.

She glanced towards the door again and then took Lucas's cell phone off the night stand. Popping two more pills, she started scrolling through his text messages.

She found something strange. Lucas had been texting someone named Sarah. She opened the conversation, and the first thing she saw was pink flesh. It was a naked picture of a young white girl lying on her bed, her legs spread wide showing off her pussy, and her head turned to the side, giving a cold sexy look at the camera. Her arm was out of frame because she was taking the picture herself. In the background there was a white stuffed horse sitting on a bookshelf. It was Sarah. Morgan's cousin Sarah.

What the fuck?

Now she remembered, them getting all chummy at the zoo. Sarah touching his arm when they left. Sarah telling her "he seems like a great guy, and he's super cute too." She thought Sarah was happy for her. So stupid. How could Sarah do this? No. How could Lucas do this? That fucking bastard. That sick fucking piece of shit. She popped two more pills. That makes seven.

Lucas came back from the bathroom in boxers and a wife beater. He was smiling his stupid squinty-eyed smile, but when he saw her, immediately his face dropped. She was holding his phone up with the picture of her cousin.

"Morgan, I—"

"What the fuck Lucas!"

"You were going through my phone?"

"She's sixteen years old!"

"Listen, I didn't even ask for that. She sent that to me on her own."

48

"She's my cousin, Lucas! That's Sarah!"

Morgan was crying, her eyes were dilated. Things were getting blurry and salty and stinging. All she had was anger. Anger at this human shaped blob in front of her.

The blob approached. "Listen, Morgan. It's not what it looks like. I—"

Morgan flailed at the blob. She threw the phone at him but it just bounced off. He winced a little and she grabbed the pill bottle and pushed past him into the hallway. She took two more pills and stumbled into the kitchen. That's nine.

"Morgan!" Lucas called after her. "I'm sorry!" He followed her into the kitchen and found her sitting on the floor sobbing quietly. "Morgan?" He approached her cautiously. "Morgan. It was just one picture. I didn't even ask for it. She just sent it to me. It freaked me out. I don't talk to her anymore."

Morgan didn't acknowledge him. She just stood up with drool hanging out of her mouth and looked at him. Her eyes were red and wide and dizzy.

"Morgan. I think you need to sit down." He moved towards her, and tried to put a hand on her shoulder, but she jerked her arm away and mumbled something unintelligible. "Morgan! You need to sit down." He grabbed her by the shoulder, and she started pulling away, so he held on tighter. She started yelling. "Morgan! Calm down! It's okay." She started slapping at his chest, and he grabbed her other wrist, trying to push her back towards the kitchen counter, trying to subdue her. "Morgan…calm…down." She was kicking at him and yelling, and squirming around. They were pressed against the counter now. Somehow in the struggle Morgan's left hand got free, and as he was trying to grab it again Lucas saw a flash of silver. She had grabbed a knife from the block on the counter. "Morgan, don't—"

He stumbled backwards in reaction to her sudden movement,

falling on the tile floor. He thought maybe she had missed him, but then felt a wetness on his stomach, and looked down to see a dark red splotch growing on his shirt. Then there was a throbbing in his stomach, which slowly increased in intensity until the pain was unbearable. He was backing away as fast as possible, his heart racing, until he bumped into a wall. He grabbed his stomach trying to make the pain stop, but it just kept getting worse. He looked up and Morgan was gone.

She was out in the driveway, a cool breeze blowing on her skin. She had the knife in her hand and was not crying anymore. Now her eyes were just pounding and everything was blurry and shifting in front of her. She found Lucas's car in the driveway, that stupid beat-up white Prizm. She gripped the knife tight in her hand, and thought about opening the scar on her arm and painting the car with her blood. But then she imagined him coming outside and finding her dead on the ground, stepping over her body, getting into his bloody car, and driving away to go meet some other girl across town, smiling his stupid squinty-eyed smile the whole way. So instead, she crouched down and jammed the knife into the front tire. There was a sharp hissing noise as all the air suddenly escaped. She repeated the process with all three other tires.

Lucas was on the floor yelling now, because the shock had gotten through his system, and he was trying to sit up without passing out from the pain, when he saw Morgan come back into the kitchen, her eyelids drooping, and the knife hanging limp in her hand. At this point he didn't say anything. He just watched as she dropped the knife, and with one last sad twinge in her face collapsed on the ground. The pill bottle popped open as it hit the ground, sending a cascade of little blue pills scattering across the floor. Each with their own serial number etched in the side.

Lucas winced as he climbed to his feet. He thought about leaving, about getting in his car and just driving away, but he saw Morgan's eyes fluttering and he felt his own eyes start to close involuntarily. So instead he walked slowly back into the bedroom, bent down with great difficulty and picked his cell phone back up off the floor.

And the first thing he saw was the picture that had caused so much trouble: Morgan's cousin, Sarah, sprawled spread-eagled on her bed. Lucas swiped the picture away with his finger, and dialed 911.

As he was waiting for the ambulance to arrive, he found the picture of Sarah again. Sarah who was sixteen, who had claimed to be a virgin, who was a little white girl, and he a big black man. Suddenly he regretted calling 911. He deleted the picture, and scrolled up and deleted the whole conversation. She had started it, but he had asked for the picture. It wouldn't look good at all. Get rid of it. *Morgan was crazy and on pills anyway. They wouldn't believe her, would they? No. She had stabbed him. She was the one who was screwed. She really fucked up. Goddamn it. I hope she goes to fucking jail. Fucking stabbing people. Fucking shit. Crazy.*

51

BECAUSE OF DANIEL
VIRGINIA BAKER
COLUMBIA COLLEGE

DANIEL DRAGGED ME TO THE JAZZ CLUB down the street because, according to him, I wasn't getting out enough. He wasn't getting out enough either, but I guess he was the one who was beginning to take initiative and do something about it. While I sat on the couch, Daniel kneeled by the door, lacing up his boots.

I didn't want to go. I'd grown so used to staying holed up, hardly doing anything besides sleeping and going off to serve rich folks at a country club on the northside, the job I fell into after quitting my minimum-wage job at Cinema 9. Five days a week I put on my shirt, vest and tie and placed three-course meals before bougie people I addressed as "Mr." and "Mrs." I was bored and terrified and the only company I had was Daniel. And we were good for each other. He was lost. I was lost. He was sad. I was confused. We were two blind children, searching the city for something to salvage, something to cling to, so we latched onto each other. He was heartbroken and hard. I was timid and unsure. In the past six months, we had grown to be

52

best friends, but I didn't know whether it was because we wanted to or if it was due to some default setting. Either way, Daniel was my only friend. In this whole fucking city, Daniel was all I had.

And for the past few months Daniel and I were stuck, frozen into our habits and mindsets. Any time we weren't working, we were together. Maybe it was the Chicago winter, my first, his fourth. I tended to blame a lot of things on the winter. The days when we didn't have to work at all, we slept through the afternoon, waking up as the sun went down. Some days I spent the night at his place, and we would continue through the next day, picking up right where we left off. If I woke up in my own apartment, it was only a fifteen-minute bus ride on the 151 before I landed at his front door and we started all over again. We stayed up too late, drank too much whiskey, said too many of the same things. We had the same conversations, over and over again, repeating the same stories and memories, as if reading lines off of a script. I started to lose track of time, started to sound like my mother when I said, "It's all happening too quickly. I can't keep up." It was predictable. I knew exactly when Daniel would announce that he was going out to smoke a cigarette. He'd wave the pack back and forth in front of me, to try and entice me, as if he was waving a string in front of a cat. I'd take a moment to consider if I actually wanted one or if I was just playing along, but still, I'd pluck a cigarette from his pack and follow him out to the fire escape, where we'd shiver and smoke and look out at the city, the one I didn't belong to yet, the one that didn't feel like home, the one I feared might never feel like home.

It had been almost six months since I left New Jersey, almost half a year of my life. I left because of a compulsion. It was either I would stay and do nothing, or leave and do something. But I didn't know what my something was and so all this time had passed and I had nothing to show for it. Each day I woke up with anxiety gnawing at my body. A feeling of dread, the pulse to *do* something, but not knowing what to do. Sometimes it was paralyzing. I thought I might shrink, that one day I might evaporate and my landlord would knock on the door and find my apartment empty.

Daniel and I took our frustrations out on each other. I was tired of the monotony, the way I knew exactly when he would talk about Sarah, the ex-girlfriend, the one who tore him apart. Sarah left him just weeks before I first met him, when Daniel and I happened to sit beside each other on a bench facing out towards Lake Michigan on Hollywood Beach. The Daniel I met was a skeleton. I often tried to picture who he was before I met him. I liked to imagine that he was happy. He probably smiled a lot and said hopeful things, not like the constant negative commentary he had on loop, about climate change and the apocalypse and oppression and all of the other things that kept him tethered to the ground. That Daniel probably didn't smoke or drink as much. He probably got a healthy amount of sleep and ate better.

I liked to imagine that kind of Daniel, before I knew him. But I know that version of Daniel and I would have never become friends, because if Daniel had something, he probably wouldn't have needed me.

HE GRABBED MY WRIST and pulled me up from his couch. "Let's go."

"But, Daniel—"

"C'mon, Annabelle. We need to get out of this apartment. We need to go."

He was right. But I hadn't been out to a bar or a club in a long time. I didn't even know if my fake ID worked anymore, or if it had expired. I tried to think up a good excuse, but couldn't.

"Please, Annabelle," he said, his eyes polished like obsidian, warm breath I could feel on the tip of my nose. "*I need this. It's been too long.*" He was talking about jazz. The biggest reason he moved to Uptown was so he could be close to the Green Mill. Jazz music was one of the few things he loved. CDs by the greats like Louie Armstrong, Chet Baker, and Miles Davis were about the only possessions Daniel owned. Towers of CDs were piled in the corners of his loft, stacked up on his kitchen counters, and once I even found one in the bathroom cabinet. He had big, coffee-table books on the history of jazz and could tell you any kind of trivia you wanted to know, like the first venue Fats Waller played in New York City, or on which street Louie Armstrong grew up. He dreamed about going down to New Orleans, to the birthplace of jazz, but so far he hadn't made it.

I never questioned or understood most of it. Just accepted it as a part of him and tagged along whenever I could, even though it didn't mean as much to me. But when I'd catch a glance of Daniel staring off, far beyond where the music came from, looking out at something I couldn't see, I'd start to feel it. Some kind of tingle, like being caught by stinging nettle. And I'd start to wonder who Daniel might really be, if he had never met Sarah or if he had stayed out on the West Coast by his family or if he had finished med school and become a doctor. Only jazz made him look like that. Only jazz made me start to wonder.

I WAS SLOW TO GET DRESSED and follow him down the stairs. The whole time we were walking, Daniel was two steps ahead of me and I was trying to slow him down. His lips were set straight and hard on his face, hands shoved into pockets, shoulders pinched up to his ears.

We walked west on Lawrence, going under the shadows of the L tracks. The red line train rumbled overhead, stopping at the platform and then heading further up north. I didn't see anyone there, but then some coins started jingling inside a styrofoam cup, and I saw a figure hunched in the shadows. I kept my eyes focused straight ahead so I didn't have to look at him, but Daniel went over to him. The man was wrapped up in torn clothes, sitting on newspaper. How did he survive? How did he even *want* to survive when he went around every day in this city with absolutely nothing? It made me feel as though I had it all, a roof over my head, a kind-of bed (an air mattress wasn't the best), and means to buy food. It made me feel guilty for feeling so shitty.

Daniel pulled a dollar bill out of his wallet and dropped it into the cup. The man tilted his head up and nodded. As Daniel walked back over to me, the cup jingled again.

"We're lucky, aren't we?" Daniel said. It sounded foreign, coming from someone who was constantly bemoaning about everything he had lost and everything he didn't have.

"You think?" I asked.

"Yeah, I do. I mean, sometimes I forget it. Sometimes I forget how lucky I am." The streetlights created a glowing outline around him. I couldn't make out his expression, but I could tell he was chewing the inside of his bottom lip, thinking.

"I don't even know what luck means."

"Just that we have something, you know? Some sense of belonging to *something*. However vague that sounds. We have it."

My neck felt itchy, and I felt like I was wearing too many clothes. "Oh, yeah? What do we have?"

We stopped at the corner of Lawrence and Broadway, and he squared his body towards mine. "We're not alone."

My cheeks felt hot, despite the wind that was tunneling through the intersection, and I almost told him he was making me blush and I didn't know why. But I was embarrassed, which seemed ridiculous.

This was Daniel. I'd thrown up in his toilet and recklessly cried on his lap and *now* I was embarrassed.

I thought back to a conversation we'd had last week. We were sitting on the fire escape, our legs dangling towards the ground, three floors below us, each of us smoking a cigarette. Daniel always looked so good with a cigarette. When he had one between his lips, I could see him as someone else might, the way my coworker saw him when Daniel met me at work one day. For weeks afterwards she asked me what was going on between us, and every time I told her that he was just my friend and that I didn't see him that way.

But something happened when he smoked. He narrowed his dark eyes, and the sprouting gray hairs on the back of his head made him look prestigious, like he could have been a good doctor. As I was sitting on the fire escape with him that day, I noticed that he had shaved recently, within a day or so, and his jawline looked like porcelain. The outside of our thighs were touching and the wind was calm for once, one of those winter days that almost felt like spring.

"Daniel," I said, "I don't know what I'm doing."

"Me either," he said.

"I feel like a fuck-up."

"You're a fuck-up? Please. At least you're still young. I don't have that excuse anymore."

"Oh, c'mon. You're only twenty-six," I said.

"Yeah, and you're only nineteen. What do you know?" He nudged my shoulder with his.

I rolled my eyes. "Fuck off. I'm tired of you talking about my age."

"Okay. I know. I'm sorry. It's just—you're not a fuck-up. You're fine. We're both fine."

"What does that even mean?"

He pinched his lips around the cigarette and breathed in slowly.

"Well, at least we have each other, right?"

I nodded. "Yeah. I guess so."

He flicked his cigarette down onto the street below and in one quick motion his head was resting on my shoulder and his hair was brushing against my cheek. "I'm glad you're here. These past few months, I don't know what I'd done without you."

"You would have been fine," I said.

"You came at a good time," he said. Warmth spread like goosebumps throughout my body, and I didn't know what else to say.

Daniel had rested his head on my shoulder before, and I'd done the same to him, usually when we were watching a movie or after we drank too much, and every time, I always imagined it was someone else. It was someone else's head or someone else's shoulder, someone I really wanted, someone I might've loved. And I always thought that Daniel did the same thing, that maybe he imagined I was Sarah, that she was back, that she had never left him. I would've understood.

But this time, when he rested his head on me, I didn't imagine anything. I just felt him there with me. And it felt good, to have something concrete.

THE GREEN MILL WAS DIM AND SHADOWY. Music filled the room like mist, and I waded through it as I followed Daniel over to a small table propped up against the wall. We stripped off our coats and unravelled our scarves. Tables were wedged together tightly like a Tetris game. Most of them were filled with men and women, making eyes at each other, knees grazing underneath the table, fingers resting gently on top of elbows, touching each other in some sort of reassurance. The band was propped up on a stage before us. Four men dressed in black; one sitting down at the piano, another with a stand-up bass, one with a saxophone, and another behind a drum-set.

A waitress came over to us, and Daniel ordered two drinks. She nodded without smiling, and when she came back, she placed two tall glasses on the table. I picked one up and smelled it: whiskey and ginger-ale, Daniel's favorite. Across from me, he raised his glass and clicked it against mine, and I realized how serious he looked in the candlelight.

Whenever Daniel asked me what I thought about jazz, I never really knew what to say. I didn't know much about it, hardly knew the names on Daniel's CD cases, but I still liked hearing it, whenever it found its way into my life. My dad used to play it on the stereo every Sunday, as he made pancakes. I always wondered why there weren't any words. "Because sometimes you don't need words," my dad said. "Sometimes you just need to feel something." That was a long time ago. Before he left my mom and my sister and me. Before things started to crumble.

Jazz was one of the reasons Daniel came to Chicago. I came because I wanted a second chance. I wanted to start again in a city that revived itself, that rose from the ashes after it had been burned to the ground. It sounded limitless, like it couldn't be defeated. But Daniel came for the music, and for med school. He never made it through med school, but the music stuck.

There were people standing off in the corners, propped up around the bar, gathered around the tables. Some were alone, some were in groups, some of them had their eyes closed, head tilted back, lips pinched together, and I wondered what they were thinking. The saxophone player started making long, low sounds, and as I breathed, the music crawled inside of me, and it was like all of the thoughts I wanted to suppress were ballooning to the surface, levitating in the space before me. I took a long sip and tried to swallow them back down, but they slipped out of me in fragments.

The time my sister and I had tried to jump across the creek in the park in our hometown and she ended up falling in and getting all wet and I ran with her all the way back home. The time I found her in her room, crying over some boy who had made fun of her acne. I smoothed out her hair and told her it was okay, they all did that. The time she drove me to the train station, the day I left. She sat in the driver's seat, staring out the windshield. "I can't believe you're leaving," she said, and it felt like my chest was an hourglass and the grains of sand were leaking out one by one.

"I'm sorry," I told her. "I have to do this. I have to leave." But she wouldn't look at me, and if she did I probably would've started to cry. I wanted to tell her I loved her, but I didn't know how. I didn't know how to tell my sister I loved her because I didn't think I'd done it before.

"I'll see you soon," I told her, not knowing if it was true or not. She nodding, without turning to look at me. I got out of the car and stood on the curb as she drove away and I could've sworn I could see her eyes in the rearview mirror.

When the song ended, Daniel eyes met mine and he smiled. His hand was resting on the table, and I had an overwhelming urge to take it in mine, to grab it and stick it in my pocket and claim it as my own. The band started to play a quiet number that sounded like foggy grey days, when the clouds covered the top of the Sears Tower. Daniel shifted back to look at the stage, and he suddenly looked so far away, as if I was looking at him through the wrong end of a pair of binoculars. I wondered what I would think of him now if I didn't know him, if he was a stranger. I stripped away his dark hair and the stubby whiskers that clung to his cheeks and jaw. I peeled away his fears and insecurities, and started to imagine he was different. What if I didn't know about his bad dreams or his heartache? What if I didn't know about his anxiety attacks, the times when he would clutch his chest and stagger his breaths to try and slow his heart rate? Maybe he would be happier, healthier, stronger. Maybe he would be something.

But it wouldn't be Daniel. That person wouldn't be the Daniel I knew. And it was all of those things I liked about him. It was all the holes, all the sadness, the way he sighed in his sleep, the way he clenched his fists, the way he was beginning to chip away, like old paint. Because it was Daniel. And I *knew* Daniel. Probably better than anyone I'd ever known.

The music seeped into me. All of the instruments echoed and the sounds weaved together and I wanted to hold them all. I wanted to catch them and bring them close to my body and never let them go. And maybe that's what Daniel had been talking about this whole time.

"Jazz is life," he told me once, when he was playing an album by Bill Evans. We were lying on our backs on the floor of his loft. The lights were off, and he told me that I wasn't allowed to talk, I wasn't allowed to say anything because *Young and Foolish* was *his favorite song ever*, and conversation would ruin the moment.

"Improvising. That's all it is. We all try to pretend that we know what's coming next, but we don't know. We're just trying to figure it all out as we go along. That's jazz. That's life."

It didn't make sense to me then, but it did now. This whole time I'd been in Chicago, I had no idea what I was doing, what I wanted, what my next step was. I was treading water, trying not to plummet. Maybe the only thing keeping me afloat was Daniel. He was my only witness, the only proof of my existence.

The song ended and Daniel drank down the rest of his drink. As the music started up again he stood up, took a step toward me, and reached out his hand.

I didn't dance. I didn't ever dance. But he looked so nice standing before me, candlelight flickering against his skin, arm outstretched, palm open. I took the last sip of my drink, placed my hand in his, and let him pull me up from the chair. He snaked his arms around my back, and I blended into his body, my face fitting just below his shoulder, my hips squared against his pelvis, our legs mashed together. His cheek pressed into my hair, breath pooling in my ear. I stuck to Daniel like a gnat pasted to flypaper.

He smelled like hot summer days, the moment before it might rain. We stood beside the table, pressed together, the closest we had ever been. Music spun like filaments of silk. I wondered how everyone else saw us. Maybe we looked like we were happy, like we were together, like we were in love. I squeezed Daniel, burrowing closer into him. What if I could slip inside of Daniel and rummage through his body? What if I could pull out all the pieces of him and arrange them on the floor before us? What if I could fish inside of him and take out all of the things that made him sad, all of the things he didn't want to remember anymore? What if I could stack them up in a pile and light them on fire so they would turn to ashes and he wouldn't be so sad anymore?

Each note from the piano made it feel as though there were fish hooks stuck into my skin and they were pulling me in different directions. I felt like I might melt, like I could trickle down and spread across the hardwood floor like wax, and in the morning, the maintenance worker would have to pick me off the ground with his fingernail.

The song ended in a whisper. Claps circled around us like cicadas, and Daniel and I stood there for a moment before unsticking our bodies. We sat back down at the table, and I tried to focus on sitting correctly, on breathing correctly. But my skin was peeling like a clementine, and I couldn't keep track of all the things falling out of me.

"DANIEL," I BEGAN, when we were back in his apartment, as he kicked off his shoes, as he grabbed a glass from the kitchen cabinet and held it under the faucet. "Daniel, you're right, you know."

He twisted to look at me, squinting, pursing his lips together. Water ran over the sides of the glass. He switched the sink off. After a long swallow, he set down the glass.

"Oh, yeah?" he asked.

"Yeah."

"About what?"

I looked down at my feet. My big toe was poking through a hole in my sock. I hadn't trimmed my nails in a long time. "About being lucky. You're right. We are."

He walked over sat down on his bed, just about the only furniture taking up any space in his loft. I lowered myself down next to him.

"Thank you," I said.

"For what?"

"I don't know," I said. "For everything, I guess."

He placed his arm around my shoulders and pulled me into him. I could feel his chest beating. "You know, kid," he said, "I think we're gonna be all right."

A LITTLE LIGHT LOOKS THROUGH
LAUREN T. SILVERMAN
DEPAUL UNIVERSITY

A MID-DAY PHONE CALL FROM ROX interrupts the strangest dream I've had in months.

"Leonard's daughter is sick again, so I'm taking his six-o'clock to midnight," Rox says in lieu of "hi."

This is nothing out of the ordinary. She picks up extra shifts all the time. But it'll be the third gig she's missed in a row, and I'm not sure I can fend off Jolene much longer.

"Band goes on at nine, Rox," I say, yawning. I glance over at the alarm clock. One of Rox's socks is draped over it. I move the sock and see that it's almost noon, which means that she's probably on her lunch break. Or maybe she's just on a cigarette break, I forget. Lunch breaks at grocery stores happen at noon, five, even midnight if it's one of those all night joints. Luckily, Rox got in with a good one. It's organic, which means they treat the employees with kid gloves (organically sewn, no doubt). I'm pretty sure there's aura cleansing every half hour too (or maybe that's just in my imagination). Plus, nobody cares about the streak of pink in her hair.

"Jeremy, if you decide to bring in some extra cash, I'd be happy to take off work and come to your little jam session."

"Whatever, I'm not doing this," I say. I'm already wishing I was back in the sanctity of my twisted mind. "You're in a mood today."

"Hey, fuck you," Rox says, but the air is out of her tires. She pauses. "I got a call from Naomi this morning. She sold three paintings at the Damen Art Fair yesterday."

I don't say anything.

"You there?" Rox asks.

"You know what I'm going to say."

"Yeah," she says, "but I'm not exactly inspired bagging groceries."

"Now that's not true," I say slowly. "You don't bag, you cashier. That little punk with the piercings bags. Shit, that reminds me. I had the strangest dream this morning."

"Cig break is over. Gotta go." And with that she's gone. No more of a goodbye than there was a hello. I listen to the dial tone a few seconds longer. In my hazy state, it's my only proof that this conversation actually happened.

IT'S ALMOST NINE P.M. and Jonesy, Martin, AJ and I are in Tony's back office. The sound of a hundred or so people in the front of the bar is fantastically deafening.

"Fucking unreal," Martin says. He is bouncing around the room like a six-year-old on pixie sticks.

Maze, a bar the size of a large living room, doesn't have dressing rooms. Tony Toluca, the small, furry little bar owner, always lends us his office in the back. Our singer, AJ, is sitting behind the desk, looking like Trent Reznor on a job interview. The rest of us (minus Martin) are leaning.

"Did you see it out there?" Martin asks. "Have we ever played for this many people?"

There's a part of me that wants to remind Martin to play it a little cooler, but who am I kidding, this is the biggest crowd we've ever had. Somehow over the last few months, we've developed a following. And not the following we had in college, comprised of our buddies and their buddies. An actual paying-crowd following.

"Panties will be dropping when I launch into my solo on 'Malleable Moods'," Jonesy says. "You watch the floor for that one."

"Dude, you are *such* an asshole," AJ says, laughing.

"Malleable Moods" is our most well-known song. We were hanging out in Martin's dorm room freshman year, bombed off a shared bottle of Captain, when AJ started slurring, 'I'm in a malleable mood, man.' It was one of those great 'how the band got started' stories, one I hoped to tell on VH1 some day. VH1. Fuck, we're getting old.

"Yeah, come on, buddy, panties dropping?" I say. "What are we, Poison in the '80s?"

"We could use a few groupies," Jonesy says. "Who's got the band's creed? Somebody add it in there. No backstage pass allowed with top on."

"Great, we'll get a bunch of shirtless dudes hanging out with us in this cubicle," I say.

"Speaking of groupies," Martin begins, turning towards me. "You see Jolene yet?"

Jolene. Bartender at Maze and orchestrator of my current dilemma. Tight little body, freckles and long wavy red hair. We didn't really talk for the first nine months the group played here. Just exchanges of head nods and hi's, smiles and sometimes fuck-me eyes when the hour was late and the whiskey was flowing.

That all changed after last month's gig. All the guys headed to some makeshift party at AJ's cousin's house, while I stuck around for one last drink and found myself walking Jolene home. She lived eight blocks away. We didn't talk about anything big, but when she said goodnight at her door, she glanced at me two beats too long. I spent my walk home picturing her long red hair splayed across my pillow.

"Yeah, she was having a smoke outside when I came in," I say, taking a swig of my Heineken, already warm from my sweaty hands. I always give Rox shit for her habit, but I stayed out with Jolene for two. "See you after the show?" she had asked. Without thinking it through, without my mind and mouth agreeing upon the terms, I found myself saying, "I'll look for you." In the four-plus years we've been together, I've never cheated on Rox.

"Chick's got it bad for you," Jonesy says, with an exaggerated whistle.

"What's up with Rox anyway?" AJ asks. "Haven't seen her around lately."

"I don't know," I say, and it's true. I decide to change the subject. "Let's talk about 'Twine.' I have an idea for the second verse."

We are in the midst of sorting through lyrics when Tony pops his head in the door.

"You're up."

There's a muffled announcement and the sound of the crowd cheering. This might as well be a dressing room at Madison Square Garden. We leave the office feeling like rock stars.

WE ARE IN A FIELD, ROX AND I. A field with a million sunflowers. Her long blond hair falls just past the straps of her white dress. She is barefoot and laughing. All of a sudden, the sky darkens. Rain begins to fall. We are running towards something. Shelter? Safety? Then everything changes. Rox and I are looking at each other across a crowded train. There is a sea of people between us, and their faces are all ugly and distorted. Like aliens. A stop is called and Rox is exiting. I try to follow her, but I can't move. I'm stuck between the creatures. I yell out, "I'll meet you, I'll find you." Rox shakes her head no. Then she is gone.

IT WAS THE LONG HAIR THAT GAVE IT AWAY. That was the Rox I first met. Back when she was Roxanna, a girl from a small town in the middle part of Michigan. She was a sophomore then, a transfer student from her hometown community college. I was a senior. She came to the university to study art. Mixed media, she said. I noticed one of her paintings before I noticed her. It was at a student exhibit second semester. A petite girl, a sprite with long blond hair, had sidled up to me in front of a picture of a young girl in a field beneath a star-filled sky. I thought of nights spent on my grandparents' farm in Ohio. "You like it?" she had asked. "It's incredible," I said, and meant it. She hopped from one foot to the other and gave me a small smile. "It's mine." I fell in love with her instantly.

When graduation came, Roxanna moved to Chicago with me. She would work on her painting. I would work for some corporation by day and play in the band at night. We would live on wine and ramen, sex and sunrises. Roxanna took a job at the grocery store. Somewhere between all the wine and sunrises, I lost my job. I started taking odd jobs moving equipment for bands. Roxanna lost part of her name and long locks. Her desire to paint soon followed.

And here we are.

SOMETIME MID-SHOW, I knew this was going to be good. I was in a groove—we were in a groove—and I could feel the crowd was digging it, too. We had just started "Martyr" when it happened. As illogical as it sounds, my first thought when I saw the smoke was, *We did this. Our smoldering intensity of righteous music created this.* It was only after the alarm went off and the fire trucks came that "grease fire" truly registered.

"FUCKING UNREAL," Martin keeps saying. He's unsteady on his feet from the weight of his snare drum. I only have to carry my bass, and that's plenty. I'm actually surprised this hasn't happened sooner. Their burgers always give me heartburn.

We are mixed in with the other displaced patrons milling about outside the bar. There's a touch of excitement in the air. The same feeling as when class would get called early for a fire drill.

Most of us are standing just across the street. It was only a small fire, but there's a fire truck and police car anyhow. I don't see any actual smoke, but the air still smells of sulfur.

"Do you think it's safe to get the rest of our equipment?" Martin asks.

"No clue," I say in response. I feel tired. I look around. Jonesy and AJ are talking to a group of girls.

"Singers and guitar players get all the glory," Martin laments. I see his eyes move to a place just behind me. "Looks like you still have a fan."

I feel her slide up next to me. Her long red hair is up in a ponytail and I can smell the mix of sweat and perfume on her skin.

"Tony told us to take off for the night; he asked us to come back in the morning to help clean for double pay," Jolene says, looking right at me and ignoring Martin.

"Sounds good," I say. I'm stalling.

Martin is still standing there, witness to this. He gives me a wide grin. I look at him pointedly and he retreats.

"All right, I'm off like a prom dress," Martin says, leaving in search of chicks who dig drummers.

Jolene cocks her head to the side. "Walk me home," she says.

"I might be heading to another bar with the guys to commiserate…"

Jolene stands on her tiptoes and whispers in my ear. "Walk me home, Jeremy."

She puts her hand in mine. I take it.

We begin moving away from the bar, away from the crowds. In that moment, I convince myself we are moving forward.

I AM STANDING IN THE DOORWAY of Jolene's apartment. She busies herself with putting her keys in a basket and filling a bowl with cat food for a cat that has yet to emerge.

I survey the apartment I've spent hours picturing. A blue fabric thing hangs on the wall over a worn beige couch. Small, framed black-and-white photos of flowers and friends and foggy bar scenes occupy the remaining walls of the living room.

"Did you take these?" I ask.

"My ex," she says.

It's only for a minute, but I feel her presence. Rox is with me. I look to Jolene to see if she feels it too.

"I was hoping we'd end up here tonight," Jolene says. And she smiles.

It's a smile of hope. It's a smile I recognize from so long ago.

My ex, I think.

ROX NEVER CAME HOME LAST NIGHT and I have yet to sleep. When she finally emerges, it's eight a.m. She's still in her work uniform and there are tears in her eyes. My own eyes begin to swell.

"Don't even talk to me, don't even fucking try to talk to me—I just came for some clothes and then I'm fucking out of here."

I go up to her and gently grab her shoulders. I'm so tired, so tired of fighting, but not too tired to fight for her.

"Rox," I say, uncertainly. "What's going on?"

"I saw you," she says, shaking. "We were slow and Aaron let me off early. I went down there to see you and I…saw her."

For a moment, my mind shifts to Jolene. After I told her that I couldn't do this, that I was sorry I got her mixed up in all this, she looked up at me with a sad smile. 'Whatever' was all she said.

"I was a fucking asshole, Rox," I say. "I held her hand and I walked her home. But nothing else happened, I swear to Christ nothing happened." She looks at me. I can see she believes me, but it doesn't matter.

"You were going to sleep with her," she says, quieter than I've heard Rox speak in a long time.

"I was going to sleep with her," I say. "But I didn't. I couldn't."

Rox is silent.

"I kissed Ramón," she says.

"Last night? You fucking kissed that punk bagger last night?"

"No, it was at a work thing about a month ago. Anyhow, what's the difference…" she says. Her voice is weary.

"Where were you last night, Rox?"

She doesn't answer.

"Jeremy, we can't do this anymore." She walks over to her dresser, and takes out a stack of shirts to start packing, but then pauses, a shirt in mid-air. It drops. Rox begins to cry. I come up behind her, put my arms around her waist and kiss her neck.

"Lie down with me," I say.

"No," she says. She is breaking my heart. Or maybe I am breaking hers.

A little light looks through our bedroom window. I grab her hand and lead her to the bed. As soon as we hit the sheets, we are one. We are kissing, kissing and reaching for each other with abandon. She's under me, and I'm in her. And we're holding each other tighter than I would have thought possible. When it's over, she is lying down beside me, back facing front. Spoon in spoon. I hear a phone ringing in the distance. We stay entwined, neither of us speaking. Then, Rox does.

"This doesn't change anything," she says softly, not turning around. "We can't just fuck our way all better." There's silence again. I am hoping we can.

"Hey." Rox's voice is now a whisper. "Tell me about your dream." I know her eyes are closed.

I run my fingers through her short spiky hair. Hairspray and gel are absent. There's a softness I haven't felt in a long time.

I will tell her, I think. *And I will ask about hers. I will tell her all the dreams I can remember. I will breathe them into her until the moment her eyes blink open.*

WAKE ME UP WHEN IT'S GREEN
NICOLE MONTAVLO
COLUMBIA COLLEGE

THIS MAN IS GETTING WASTED ON THE METRA. He has a giant suitcase with a straw hat on top of it. I'm giving him dirty looks like I've got the upper hand, but I'm bluffing; I'm scared of him. I'm so glad this man is not my father.

This man is getting wasted on the red line. He is wearing baggy jeans and a big brown jacket. I politely laugh at his off-color joke like I think it's funny—but I don't; I'm scared of him. I'm so glad this man is not my father.

I let go of the Tooth Fairy and Santa long ago, but I carry one delusion into adulthood with me: My father is perfect and invincible.

The first time I saw Daddy enjoy a drink despite Mama's eye-rolling was when I was seven and I was the flower girl at my cousin Chickie's wedding. My dad and my grandmother, who everyone calls "Ma," enjoyed sangria or orange juice cocktails or something sweet like that while my grandfather, who everyone calls "Pa," and my mom drank water and shook their heads. We're Pentacostal Christians, so

73

even light drinking is considered sinful. Mama is a Republican from Kentucky and Daddy is a Mexican ex-Catholic-turned-Pentacostal liberal and an artist. Two clichés in one: high school sweethearts and opposites that attracted. It's amazing my parents are still married. That night Daddy taught me how to dance to Ranchero music and began teaching me the difference between getting drunk and enjoying a drink.

Daddy doesn't drink and drive. His problem is much more serious than that. Drinkers can go to rehab, but his disease is incurable. He sleeps and drives. He has sleep apnea. Those fuzzy memories I hold of my dad's driving days revolve around a rusty, small brown truck. When it was just him and I in his truck together, he would take naps at red lights and he would say, "Wake me up when it's green." And I took that job very seriously. I was so proud to say "it's green."

On the Metra, on our way downtown, my first week of college, my dad sleeps while I look out the window. The sound of a snore and then silence and then finally another snore is both alarming and comforting. As a child, I had trouble sleeping alone. My dad would lay next to me until I fell asleep and with every snore, silence, snore, my heart would drop from fear and then beat even again. Death has followed him closely since he was a teenager. New pastor after new pastor at our church learned that his naps during sermons were unavoidable and my family has learned to just laugh when he falls asleep standing up. Still, he reminds us, *a sleeping tiger is no less dangerous.*

THIS WOMAN IS STARING AT EVERYONE and at no one on the Metra. She is wearing a trendy modest top with sparkles on it or something like that. What I presume to be her granddaughter is sleeping next to her. I pretend like I don't see the sadness in her eyes—but I do; she looks bored, scared, and stuck, or just completely out of place. She's blond and wearing just enough makeup in just the right spots. Like my mother, this woman is much too classy for the train, which is both an admirable quality and a flaw. This woman is my mother.

This woman, numerous times, is smiling and warm towards me in a Western-style restaurant in China. I only know that she works in this restaurant, or maybe owns it, but she smiles genuinely and I believe, somehow I know, that she is internally beautiful, strong, and caring. I only barely speak Mandarin, so I mostly just smile and then leave with my food—but I appreciate her kindness more than she will ever know; I love her. This woman is my Chinese mother.

TRYING TO CLEAR THE FOG from my childhood memories of third, fourth, and fifth grade, I don't remember much of the sadness; I can only blow the dust off of bits and pieces. I don't remember Mama's sadness during the low point of my parents' marriage, although I probably should because she claims that's when her frown lines became permanent. Although my parents toughed it out and stayed together, the healing process may be forever ongoing. And I only vaguely remember her frowning when my sister would get herself into trouble with a drug addict boyfriend/abusive husband. Mostly I remember Mama's boredom, unhappiness, and disapproval because I have always taken responsibility for it, because something in my nature is always-sensing, always-feeling, and always-guilty the same way something in her nature is.

My mom has to dye her hair now because it is graying but is a natural blond with giant blue eyes and a small frame. The thought is weird for me, but I imagine my parents were the hottest couple at their high school—even with their high school being rich, suburban, and mostly white with graduating classes of a thousand. My mom has never smoked, drank, or even spoken a curse word in her entire life, and my dad absolutely adores that about her. Her wholesome being is something to be admired, as is her magnetic, inherent charm and her strength. She may seem unsatisfied a lot of the time, but life has given her reason to be unsatisfied—she is strong, always relying on God and trusting Him in a way I look up to, but I wish she could be strong for herself too and not just for us.

MY DAD IS A SHORT but muscular Mexican man. By IQ and test scores, he is a certified genius. My mom is smart, too, but she doesn't know it. Starting college on a full-ride scholarship studying physics and history, he dropped out because he got bored. My dad and I bond through political conversations and talks about different pop-culture happenings and literature. We love to banter. He cuts the sleeves off all his shirts, showing his four tattoos. The most notable are a pearl that has my mom's name under it on his arm, and a tiger on his arm that has lettering underneath that reads "a sleeping tiger is no less dangerous," the slogan he used for every political campaign he ran for different positions in the UAW local 588. He also has a chili pepper with a spear through it on his neck and lettering underneath that reads *el amor duele*, or "love hurts." We got our chili pepper tattoos at the same time (although mine is just a skinny pepper on my thigh), a few months after my 18th birthday, a few years after my sisters got theirs and about a year before my brother got his. Like their difference in opinions on social drinking, my mom also disapproves of tattoos.

My mom often hands my dad the phone when I call because she knows I will be more calm talking to him than I will be talking to her, something I try to keep from being true but usually is. He was never touchy-feely, never an arm-around-you or baby-you're-beautiful dad. His compliments were always clever and hidden which makes them all the more touching; his love language is jokes and wit. Before I left to study abroad, my dad hugged me and kissed me on the cheek, reminding me of the very few other times he had done so before, such as when a boy broke my heart in high school or before I left for summer camp every year. These moments are few and significant, but they are not the most important. While he has never been very physically affectionate with his children, he has always made me feel like he could get me out of any bad situation, could solve any problem I had. I wish Mama had the faith in Daddy that I do. Daddy always works everything out; Daddy never complains; Daddy makes life a party. He has given Mama his whole life.

MAMA HAS GIVEN US, her children, her whole life. I don't blame her for living her life this way—I only feel guilty and wish she had let herself blossom instead of babying me—but I respect and appreciate her. This is the part where I emphatically express my guilt for not being a better daughter, for criticizing her, and emphatically express my wish for her to just finally be happy. All she ever wanted was my happiness and all I ever wanted was hers, but here we are.

MAMA. WANTING. ALWAYS WANTING. Never satisfied. Mama usually lives in the past. I want to make her smile. I want her to be self-actualized. She really tries to be content, but I believe she's trapped in darkness in a chemical-imbalance or spiritual-warfare way. She is tormented by her own mind. This has its pros and cons, as my mom's very real deep spiritual infiltration is seen through her ability to discern a person's character immediately after meeting them, a gift I've seen proven real again and again.

The innocent flirty-ness she perfected in her youth never left her. My boyfriends are always charmed by her. She is wild and beautiful. But she is trapped by her own mind.

I want to be Daddy and I am, but I am also Mama. I often feel the darkness my mom feels, that sadness that hits like a cold, salty wave unexpectedly, that unsatisfaction, that desire to criticize, that feeling of having no control over my facial expression or my body movements or even my words in moments of extreme attack. Once we get past our initial nonsensical fighting, my mom and I have the most deep, spiritual, emotional, overall beautiful conversations—but we have to fight past the storm our mini dark clouds form when we come together.

THE MAN I HAVE FALLEN IN LOVE WITH is just like my dad, with the same eccentricities and manliness. Both with a love for gift-shop knickknacks, music, art, pop culture, knives, cooking; each with an an intense curiosity about life, desire to learn, go-with-the-flow flexibility, and ability to seem like there is no obscure fact that they do not know. Neither taller than 5'6", they both somehow manage to give off a feeling of ultimate machismo, sometimes seen most clearly though their ability to claim completely unmanly things as manly, such as my dad's obsession with jewelry or Erik's obsession with his own hair. I always thought, hoped, I'd end up with someone tall, yet somehow this man still feels tall to me.

Erik, however, is physically much different than my dad, which I am thankful for. He has olive (not brown) skin, big (not small) brown eyes, a tiny (not large) nose, and big (not small) lips. The only physical similarity would be their full heads of curly, black hair.

More of their good similarities include: Their artistic spirits; the way they tell stories in an organized way with the audience fully in mind; their desire to buy me a dress rather than just outright say "I love you;" their forgetfulness and tardiness; their never-ending hidden tricks that save us just in time; my feeling that I will always be loved and taken care of by each of them; my feeling that my humor and talents and intellect are being recognized by them in a way they are not by anyone else.

They do also share some dark similarities. Erik is my dad if my dad had been raised without liberal, loving parents from Brownsville, Texas. He is also my dad post-midlife crisis, crashing a bit earlier but rising back up just as well. If my dad had made the choice Erik did, which he easily could have, Erik and I wouldn't be together. It was a bad mistake, but it all worked out for the best. Erik left his first wife; he was a different person, an artist suppressed and a man not yet quite mature or confident enough, when he was with her. My dad was a different person at the start of my parents' marriage than he is now. I have seen God radically change someone so I believe Erik is also radically changed, although the situations and results are different. My mom and dad started over and made it work—not through my mom forcing my dad to change but through a personal transformation on his part—but they have always been right for each other. Erik and his first wife were never right for each other, a sentiment spoken in different words by many people before I was old enough to fully understand a thought so complex. He is starting over with me and, in a way, I am starting over with him. The crash has already happened. The change has already been made. I am unafraid. This was not something forced on him, this was a personal transformation. People can't change people; God changes people and only when they choose to let Him.

But still, for Erik, there are residual effects that are deeper than a marital split. Still affected by a single mother who had five different husbands and then further suppressed by his business-woman first wife, he has been silent and numb for far too long. A Gemini with a troubled past, he often recounts stories of the "bad boy" lifestyle he lived as a teenager. Naturally outgoing, musically talented, and intellectual, his bad marriage is more a symptom than the cause of his many years of unhappiness. I don't believe I've fixed him; I believe he finally made the choice to fix himself and I helped. Erik, unlike my father, has been extremely damaged and buries his emotions. When our love first began to sprout and bud, during our long text conversations on my ride home from work each night on the Metra, all of his walls came down in a way they never have before—they came down in a way they never did with her. Although our connection is deep, we often find ourselves sitting in his car fighting because he won't tell me how he really feels, because he can't express his emotions, because I want to be there for him and he won't let me, because he forgets who I am. I am the one girl who made him feel safe to open up, the one girl he truly let in—but he forgets. The word "girlfriend" carries a different kind of weight than "exciting new friend I'm falling in love with," and I want him to always remember that behind the heavy word is the exhilarating but safe phrase.

WHEN I CAME BACK from my study abroad in China, before Erik and I were officially an item, after the beginning stages of the divorce and the rumors and the family hurt, when all the pieces finally fell into place, Erik gave me a white lace dress. I had tried on the dress and sent him a picture months earlier.

The first time I wore the dress was the New Year's Eve that our relationship began. It was crisp white, tight on the top but flowing on the bottom, about mid-thigh length, and paired with winter-purple tights. When he saw me, he gave me that stock "wow" look you can morph onto any man's face to create the perfect picture of a man loving a woman, a look I've gotten many times from many men that I've later made cry. The only difference about the look this time was that I finally appreciated it. I thought it was the first of many.

I DUMPED A BOY AT HOMECOMING, in a strapless periwinkle dress with black over-lay, with cat-style eyeliner and dark lipstick, dancing with my comforting female friends. I dumped a boy at Homecoming then tried to disappear into his car's backseat while he drove me home with tears in his eyes. I was told once by a different boy that he had always regarded me as a spoiled brat who always got what she wanted. Being this girl is my biggest regret. This will be my last relationship and this one will be right. I am different now and this is like nothing I have ever experienced before.

THE SECOND TIME I WORE THE DRESS, it was summer and we were going to church. I received a small, sweet smile. He ran his hand over my freshly shaved legs while he drove.

I cheated on every boyfriend I ever had—before Erik.

I CHEATED ON HOMECOMING-BOY with my first love and then I cheated on who I later regarded as my true first love with my actual first love and then the chain of the story is so much longer than that. Flirtatious and free, a tease by most definitions, I always got bored so I always broke hearts. I had an innocence and naivety that got me into trouble, but I was also selfish. This time, I will not get bored. I have always been accepting and nurturing, but had so much trouble fully connecting with people. Usually a great listener but often a horrible talker. My view of relationships, friend and romantic alike, was strange and untraditional and based on some kind of formula I had made up. I was always trying to find friends and boyfriends alike who I could actually connect with, could actually open up to, people with whom I felt something I couldn't explain with a single, simple phrase. I now understand that I didn't then understand the reality of living that way, didn't understand how detrimental it was. I have found my last, most real, and only permanent magnetic, not-easily-explainable connection.

THE THIRD AND FOURTH AND FIFTH TIMES I wore the dress, I had to prompt a reaction. The reactions got less and less enthusiastic, unmemorable reactions burned into my memory. The dress went from crisp white to a dingy almost-yellow and now houses one or two coffee stains. The dress has stopped feeling fitted and the shortness has become uncomfortable.

It's not my fault, not this time, finally it is not my fault. But it's not his fault, either. Criticizing is so easy, talking of ideal love is so easy, but reality and living out your principles are not. At the end of the Era of the White Dress, the loss of a job had drained Erik, and reality had taken our fantastical relationship through more than it could stand up straight under. I wonder if the loss of a driver's license has drained my dad.

Relationships take work. Both Erik and I have proved ourselves quitters and hiders many times in other relationships. My family often warns me that he may leave me one day. Likewise, they are always telling stories about my past boyfriends to him. These are knives that dig deep right into our chests. But those people, the people we used to be, are not the people we are today—we have to remember that. No more quitting and no more hiding. God can radically change people.

A NEW DRESS IS BOUGHT FOR ME. We go shopping together and Erik buys me a black and white floral dress for his sister's wedding. The wedding is mostly awkward, but I chase his six-year-old daughter around in this new tight, short, flowing dress and heels and I feel his secret, loving glances on me all day. A few times, when we have seconds alone, he looks me over obviously and says, "mmm, you look so good" with that signature smile on his face.

This is the second wedding we've attended together. The first was his cousin's wedding where I drank wine with his mom, wine bought for us upon her request by her latest husband. Erik knows I'm kind of getting drunk even though I'm not sure if she does and he laughs at me half with adoration and half with worry. He often jokingly calls me a "lush" or a "whino" or even an "alcoholic," partially because he knows that will push my buttons, because he knows I am struggling to find my place between abstaining from alcohol and party girl, because he knows it's far from the truth, and partially because he is always worrying about me even when he has no reason to.

MY DAD BUYS O'DOUL'S non-alcoholic beer from Mariano's because he likes the taste, a bottle of sake at a sushi restaurant to make the non-Christians at the table more comfortable, and a glass of sangria when it comes in a keepsake cup. Mama tells us she's never taken a drink for fear of enjoying it too much, says none of us would exist if she had picked up drinking as a hobby in the 18th year of her life (her last year of being unmarried). Erik only drinks the darkest of ales and White Russians. I exchanged the recommended citrus beer for a black-colored, thick Robert the Bruce on my 21st birthday at the expensive locally-brewed-beer downtown bar. Mama would be crying if she knew her baby daughter spent her 21st birthday in a bar. Mama believes that Christians don't drink and Christian women definitely don't drink.

Erik has helped me "find my place." Whether he initially realized it or not, he took on a lot when he took me on. He pursued me relentlessly (as men like to do to women), took on his challenge at full speed, never for a minute doubted that we were each other's closest resemblance to what a soulmate would be if we believe in the concept. I was hesitant at first, wondering if he was only attracted to the idea of me, warning him I was less glamorous than he thought, but we got past his initial attraction to the idealized version of me and he proved he was genuine. Sometimes, Erik and I drink Fancy Pants wine at his apartment or go to bars and drink 3 Floyd's and enjoy being "young" and in love.

But sometimes, he doesn't want to drink wine with me, and that is when I know he is retreating to his familiar cave of hiding again, when we are less close, when we are, essentially, having less fun together, not because of the alcohol itself but because of my asking and his saying no, because of what this state represents. Life with the man who bought me the white dress will forever be a battle. We will forever be fighting for hope and affection.

WITH EVERY STEP FORWARD, we are pulled back. I became his hiding place once. I want to be his hiding place forever. I will forever be pulling his chest apart so that I can crawl inside for a few hours at a time, weeks if I'm lucky. Then his body will spit me out again and the process will restart.

But the battle is two-fold. Sometimes I am the one being loudly silent in his car while he is the one fighting (or not fighting) for communication. I will forever be locking myself in the darkness of my mind, in my fears and doubts and negativities that I constantly fight, and he will have to choose whether to reciprocally retreat or fight for me the way I often fight for him.

Laying in his bed, holding each other on a summer Sunday afternoon, I start to feel sad suddenly and for what seems like no reason at all. I can't tell if he can tell, but then he pulls me closer and says, "You know what I like? I like that you're my best friend." The sad tears that were going to fall before turn to happy. We will never be the version of Mama and Daddy that is the unhappy criticizing woman and the beat-down never-good-enough man. We will be the version that is the undying love team.

METACOGNITION
MATTHEW MORLEY

Having woken up early to an echo
balancing on the edge of my mind—
an empty glass tipping, tempted to jump
to the floor below—I wonder if I will
remember this cool spring air of 4AM
or the weakened roars of elevated trains
on tracks the next street over, of taxis without
purpose gliding over wet concrete.

Will I remember this softened
paralysis of sleep or the yellow-grey
pre-Sun sky behind the silhouetted scene?
And looking back, ages and ages hence,
I might be tempted to liken the color
of this sky to a gentle gold, a dust cloud
full from implications: a million kilowatts
burning from a city below.

But for now, there is still so much to contemplate:
the leaky bedroom door, the extra, black comforter
that I will retrieve soon, and above everything this year,
the worst thing that could happen, which happened here.

QUIET DEATHS
AUSTIN ESKEBERG
COLUMBIA COLLEGE

I WAS SEVEN THE FIRST TIME I SAW DEATH. I'd seen it before, on television, in movies. I was aware of it, as a thing waiting somewhere in the wings. I knew about it in the way a child knows that they're seeing something they aren't old enough to process. It was an abstract concept, similar to growing up, getting married or falling in love with a girl. You knew these things happened, but you didn't have the ability to properly contextualize them, to have them make sense to you. I think the only way to understand death, to truly get what it is about, is to see it yourself. Small deaths, big deaths. It's all the same, only the circumstances change. One second you're here, living, breathing; the next? Well, the dead tell no tales.

I was standing on a street corner when it happened, downtown Chicago, on the Mile. I don't remember why. I don't think it really even matters. Coming back from dinner, running errands, I don't know. My mom was standing next to me. She'd insisted that I hold her hand while we crossed the street, like that would've protected me if a car decided not to stop. But at seven it was enough. At that age, your parents are invincible. Until they're not. There's a certain irony to that.

It was a warm, vaguely summerish day. I remember that much. Shorts, t-shirt, sandals-wearing weather. Even though it was edging towards nightfall, clouds were hanging in the sky, dark, swollen and pregnant with rain. You could see them, just out of reach, watching, waiting to drop their precious cargo. Shadows stretched, splaying out over everything. We were standing at the corner of this street, waiting for the light to change, cars streaming by so close that their slipstreams whipped my shirt left and right, aching to go with them. My mom's hand, gigantic to me then, clasped my hand tightly; warm and slimy with sweat, like how I thought a lizard would feel. I wanted her to let go.

A woman was standing next to us. She was wearing this green tank top, the color of pond scum, or seaweed. She'd pulled a visor over her eyes, obscuring them. It was the same color of green as the shirt. Her chin jutted outwards in an extreme underbite, which coupled with the visor made her look vaguely gator-like. I couldn't help but stare. She glared when she noticed.

The light changed, and I was being pulled along by my mother into the crosswalk. The timer said twenty seconds, counting down. On the opposite side of the street there was this kid, probably sixteen or so, the same age I am now, riding a skateboard. Heading towards home, maybe. I don't even know why I refer to him as a kid—he was almost a decade older than me. He was wearing a t-shirt printed with some graphic that I couldn't read, along with a pair of baggy jeans. He had headphones on, long blonde hair streaming behind him like motion lines in the old comic books I'd found in the attic one endless summer day.

My mother and I were halfway through the crosswalk when

the kid jumped, pushing off from the curb, flying through the air. Seven-year-old me was entranced, in awe of the way he seemed to be suspended by nothing, arms parallel with the ground, knees bent. I watched the board, wheels spinning in empty air, over and over again. He landed. His weight distribution must have been off, or maybe he didn't get the traction he needed, I don't know. It could have been any combination of disparate elements. The board flew out from under him and he fell backwards, the back of his head slamming hard, too hard, against the edge of the curb.

I hear the sound sometimes he made when I least expect it, when my mind is on other things. The meaty thump, flesh against concrete, the quick gasp of air as it is exhaled, and it jerks me backwards to this moment, a fish on a line.

Thump. That's all it took, one little thump. *Thump* went his head, and his body went slack. *Thump*, the skateboard came skittering off the ground, scratching its way over to me. It hit my shoe as it rolled to a stop. *Thump*, my mother let go of my hand, both of hers shooting upwards over her mouth.

The kid—I never found out his name—looked like he was asleep. I guess I tried to tell myself that, to avoid having to deal with something I didn't have a frame of reference for, but it was a cheap lie, small and flimsy like most are. It didn't cover the whole of what I was seeing.

The gator woman pushed past us, running over to the kid. I remember looking up at the timer on the streetlight, sure we were about to get hit by a car at any second. A giant ten blinked back at me. The gator woman had knelt down when I looked back; she was bent over him, doing what I realize now was mouth-to-mouth resuscitation. She came up for air, but it looked like she was eating him, visor and chin wide open, teeth flashing, gleaming, leaning back down for another bite. The timer counted down further. He wasn't moving. Cars were honking, headlights bright, pronouncing the time of death. We were out of time.

My mother's hand, a lizard's no longer, grabbed me and pulled me in the opposite direction. I watched the scene, crowd gathering, getting larger and larger, people standing and staring, cars honking, until we turned a corner, whisking the scene out of my view. Raindrops started to fall in ones and twos, then in numbers too high to count. In the distance I heard sirens gathering, loud and shrill, and there was the feeling of something irretrievable slipping away.

ON THE HUNT
CHARLIE HARMON
COLUMBIA COLLEGE

PETEY HADN'T EVEN WANTED to go out that night, but Chad had been relentless. He needed a "wingman," he'd said; he couldn't go out on the hunt by himself, he'd said. "On the hunt"—like they were apex predators, the top of the food chain, and not a couple of art school dropouts who were going to find some passed-out drunk or helpless old lady to roll so they could score some Oxy, maybe some Adderall. The physical encounters, the shit with the potential to get violent, that all made Petey very uncomfortable. Cashing bad checks, maybe a little panhandling, that was more his speed, but Chad had made it very clear that if Petey didn't back him up, he wouldn't be sharing in any of the spoils of "the hunt," and that had clinched it.

So here they sat on the red line in the middle of the night, waiting for an opportunity to present itself. They were seated across from each other in the middle of the car, Petey in jeans and a faux-vintage Aquaman t-shirt, too small and skinny to present much of a threat to anybody. Chad was bigger, burlier, wearing a ratty leather jacket and steel-toe boots; he didn't look so much like a guy who might try to rob you as a guy who might start some shit for no reason whatsoever. It didn't help that he was fidgeting, bopping his head and slapping out an arrhythmic beat on his thighs, inspecting everyone who entered the car a little too intently.

They'd been on the train for two hours when it happened. There was an abrupt mass egress at Cermak-Chinatown and when the doors slid closed, they found themselves alone in the car with a man who had to be at least sixty-five or seventy. He was tall and thin, almost emaciated, and the kind of pale a person gets from working a night shift his entire life. He was wearing a nondescript navy suit with a matching porkpie hat and had a worn-looking, powder blue bowling bag resting on his lap, his fingers looped loosely through the handle. He didn't even seem to notice Petey or Chad.

"Sox-35th is next," said the canned voice through the train's speakers.

Chad's hands, which hadn't stopped moving since he'd sat down, came to a rest on his knees. He waggled his eyebrows at Petey and jerked his head at the old guy a few times. Petey felt cold pinpricks of sweat breaking out across his scalp. His stomach churned. He hated this shit, just hated it. *Are you sure?* he mouthed at Chad, his hands still in his pockets. Chad responded by standing and glaring down at Petey until he followed suit. Chad reached into one of his jacket pockets and shoved something into Petey's right hand, something too dense and cold to be anything but a gun. Petey held it in both palms and stared at it, not wanting to take possession. It was dark and compact, with a short barrel and a wooden grip. *A revolver*, Petey thought, the kind of gun that a thug would carry in a Raymond Chandler novel.

"Let me do the talking," Chad said in a low voice, eyes on the old guy, his big mitt still wrapped around the hand holding the gun. "Just stand behind me and make sure he can see that you have it. I don't even want you to point it at him, not unless he tries to give us trouble."

Petey's eyes were burning and he blinked furiously, mortified by the idea of crying in front of Chad. "Where did you get this?" His voice was so high it was almost a squeak.

"My brother gave it to me the last time I was in Durham," Chad said, still watching the man. He took a quick glance at Petey and snorted. "Jesus Christ, suck it up—it's just to scare him." When Petey didn't respond, Chad's hand tightened around his. "Hey, Petey—you with me? I need you backing me up here, man."

The old man was still staring straight ahead, seemingly oblivious, and Petey took a long, shaky breath and nodded. Chad clapped his hands on Petey's shoulders once, then walked toward the old guy, arms swinging convivially, like he was just heading over to say hi. Petey followed, favoring his right side, though the gun couldn't have weighed much more than a pound.

"Hey, mister!" Chad called, almost singsong, as he came to a stop in front of the man. "My friend and I are gonna need you to hand over your money and any other valuables you might be carrying." Petey bent his arm at the elbow and flared his gun hand out to the side a bit, trying to make sure its presence was apparent.

For a moment nothing happened, and Petey felt an odd twinge of guilt as he wondered if the reason the man had been ignoring them was because he was deaf, but then the man looked up at Chad. His eyebrows drew together, his jaw set, and his head tilted slightly to the side. The change in the man's affect was so dramatic that Petey found himself taking an involuntary step back. "Or what?" the man asked in a high, soft voice. "You'll hurt me?" Goddamn if the creepy old shit didn't look like he was trying not to laugh.

"That's right," Chad said, though he seemed suddenly unsure. He glanced back at Petey, as if to make sure he was still there with the gun. "We'll fuck you up."

The man drummed his fingers on the bowling bag, never breaking eye contact with Chad. He reached his right hand into an inside jacket pocket, keeping the left curled tightly around the bag's handle, and pulled out a plain, brown wallet that looked to be thick with cash and credit cards. He tossed it up in the air, forcing Chad to fumble to catch it. "Take it," he said in that high, breathy voice. "And consider yourselves lucky I'm in the middle of something."

Chad, whether he was emboldened by the fat wallet, which had to have at least a few thousand in cash in it, or just angry at how quickly he'd lost control of the situation, stared at the man for a few seconds. "No. No!" He stuffed the wallet into his jacket and said, "I want the bag." The man's expression shifted from amusement to mild annoyance, but he didn't otherwise respond. "I want the bag," Chad said again. "Gimme the *fucking* bag!" He reached for the handle, but the man's free hand clamped around his wrist. They held like that for a second, seemingly stalemated, and then the man twisted Chad's arm and he was suddenly on his knees, yelping in surprise and pain. Petey just watched, dumbfounded, until Chad shrieked, "The gun, Petey, use the gun, Petey, use the *fucking gun*, Petey!"

Petey was almost startled to find himself pointing it at the old guy, his stance wide, supporting his gun hand with the other like he'd seen in the movies. Of course, he was shaking so much he wasn't sure he could hit the man even from three feet away. "Luh-let him go," he said, his teeth chattering. The man just sneered at him and took his left hand off of the bag, reaching into the other side of his jacket. Almost without thought, Petey pulled the trigger. There was more resistance than he would have expected, but he gritted his teeth, forced it back, and almost fainted when the hammer fell with nothing more than a loud *CLICK*.

"Ha," said the old guy, pulling something small and dark from his pocket, revealing it, with a practiced flick of the wrist, to be a straight razor.

Still operating entirely on instinct, Petey hopped forward awkwardly and clubbed the revolver against the side of the man's face, connecting solidly enough to knock the hat from his head. The man looked more surprised than hurt, though blood flowed freely from a wide gash over his cheekbone and he was dazed enough to let go of Chad's wrist. The man seemed to be finding his focus pretty quickly, so Petey hit him again, a big looping roundhouse blow that he felt all the way up to his shoulder. "What..." the old guy said. "What are you..." and Petey hit him one more time, swinging his arm like a hammer and bringing the butt of the gun down on the crown of the man's head with a *THUNK* so loud that Petey couldn't help wincing. The man said, "I...I..." but then his eyes rolled back and he slumped to the side, the shift in position dumping the bowling bag onto the floor.

Chad was still down, though he'd scooted a few feet away. He tried to push himself off the ground, but the twisted arm gave out as soon as he put weight on it. Petey tucked the pistol into his pants and, after some heaving and struggling, managed to hoist Chad to his feet. Before either of them had time to say anything, the train began to slow and the canned voice announced, "This is Sox-35th."

Chad, waxy and pale under the harsh fluorescent lights, said, "We have to get out of here right now." He stumbled to one of the sets of doors. In a flash of inspiration, Petey grabbed the porkpie hat off the floor and arranged it on the old man's head, covering as much of his face as he could. There were also bright, wet patches of blood collecting on the man's white shirt, and Petey used the suit coat's lapels to pull it tighter around him. "Petey!" Chad said as the doors slid open, his voice higher than Petey had ever heard it, almost whiny. "Come *on!*" Petey moved to follow him, then stopped. He scooped the powder blue bowling bag up off the floor and hurried out into the cool, dry night.

There were a few people on the platform, but none of them paid Chad or Petey any mind, not that late. Chad walked briskly toward the station's northern entrance, shoulders hunched, hands jammed in his pockets, looking like nothing so much as a man who'd just committed a serious crime and hoped no one will notice him. Petey struggled to keep up, and they were almost to the street before he realized the butt of the gun was still sticking out of his pants and pulled his t-shirt over it. When they stepped out onto 33rd, Chad said, in a loud, hoarse whisper, "We should split up for a while."

Petey didn't like the idea, didn't want to be alone, but he didn't have the energy to argue. He felt like he could sleep for a week. He did, however, have the presence of mind to say, "What about the Oxy?"

Chad looked over both shoulders before saying, "I told Dave I was coming by tonight." Dave was a UIC student who worked part-time as a pharmacy tech and seemed to have access to an unlimited number of pills.

"Great," Petey said. "So why don't we both go?"

"If the old fart comes to and calls the cops, they're going to be looking for two of us," Chad said. Petey's mind flashed to the old man's lack of fear, to his aggression, to that goddamned straight razor, and the idea that he would call the police seemed unlikely at best. "You go back to the apartment," Chad said. "I'll hit Dave's and be home by dawn." Petey was still skeptical, and Chad rolled his eyes and pulled out the man's wallet. "Here," he said, pulling out three crisp, smooth hundreds. "Get some cigarettes and booze to tide you over 'til I get back. Oh, and..." He stepped in close like he wanted a hug, looked up and down the street one more time, and fished the revolver out of Petey's waistband, dropping it back in the pocket it had come from. "You did good, Petey," he said, before turning to walk eastward.

It took Petey almost an hour to find an all-night convenience store that'd take a hundred, and another hour to find a cab and make the trip back to their place in Uptown. It was a two-bedroom apartment in a giant, condemned building filled with art school dropouts and idealistic types, all of whom were squatting. By the time he'd made it inside, he felt the vague, unpleasant itch at the tips of his fingers and the backs of his eyes, the general sense of unease that was his brain's way of telling him that, okay, no kidding, it'd really like some drugs now, please.

He'd gone through the medicine cabinet in the bathroom and all of the drawers in the kitchen before it occurred to him that he'd never opened the old man's bowling bag. It certainly felt like it had a bowling ball in it, but you never knew—maybe it was ten pounds of Vicodin and a ham-and-cheese croissant. He grabbed the bag from where he'd left it by the front door and put it on the scuffed, dirty coffee table in front of the TV. As he opened the zipper, an unpleasant scent wafted out, something he couldn't identify: sour milk and unwashed feet and something metallic. He spread the bag open and before his brain could process what he was seeing, he realized he was looking at a severed human head.

He stared for a moment, still holding the edges of the bag. It was a bald, fat, white guy with a dark mustache. The eyes were open but they looked strange, until Petey realized that they'd been cut out. Petey wasn't an expert, but the head seemed like it was starting to spoil, and there was slimy muck pooling in the bottom of the bag.

It was the smell that brought him back to reality: what wafted out of the bag when he was opening it, but times a hundred. It hung thick in the air and made him gag. He closed his eyes, held his breath, zipped the bag shut, and carried it to the bathtub, closing the bathroom door behind him on his way out.

He drank quite a bit from the exorbitantly overpriced bottle of bourbon he'd bought at the convenience store, which helped a little, but what really helped was the Xanax he found in an unlabeled pill bottle rattling around one of his desk drawers. When his heart wasn't hammering quite so enthusiastically and he'd gotten his breathing under control, he dialed Chad's cell and was dumped straight to voicemail.

"I don't know where you are, man," he said, "but you need to get home *right fucking now*. The bag we took from that guy on the El has a head in it, and I am *not* dealing with a *human fucking head* on my own." After a long, breathless pause, he added, "This is Petey," and hung up.

He sat there, in his desk chair, and drank bourbon straight from the bottle until he could barely remember his own name, let alone think about what was decomposing in the bathtub, and then sprawled across his bed and sunk into a deep, fevered sleep.

He dreamed of Chad in a khaki suit and a pith helmet, stalking the old man from the train down a succession of dark city streets. At some point, the old man noticed Chad behind him and began to run, and Chad cried, "Ha-*ha*! Chemical intoxicants are nothing compared to the thrill—of the *chase*!" and set off after him. The old man ducked down an alley, but when Chad went in after him it was a dead end, the man nowhere to be found. He turned to discover the man standing behind him, a savage grin on his long, pale face.

"Beware of wolves in sheep's clothing," the man said, and slashed across Chad's throat with a straight razor, cutting so deep that Chad's head flopped back on his neck like a Pez dispenser.

That was when Petey woke up, still face-down across his bed. His head was pounding and his tongue felt too big for his mouth, which tasted the way used cat litter smelled. For a while, he just laid there and moaned. When he'd worked up the courage, he dragged open his right eye and saw that it was almost 7pm. His bedroom was cast in the dim orange light of the setting sun. His cell phone was on the bed next to him, and, moving as little as possible, he pointed the screen at his face and saw that he had two missed calls.

He managed to drag himself forward and swivel until he was sitting on the edge of the bed. He dialed his voicemail. The first message was from 5:23am.

"Hey, man, it's me," said Chad's voice, somewhat slurred, the quiet din of group conversation in the background. "Sorry this is taking so long, but you know Dave: first we had to smoke a bowl—then he had to make a big show of getting all his merchandise out, just in case I wanted something and didn't know it—and now a bunch of girls showed up, and, well, all the excitement got me feeling randy. Oh, the thing about the 'head in the bag': I didn't really think it was funny, but maybe I didn't get it. You can explain it when I get home. I'll try to be back by noon."

The second message was from 11:17am.

"Are you there?" Chad said, low and quiet and as sober as Petey had ever heard him. "I think—I think someone is following me." It ended there.

There were no more messages, no more calls, but maybe that was because Chad had made it home and was waiting for him to wake up. Petey crawled to the edge of his bed, intending to go looking, but what he saw froze him in place.

There was a salmon bowling bag sitting on the floor at the side of his bed.

"He was right, you know," said a high, breathy voice to his left. "Someone *was* following him."

Petey turned his head and saw the old man to the side of the bedroom door in one of their dining room chairs, legs crossed like a woman's. He was dressed in another clean suit—black this time, but otherwise identical—and white gauze and medical tape were visible beneath the porkpie hat. Ugly, purplish-black bruises pooled beneath his eyes and there was a bandage on his cheek, but he was otherwise none the worse for wear, smiling and idly flicking the straight razor open and shut, open and shut, the orange light of the sunset flickering on the blade. "Oh, shit," Petey whispered, feeling a warm gush of piss against his thighs. He couldn't think of anything better, so he just offered, "I'm sorry."

The old man stopped flicking the straight razor and just stared at Petey for a moment, and then he spat out a rasping guffaw. "You know what, Petey?" he said. "I believe you. I even forgive you. And it's in the spirit of forgiveness that I've brought you a present." He gestured at the salmon bowling bag with the hand holding the razor. "Open it."

Petey knew, as sure as he'd ever known anything in his life, that when he opened that bag he was going to see Chad's lifeless face staring up at him with hollowed-out eye sockets. Chad could be a dumbass, and he was kind of a bully, but he was also Petey's best friend. "I would prefer not to," he said.

"Come on, open it," the man said in a patient, friendly tone, like a parent trying to sell a small child on his first taste of *baba ghanoush*.

Petey reached down, took the zipper in his fingers, and mostly managed to choke back a sob. Slowly and carefully, he unzipped the bowling bag and spread it open. He frowned.

"It's empty," he said.

Then, out of the corner of his eye, there was a whisper of movement and a flicker of orange light.

BUS #146
ALYSSA FUERHOLZER
COLUMBIA COLLEGE

I'VE NEVER SEEN THE STARS. I've never seen the stars and I think this is a real problem. I mean, I've seen one or two. I've seen Orion's belt buckle and the Big Dipper and some other minor constellations. But I've never seen the *stars*.

Growing up in a suburb next to a very large city will do that to you. It will rob you of your chance to glance into other galaxies. I went to Wyoming once when I was twelve. I rode a bus through the mountains of Ireland, Wales, and England when I was eighteen. I don't remember seeing any stars. For most of my life I walked with my eyes on my feet, on the sidewalk, on the tips of my dirty pink Chucks. I don't remember ever looking up.

Why didn't I look up?

It's 10 p.m. on a Tuesday. I'm falling half in love with the brightly lit, headless mannequins in the window of Burberry on Michigan Avenue, donning dresses that cost more than my rent, and the three workers wearing matching t-shirts and jeans painting the ceiling of the Apple Store after-hours, and the little old lady with a paisley babushka wrapped low on her forehead, huddled on the bus stop bench in front of the John Hancock as we pass by, waiting for the next bus or the next. We head under a viaduct and emerge on Lake Shore Drive. On one side of me is the city: lights, lights, and more lights, and buildings—tall, taller, and tallest, a nighttime display of ostentatious illumination. And on the other side there is nothing. The lake, but I can't see it. Black, black, black. A half-bitten moon. I wish there were stars but there aren't. We whisk along, going express to Belmont, and there are no stars. The bus sways and I remember the time I was in the emergency room because I had a kidney stone, and there was an IV in my arm and the pain drifted away and my mind felt slanted to the side, all my thoughts tumbling to the left and gathering in the crevice there, while an out-of-context quote cycled between the blood in my veins: *Everything was beautiful, and nothing hurt.* I want the bus ride to feel like that. Like wonder and infinity and the strangeness in beauty. But it doesn't feel like any of that because my thoughts are sticky with anxiety and my spine hurts from the sparsely cushioned seat and there still aren't any stars.

I wish all the lights would just go out. All at once, in a mind splintering snap of an electrical cord being severed. Everything off. Even for just five minutes. There's so much light in this city, all the time, every minute of the day and night, but I can't see anything. Just five minutes, that's all. Just enough to be able to see in the dark.

"I've never seen the stars," I tell Joseph later that night when we're lying in bed, my head on his shoulder. His breath is warm and minty as it brushes my forehead. "I think this is a real problem."

"I'll take you to South Dakota sometime," he says.

So we drive to Chamberlain, South Dakota, where his extended family resides in a white house with a red front door by a river that's crisp and clean. I'm skeptical because I've been to South Dakota only once before when I was twelve and we stopped at Mount Rushmore. It was a huge disappointment. Crushing. It's not as big as it looks in pictures. Would the stars be less impressive than they are in pictures, too? Maybe I'll just go back to the city and look out the window of the bus and pretend to see what's surely there, somewhere, on the other side of all that nothingness.

"Okay," he says, leading me out of his truck. His hands are warm and I trust him. We're in a field. I didn't see the route we took. My eyes have been closed the entire drive. "You can open your eyes now."

I open them. My face is tipped down toward my feet. It's so dark I can't see anything.

I look up.

Lights, lights, and more lights.

YOUR EVERYDAY LIE
ANGIE FLORES
DOMINICAN UNIVERSITY

And I'm here waiting, just waiting.
In my red dress, red lipstick
And eyelashes curled.
I have driven through the city,
Dark sky yet my surroundings are colorful.
Out of all the lights and people
You are nowhere to be found.

You said you would be here
But you are nowhere near here.
I fell for one of your many lies.
You lie every day, yet I chase you anyways.
And still I hope that you will fix those broken promises.

Should I bother sending you another text? Another call?

Now I'm walking downtown.
All I see are couples going and coming from dates
And here I am with tears wetting my face,
A tragedy taken place outside this theatre I'm by.

I'm more hopeless than I've ever been
That I swear the next time you break a promise
I'll hurt my wrist.
Or a rope will do.
I'll embrace it around the neck you never got to kiss.

I'm done with looking at the ground.
I'm done with these excessive tears.
Let me take a look at this building here
right now looking up is the only way to keep my head high
I think it's my turn now to be your everyday lie.

FREE ZOMBIE DUST

AARON OSBORNE

DEPAUL UNIVERSITY

I STILL TOLD EVERYONE Long Room was my favorite bar in the city, but as I walked home from the Irving Park L stop I would not go inside. I quickened my pace and nodded with a nod that could be mistaken for a stretch, while I looked with a look that could be mistaken for a glance, at the door guy whose name I couldn't recall but who recognized me as I recognized him. Sitting upon its long row of stools, waiting with elbows on the wood and concrete bar top, were too many ghosts of too many good memories of my first year and a half in Chicago—when we were there and didn't need to talk to anyone else. When we could make the one-block walk to our new home, still fresh with living memories.

Long Room was the first bar I visited as a Chicago resident with a 606-something zip code and the weight of five new keys hanging from my belt loop. In Knoxville, I never needed five keys to an apartment. There was usually one to the front door, and occasionally a complex would have an outer gate that required another key. I lived in a building across Eleventh Street from the World's Fair Park that was built for just that occasion in 1982.

I remember going there to throw frisbee or just sit on the manicured lawn under the Sunsphere and think about how tired I was of the city and almost all of its people; sit there and talk to friends and roommates about the places we didn't want to go but that we went regardless. I had lived in the suburbs that make up the larger part of Knoxville since 1992 and I was well aware of it. At that time, I lived in apartment 2007, which was the year that I moved in after my freshman year of college—well before the people living in the rooms surrounding the concrete courtyard. All except my next-door neighbor in 2008, who was well into his 70s judging by the pace he would walk the single flight of metal and concrete stairs to his corner one-bedroom. My neighbor and I, the old guard of Eleventh Place. To the others, I was old because I was 23, and he was old because he was; but neither of us ever officially complained. Like me, he wouldn't speak to the neighbors unless it was of barely recognizable courtesy; and I'd oftentimes sit at my patio table and watch college students play drinking games and yell at one another.

This is the place where she and I drank beer and got to know each other. Sitting on the patio talking and laughing with someone who didn't yet drive around town with a general disgust. To her, this had been a place where she'd come to school and met friends, a place where her dead parents weren't buried. A place where she went to Urban Bar and people like me saw her and went up to bum a smoke and buy her a drink just as an excuse to talk; something I never did even though that's how we met.

She stood by the bar in the carpeted room so filled with smoke that people who didn't smoke smoked anyway. Her and several of her friends still in their work shirts from the beer bar down the street, were grabbing a drink before the 2 a.m. last call. I sat at a table with three friends—late on a Thursday but we didn't work nine-to-fives. I approached her alone and tried to make her laugh. She did without the care of purpose and I remember smiling before I joined with her laughter.

She was something bizarrely new who hadn't gone to a high school down the street. A girl from a place called the Midwest or Great Plains or something of which I had very little idea aside from a vague notion of tornadoes and fields of wheat or corn. Something I would celebrate when I first told friends about her—as if Tulsa were a magical place that spawned girls with thick dark hair wildly falling over her shoulders and face. I still imagined her soft, blue eyes behind the heart-shaped sunglasses that I would have gladly stepped on had they been anyone else's.

I'd spend every Sunday sitting at her bar while she gave me beers and food and more attention than her other customers. I never paid covers when her bar had shows and I'd stay until four in the morning and help put chairs upside down on tables. We went out to eat every night at the three or four restaurants in downtown Knoxville that we deemed appropriate for our taste and conversation.

That year, I spent Thanksgiving with her family instead of my own. After dinner, we met her adoptive brothers out for a drink. After they left, we sat on a cold empty patio and I brought up my leaving for graduate school. Something we both knew but hadn't discussed.

"You know I'm leaving. If things are going this well then, I want you to go with me."

She smiled.

ON AUGUST 31, 2012, we drove what was then our car 540 miles to a hotel by O'Hare. After tumbling into rush-hour traffic on the Dan Ryan, she nearly peed her pants trying to hold it until we got to the hotel. She didn't but she briefly blamed me, the navigator, for the ordeal; an ordeal that was quickly forgotten after dinner and a hotel room in our new city.

We woke early the next morning after having meticulously planned our route to the new home we'd only seen once. Checking that our car—packed with a TV, two computers, hopes, clothes, plants, premonitions—hadn't been robbed and after refreshing the dying plants from a bottled water, we made the long-short drive to Irving Park and Ashland. It was a quiet neighborhood aside from the constant traffic. It was close enough to the few areas we had read enough about to think we knew.

Arriving long before the movers, we sat on the curb, quietly excited. They pulled up in a loud orange semi, not nearly small enough to fit in the alley, far too large to sit on the busy Ashland Avenue for hours. They would return in three to four days, they said, after they dropped off some strangers' furniture in Wisconsin and other places I hadn't been to—the Great Migration of Knoxvillians to the Midwest, from the hills to the plains.

As the truck left, in a fleeting moment of panic, she sat on the single concrete step leading to the gated side entrance and cried as she called her uncle to tell him we made it okay. Then we met Sebin, the peculiar, jolly superintendent of our building whose sporadic shuffle and rushed tour put our problems in perspective. He swept us around the yellow building, showing us the three entrances, two laundry rooms, and storage basement. Quickly talking through his smile in a heavy accent as we smiled back and nodded while he tested key after key—removing each correct one and placing it on a ring for us.

The way the doors and locks were haphazardly replaced over the years required a different key to every entrance and yet another different key to both laundry rooms and the storage room. I suggested we get plastic color rings to designate each door so we didn't forget, which we did that day at the hardware store down the street. We bought the cheapest air mattress and folding chairs we could find for the days ahead: without a table, pots and pans, books, movies, records, couch, art.

We carried what belongings we had and dropped them in a pile in the center of the room, next to the pile we inflated the air mattress in the living room; saving our bedroom for our bed. We unfolded our chairs and I began applying the plastic colored rings to our different sets of keys. I still think it took us a few weeks to get it down. We certainly didn't know if the pink or green key opened the way to the narrow mothball-smelling carpeted stairwell after our walk back from the Long Room on that first night.

THE LONG ROOM WAS A BAR. Outside, a small yellow-lit sign hung from ornamental metal protruding from the wall. One or two Midwestern brewery neons hung in the window. It didn't have a food menu. It didn't have TVs lining the walls. Its name, an accurate description of the layout: a long, concrete-topped bar stretched down the room with dark wooden accents and about twenty or so backed stools to match. A mirror behind stretched the length of the bar with faint yellow lights on the ceiling, providing just enough light to read the drink menu but not enough to read the specials' board.
Running along the opposite wall were a few two- and four-top tables, leaving room for patrons to walk and brush elbows with one another. At the end of the tables, before the single-stall bathrooms, hung one of the only pieces of decoration: a framed, yellowed map of Chicago and its neighborhoods marking places I didn't know. The only other displays of excess were wrought iron designs at the top of either end of the bar inexplicably nautical in nature, with a couple of fake or stuffed birds among them—curiously watching bar-goers without

ever letting on what they were thinking.

Four our five booths resided in the back next to an old photo booth that still worked, before leading out onto a small enclosed patio that allowed smoking at the tables away from the door. Music played loudly enough to hear, softly enough to have to listen.

IT WAS BUSY THAT FIRST SATURDAY NIGHT but we found seats at the bar which we preferred to tables anyway. She was a bartender and liked talking about drinks with people who knew more than I did. We looked over the menu and recognized few, if any, of their mostly local and regional drafts. The woman behind the bar—satisfyingly slow moving with short, dark curly hair and glasses—came up with a smile. We all spoke. The woman's name was Dina. She and I wanted pale ales. Dina recommended a beer whose name I had imagined to life when looking over the menu: thought about its dryness, felt it between my fingers, made it into a hot-selling, yet-to-be-invented form of speed. Dina poured us two Zombie Dusts and walked on.

Later, I ordered another and she tried something else—eager to test her pallet on the unknown. After that, I ordered another and she returned to Zombie Dust. She and I told Dina we loved it. Dina said a lot of people loved it. Dina said so many people loved it that it was hard to find—that, or wasn't readily available, but mostly a combination of the two. Dina told us it was brewed in Munster, Indiana. To us, that might as well have been Chicago. Dina said that you could sometimes find six-packs at Binny's or other liquor stores but that people would call and ask if it was there. Dina even passed on rumors of waiting lists which I imagined taped behind checkout counters, scrawled hastily with the names of regulars and friends.

We drank with Dina as patrons evaporated around us.

Conversations became loose, cars drove by on Irving Park. We asked for the check. Dina picked it up.

"A welcome to the neighborhood thing."

WITH DINA, WE NEVER PAID FOR A CHECK. We would ask and Dina would either ignore us or conjure an excuse to cover the check. We usually left a ten or twenty under our stacked empty glasses when we left. Whether that money went into the register or Dina's pocket didn't matter—it usually wouldn't have been close to the cost of our tab.

After bringing our drinks, we would all catch up on the past few days. Mostly pleasantries that always required the same response. Dina would ask her about her job and try to convince her to come work at Long Room, something she had already applied for our first week in town. Dina would ask me about my classes at DePaul and tell us about Violet, Dina's art student daughter, with whom we eventually shared a drink on Violet's twenty-first birthday.

After locking ourselves out of our apartment in the cold, when she was wearing a kimono without shoes, we walked down to have a drink at the Long Room and wait for the locksmith. Dina offered to hide a key in the bar for next time, but I never made copies and we locked ourselves out again.

We stopped by to see Dina before going to concerts, sometimes after, on our way home before closing time. We stopped by to see Dina before and after my first and only Broadway show in Chicago. A Christmas present she had given me that year. We told Dina about the show and how much we had laughed and how we saw a guy shooting heroin on the Red Line.

The following Christmas, I bought her tickets to a show she wanted to see in March. By March, she had left me and Dina had left the Long Room. I sold the tickets to a stranger for half of what I'd paid for them.

IN JANUARY, I STOOD OUTSIDE THE LONG ROOM, counting rats as they made little prints in the snow on their way under a parked car. Stooping, I could see a box from the pizza place across the street, shifting with the movement of its occupants. I remembered she and I had eaten the pizza from across the street on quite a few occasions when it was the only place open, vowing it would never happen again. Pizza fit for rats and drunks, I thought.

More often, we had gone to Dinner Diner across the street where we got the same thing every time. The guys behind the counter would start making two grilled cheeses with bacon, one with hash browns and the other with fries, when we sat down. She would speak Spanish to the Latino man behind the counter and I would listen and try to make out what they were saying. I'd tell her what I thought they said and she would give me a grade. It was the most I've practiced Spanish in my life and I kept trying to listen to Spanish speakers on the bus or train, trying to eavesdrop and failing.

People who frequented Long Room frequented Dinner Diner. It never closed and I'd see the same two men there. About fifteen or so stools sat lined up under the fluorescents—the inside of the small brick building resembling the outside with its bright white glow forcing your eyes to adjust uncomfortably to features. They had no tables, but a new, digital jukebox sat awkwardly against the end of the wall and gave patrons something to keep them busy if the counter was full.

I would sometimes put on universally hated music before paying my bill and walking home to where her clothes were still in her dresser in my bedroom and closet; her pink and white '80s road bike locked on the outside of the rack next to mine; some of her trinkets in a box by the door. Things she hadn't moved out even though she was staying with a coworker less than a mile away. Things she said she couldn't move out because our car was only mine. Everything was there but her. The music at Dinner Diner a cruel prank in which I was never witness to the pay off, but felt confident in the fact that someone was upset with something I'd done.

I LEARNED FROM THE BAR BACK that Dina was gone after something like twelve years at Long Room. The owners say Dina quit, but the bar back didn't think so. He said it wasn't about Dina drinking behind the bar; it wasn't about Dina giving away drinks. He said the owners simply wanted fresh faces. I considered asking around to find out where Dina was working, but they probably wouldn't have had Zombie Dust and it wouldn't have been the Long Room. Still, I thought about Dina behind the bar calling customers by name and buying them a shot—joining with a shot of wine if it was too early for liquor.

James was one of the bartenders at Long Room who still knew who I was, and I went in some nights when he was working. He knew I wanted Zombie Dust but would usually ask what I wanted in case it changed, or on the occasions they were out. James might not have charged for a drink or two, but he never picked up my tabs and I didn't expect him to. He was tall and slim and always wore things somewhere between a shirt and sweatshirt. He taught yoga and looked comfortable and sometimes ate Thai delivery behind the bar as we talked about his upcoming band project or whatever music was softly playing overhead.

I usually went in by myself after work or class and would have a beer or two before going home. I knew who some of the regulars were and would talk to them without ever getting to know them— enough to only barely acknowledge one another until someone felt comfortable moving down seats to have a conversation. The conversations were understood to last only as long as the next word.

Most of the time the clientele was couples or small groups of people in their twenties and thirties, talking about beer or their jobs or their relationships. I sometimes would talk to people who sat next to me who I didn't know. That is how I met a young lady with reddish bobbed hair and glasses who was there with a friend. The young lady's name was Kelly who talked endlessly about her psychology graduate program and the professor with whom Kelly went to church every Sunday. Kelly laughed at times when I didn't know I should be laughing. I caught myself watching the laugh, only joining in when it was too late and forced and obvious I wasn't laughing.

The friend's ball cap succeeded in covering half of the face and nearly all of the dark, straight hair. The friend disliked me. I knew because the friend told me. What little I had said had been enough. So I told the friend I didn't like the hat and that it was too pulled down too far. A childless comeback based on no merit aside from the fact that I already knew I didn't like the friend either.

Kelly talked; talked to me; talked to the friend; talked to James who also talked to everyone. Kelly said they were regulars at Long Room and didn't know the bartender's name. I told them "James" and James said his name was Chris—a detail I told myself to remember for the next time I went in.

Kelly and I later went to Dinner Diner and Kelly sat a few stools down and bet the guy at the next stool to finish their famous "Slinger." A plate which came with nearly everything the diner serves. Kelly finished it. The Latino man behind the counter brought Kelly a pancake made in the shape of male genitals, something I've seen them do on a number of occasions. Kelly yelled at him, I paid our bill, and Kelly and I left. I could understand that not all people find it as amusing as the standard fare at Dinner Diner.

Kelly came to my apartment to listen to records I hadn't put on in years. The records of bands from six or eight years ago that everyone knew but that I would never listen to alone. Stale music from the past flowing through the apartment where her dresser had been moved out, and my room was rearranged as much as the space would allow. The closet where my sweater hung instead of her green polka dot top on which my mother had sewn up a rip. The storage room where my bike was now locked in her old spot on the outside of the rack, within easy reach.

Kelly and I exchanged numbers and we met once more to only confirm that Kelly and I should no longer have beers together at Long Room.

I WALKED BY LONG ROOM RECENTLY without glancing at the door guy whose name I didn't recall—afraid of seeing Kelly and the friend in the ball cap sitting at the bar. Ashamed to see Chris because I thought his name was James. Except I was not really afraid or ashamed of either. I didn't think about Kelly and doubt Kelly thought about me. I would have politely waved or given a small tilt of my glass in Kelly's direction on the way up to my mouth.

Chris would have said hello and offered me a Zombie Dust if they had it tapped; even maybe laughed about the fact that I called him by the wrong name. Chris was moving to Boston soon with his girlfriend, and he offered to buy me a beer the next time I came into the Long Room. Maybe I would go back and sit with my elbows on the bar and read over the draft list, even though I knew what I wanted.

CHICAGO AFTER DARK
FRANCISCO ESPINAL
WILBUR WRIGHT COLLEGE

THE CITY CARRIES A LOT OF GUILT on its broad shoulders. Prohibition has not prohibited anything. Policemen all have a price tag to look away. Judges are easily bribed with booze and money. Alcohol is more valuable than gold. The nights are deceitful. Everything seems very peaceful, but below the elevated railways and between the glare of Chicago's night lights something is brewing. This is the untold story of how a cast of improbable characters known as "The Untouchables" capture Al Capone.

In the Loop, people are entering the Four Deuces speakeasy through the back. Men disguise themselves in long coats and strap their guns to their suspenders. Gold plated pocket watches are not for time but for gambling. Women nowadays no longer have shame. They too wear long coats to hide their short skirts. They wear head bands with feathers and false pearls to pretend wealth. They use their barely covered breasts and thighs as currency to enter any speakeasy, to buy enough for one night of drinking. The women walk with no posture as if they were men and puff smoke like steam engines. On the dance floor, women flap their arms up and down trying to fly.

Men and women alike enter the club with one purpose: moonshine. The bartender, De Marco, goes to the back and mixes a dangerous cocktail made from methyl, brucine, and kerosene with alcohol. He has been doing this for a long time now. His buddy Vitto was already arrested, but if they go to jail again, good old pal Al will bail them out, so he mixes the alcohol in the tub and takes a sip. It's ready. This new drink fusion has killed many in Chicago, but they still take the risk. There is no purpose in life if you can't thin out your blood a little. No amendments can change their minds, not the first, second, third, or even eighteenth. De Marco brings the alcohol to the bar and serves it. Bodies are being washed by alcohol and De Marco is drowning in cash. Jazz plays throughout the night and the revelry is only paused when someone dies. Just kick the body to the side; someone else will take care of it. The law has turned angels into criminals, and gangsters into idols.

Inside the illegal tavern at the last table sits the crème de la crème: Alphonse Capone, John Torrio, Big Jim, and Jack "Machine Gun," among others. Al Capone sits like a fat cat. He is always well groomed, with a nice black coat, and very fat from overeating the best steaks Chicago has to offer. Al Capone is the biggest gangster in Chicago and has been labeled public enemy number one. This title excites Al; he likes the attention. Big Al, as he is called by his buddies, is five foot ten and weighs two hundred pounds. He is originally from New York but has made the Windy City his new home. This used to be unmarked territory until Al Capone put his name all over it. He has become a millionaire with the help of Congress. Congress could not provide alcohol, so Big Al took on the heavy responsibility. He has created a web of businesses all over Chicago, Cicero, and northern Indiana. He caters to the best vices of life: gambling, alcohol, and women. Capone and the guys sat and discussed how to celebrate Valentine's Day. Whichever way they celebrated, it was going to be a blast.

Al Capone is sitting holding the *Cicero Tribune*, reading about the last pineapple primary. Al completely dislikes the *Cicero Tribune* more than the *Chicago Tribune*. His dislike for the *Cicero Tribune* comes from a journalist named St. John. He would reveal many of Al Capone's secrets and rightfully accuse him of many deaths around Cicero's neighborhood. St. John wanted the city to clean up the mob mess, but the policemen were funded more by Al than by the government. Most recently, St. John had written a column about the pineapple primary. Unfortunately, St John was killed for using his head too much. Al Capone had ordered a bombing on a voting site to discourage voters. Big Al funded a candidate he could trust to introduce more brothels into Cicero. His sponsored candidate had to win at all costs, even if it meant throwing some pineapples.

"The Pineapple Primary worked; bombing the voters during the primary election scared everyone away. Now Big Bill Thompson can win the election, and we can start bringing in more girls from the south. How much can we give this guy, Big Bill Thompson?" asks Al Capone.

"We gotta give him a little more this time so he can look away and take care of all the rumors. How about three thousand dollars and a bottle of whiskey?" responds Jack "Machine Gun," as he eats his Spaghetti á la Coloismo, the speakeasy's signature dish.

"Three thousand sounds good. Give him a case of whiskey, enough to forget what he saw. Is anyone else getting calls from Uncle Sam? The IRS keeps calling me. 'Hey are you paying any income tax?' No, Uncle Sam, I ain't got no job. Last job I had was a paperboy. You wanna tax a 'lil paperboy? Uhh Uncle Sam?" The small crowd laughed. Recently the Supreme Court made a landmark decision. The IRS can in fact collect taxes from a person or institution that collects income from an illegal establishment. Al Capone's money was dirty, but the IRS still had power to tax his illegal brothels and speakeasies, though paying taxes on an illegal establishment compromises your innocence of running an illegal establishment. If Capone paid taxes on a speakeasy he was basically incarcerating himself, and Al Capone understood this.

"Don't worry, just don't pay anything with a check and nobody is going to trace you. We got a new shipment Thursday. Do you wanna take it?" asks Big Jim.

"Yeah, I'll pay for the new booze. It better be good stuff, it's coming from Morocco. And I never pay with checks. I ain't stupid, but I keep telling my brother you gonna get caught paying for shit with checks. He just don't get it. His Italian cannoli is going to end up in jail," says Al. The men smoke their cigars and drink hooch while mocking the authorities until the end of the night. The booze blurs them from foreseeing the future, which is dwindling to an end. Al has been watched for a long time now. The FBI is setting a trap to bring down the Big Cat.

On the other side of town William McSwiggin, the Assistant State Attorney, is discussing plans with an FBI agent, Eliot Ness. Mr. Ness is not a newcomer; he is well-versed in the spying business.

"I need you to take your best men and capture Al Capone immediately. I have direct orders from Hoover, and he wants this man behind bars as soon as possible. Can you do this or should I find a new man?" asks McSwiggin.

"Yes, I can. I have assembled the best team. Here they are," Ness says as he opens the door to a larger office space labeled "The Untouchables."

"Is this a joke?" McSwiggin responds.

"No sir, this is my team. We have brought down a lot of men and women, and had them prosecuted with substantial evidence. First, we have Mrs. O'Leary. She is more than a milking cow; she is a top agent who can decipher codes in just minutes."

"Wasn't she responsible for the Great Chicago Fire?" asks McSwiggin.

"No sir, she was acquitted on false testimonies," says Ness. "Ms. O'Leary is a good spy and knows everything happening around the slaughterhouses. She is also famous for being the only cow to eat chocolate and produce chocolate milk.

"Second, we have Romberg Rabbit. He is a research specialist and evidence collector."

"Good day Mr. McSwiggin," says Romberg Rabbit, who works in television aside a goofy goose. Romberg Rabbit is a secret spy who collects information through his media connections. Romberg was close friends with journalist St. John, but has a new source of information since his passing away.

"Also we have Mr. Rodney Short. He belongs to the Rodent Investigation Bureau, or RIB," says Ness.

"You have to be kidding me," responds McSwiggin.

"I am not. He is a gun specialist and can fire a round of bullets in just seconds," explains Ness.

"Good evening Mr. McSwiggin," says Rodney Short as he takes off his hat. Rodney is adorable to look at, and he is only five inches tall. His head is fifty percent of his whole body length. Though very cute, he is a killing machine. He is very quiet with a stern face. He had served in the Marines and saw many of his comrades die in action. The only time Rodney was seen smiling was in 1908, something about his favorite team winning a world championship in a ball game. After his stint in the Marines he joined the R.I.B. It was an organization started by Franklin D. Roosevelt before his presidency. The R.I.B. was created to coexist with the League of Nations. Though the League of Nations failed, the R.I.B. became a private bureau.

"Last is Billy the Goat. Secret agent Billy is intellectual in foreign trade. Most of the alcohol used in the States comes from Africa or Europe, and he knows all of the exact locations," says Ness.

"Oh God no. I have failed this country. My reputation is over. Next thing is you pulling out Bozo the Clown out of a hat," says McSwiggin.

"Good evening Mr. McSwiggin," says Billy the Goat, as he gets up to greet McSwiggin. McSwiggin turns down the hoof shake. Billy the Goat became an alcoholic a long time ago after he was denied access to public places, like restaurants and baseball stadiums. He took the owners and managers to court for discrimination, but lost in the Supreme Court in a 7-2 ruling. The Chief Justice said that any owner can deny access to anyone with strong odor. He became an alcoholic for ten years, but eventually turned his life around and joined the R.I.B. He realized he had talent and he is a key role to bringing down Al Capone. Billy is good at following the trail of imported alcohol from Africa and Europe to find all of the perpetrators. He knows where Al is on a daily basis; the team just needs to catch him in the act.

"I don't care if you have three beavers chasing a cheesecake, Mr. Ness. I want Al Capone's head on a silver platter."

"Yes, Mr. McSwiggin. Don't underestimate my team. We will capture Big Al and his men," says Ness while McSwiggin storms out of the room.

McSwiggin is not happy about the clown show Ness has displayed, but Ness is a national hero who has a solid track record. McSwiggin puts all his faith in Eliot Ness and is his last hope to capture Al Capone. The group was dubbed The Untouchables due to the fact that they never accepted bribes.

The Untouchables are able to tap Al's phones and record secret conversations. The team is ready to confront Al Capone. They're going to do it the next night. Chicago only conducts its bootlegging at night.

The next night Al and his friends head to the Four Deuces club in their Cadillacs. They enter the party, already in progress, and sit at the last table. Outside the Untouchables are ready to shut down the speakeasy and arm themselves heavily. Ness enters and presents his badge to the crowd.

"Everyone put your drinks down, this is the FBI." Ness is unable to finish before everyone makes a run for it. Al and his bodyguards escape through the back door, but Ness' men are waiting at the rear exit.

"Stop!" screams Rodney. He's waiting in the rear exit with Romberg Rabbit. Al and his men don't stop and pull out their machine guns as they enter their bulletproof cars. Rodney pulls out his gun and starts to fire. Romberg takes cover and fires at the three Cadillacs. None of their bullets penetrate the cars' windows. Ahead of the road, Mrs. O'Leary stands and milks the pavement to make the road slippery, but to no avail. All of the men flee. The Untouchables regroup on Clark Street.

"Is everyone all right?" asks Ness.

"Yes, we're good," responds Rodney. He is so small that it is hard for him to get hit with a bullet. The rest of the team is fine, with no bullet wounds.

"We need to devise a new plan that will prove more effective," says Ness in disappointment. The team regroups back at headquarters and devise a new plan. Ness orders everyone to disperse around the city and look for more information.

Ms. O'Leary goes to the Stockyard. The Stockyard is close to the harbor where the alcohol shipments usually came in through. She eats some chocolate on the way.

"Hey Bologna, how are you?" asks O'Leary to the bull. Every bull was named after what it was going to be made into.

"Hey, what is you doing here? You best get off here before someone turns you to sausage," says Bologna jokingly.

"We are close to bringing down Al. Do you know anything? What have you heard?" asks Ms. O'Leary.

"Well, I ain't got not much time to live and produce methane gas, so I'm just gonna spit it out," says Bologna as he gets picked up by a machine and put onto a conveyer belt. "Al is gonna get a big boat here in Belmont. More booze than you'll ever see in your life." Bologna is close to the entrance of the slaughter house, where he is going to be shredded into pieces in seconds.

"When?" screams Ms. O'Leary.

"This Thursday gurl. Hey, I'ma 'bout to die. Give me some of that sweet stuff, mama," replies Bologna.

"Thanks for everything." She stands in her hind legs and squeezes some of her chocolate milk into Bolognas mouth; he catches most of it.

Seconds later, his last words can be heard: "Lord Jesus this hurts!" He dies instantly and becomes bologna.

Over by the soup kitchen Ness and Romberg Rabbit are interviewing random people on the overcrowded streets.

"What do you know, Jesse James? I know you know something. What's Al Capone's deal?" asks Ness. Jesse James is an outlaw. He is constantly in and out of jail for bank robberies.

"I ain't know nothing 'bout no one, best get out of here 'cuz you don't belong here. You know this is Al's territory," responds James. The crowd looks at Ness and Romberg and get a cop scent. They whisper to one another.

"This is government property. We can stand anywhere we want. Listen, James, we can give you some time off from jail if you collaborate with us," says Romberg Rabbit.

"I know nothing, and I don't need nothing from yous guys. Al is the sweetest guy in town and we ain't gonna let you do anything to him," responds James. The crowd joins James' anger and scream at both agents.

"What do they want?" asks a random person.

"Get out, get out," the crowd starts yelling. The crowd arouses, and, concerned for their safety, both agents leave. Since the Depression, people have turned to alcohol for temporary relief. Poverty has crippled people, both figuratively and literally. Al Capone has soup kitchens around town, about twenty. Al is very moral with food services; he would order children, women, and the elderly to be served first. He could provide what the people needed while Hoover just planted trees and rerouted water. Al mighty provides alcohol to men, food for children, and jobs to young women. There was no way people were going to turn their backs on Robin Hood.

A couple streets down Rodney is riding on top of Billy the Goat. They are heading to Al's house on 73rd street. There is no one home, strangely, so Rodney makes his move to tap the phones. Billy the Goat waits in the street and talks through a walkie-talkie. Rodney enters through a crack on the wall. He walks in with his equipment and smells something funky. A cat pounces on Rodney. Rodney avoids a claw, a second one, and a third one. He runs to the chair and jumps to the table, pulls out his sword. His sword is a light green 3" pick he took from a martini glass three days earlier. Rodney stands in the center of the table prepared with his sword turning forty degrees to the right, patiently. No cat in sight, he leaves his defensive position and turns into his attack mode. Rodney jumps to the floor quickly and the cat follows. The fight is uneven, ten claws against one sword. The cat jumps in front of Rodney and swings like Muhammad Ali, but Rodney dodges it and comes close enough to his neck to read its tag. Rodney now knows his opponent's name.

"Madam Waffles, I beg of you, please strut out of here before you get hurt," warns Rodney. She ignores his plea and attacks again.

Rodney jumps, jumps again, rolls, attacks, and swings his sword a couple of times. He breathes heavily; it turns out they are evenly matched. Rodney runs into the bathroom and Waffles again follows. He jumps into the sink and turns on the faucet. Waffles hesitates to come all the way into the bathroom. Rodney throws water at her, and she becomes angry enough to jump into the sink. Rodney is prepared and blinds her with toothpaste, and then he stabs her multiple times. She dies on the spot. Rodney puts away his sword and makes a prayer. Finally Rodney can get back to business. He taps all the house phones. Before leaving, he cleans all traces and drags the dead cat to the alley. Rodney digs up a grave and disposes of the carcass. Rodney gets back to Billy the Goat and both listen to phone conversations the rest of the night.

The team regroups and devises their new plan. They are going to capture Al Capone at the Belmont Harbor while receiving illegal contraband on Thursday night. Thursday arrives and the team is in place. Al and his men arrive and so does the shipment. The agents record the voices of all the men under scrutiny for evidence. Once they have enough clear voices on tape they go in for the kill.

"The cat is in the bag. Let's do this," says Ness to the team. The agents and cops are hiding behind crates and suddenly jump out to Al's surprise. "FBI puts your hands up." Al's men start the shooting game and the agents respond. The cops and agents work together and shoot at Al's men. Al Capone hides behind his bulletproof car and so do his men. Ms. O'Leary helps by turning over three cops' cars and barricading the agents. She turns around and fires a couple of methane balls. The men become intoxicated by the smell and jump into the lake to reduce the burning. Billy the Goat jumps out in front of the overturned cars and rams the men, and he uses his horns to penetrate each gangster while they are down. Romberg Rabbit pulls out his AK-47 and goes nuts, shooting every man on the floor. The fluffy white rabbit is merciless while conducting business. Rodney runs to the bullet proof cars and fires shots under the cars' engines. The cars explode, and it's all over. Casualties on Al's side were sixteen. Casualties on the FBI's side were two. Rodney's bravery, priceless.

Rodney lies twenty feet from the explosion. He is badly burned. Since the cars were bullet proof, he had to do something drastic.

"Rodney hold on, the ambulance is almost here," says Billy the Goat.

"It's okay, I've lived a good life," says Rodney, every word spoken more slowly. "I was going to throw the first pitch on Monday for the Cubs' home opener." Rodney dies from his very bad burns and a severe hit to the head. The Untouchables come together in agony and pray for Rodney as the ambulance takes him away. He became the greatest detective from R.I.B. agency, and later was inducted in the Hall of Fame of Private Investigators.

Al, on the other hand, is inducted into jail. Not really inducted as much as forced, for tax corruption and contraband. Chicago's mob problem is slowly going away, and the speakeasies, brothels and crime are also coming to an end, thanks to The Untouchables.

This is the untold story of how The Untouchables captured Al Capone. The secret team composed of a tough mouse, a dangerous rabbit, a milking cow, a fearless goat, and top agent might be unknown nationally, but they are heroes to Chicago. They are more than a clown show: they are cast of characters that bring justice to the city no matter how bad the wind blows. Chicago after dark is a game of cat and mouse. You have to run fast and slip into empty barrels so you don't get caught. The Untouchables still in exist in Chicago, but they only come out during night time, so that they watch over Chicagoland.

POINTS OF LIGHT
LIBBY KALMBACH
DEPAUL UNIVERSITY

IN THE DARK, Montrose Beach is the color of gunmetal. It is August 11, 2012, my friend Laurey's birthday, and I have come here with a group of her friends to celebrate. We spread out our blankets near the water line, where little waves lap incessantly at the sand and fill the air with a sweet, fresh smell. The sticky, hot day has retreated into a soft, warm evening. We make ourselves comfortable and pass around some beers.

Then we look up. It is one of the peak nights of the Perseids, the world's most famous and intense meteor shower, with around 70 meteors falling per hour. The Chicago Park District has kept the beach open late for stargazers like us, and we are sharing in Laurey's birthday tradition of meteor watching, something she's done on her birthday for as long as she can remember.

"Ah! There's one!" cries one of my friends. Meteors move so quickly, though, that by the time the rest of us turn our heads, it's gone, a momentary flash across the sky.

There are eight of us gathered on the blankets. If nothing else, it's fun to be on the beach at night, with Lake Michigan rendered secretive and mysterious, the horizon harder to spot. It turns out, however, that the city is probably the worst place to stargaze, even on a clear night like this. The urban dark is never quite dark enough—it's so light, in fact, that I can clearly see the features of every face gathered around me.

"Not exactly what I'm used to," says Laurey. She has spent part of every August of her life, save two, at her family's cottage in northern Wisconsin. For as long as she can remember she and her family would go down to the lake on clear nights, get into their boat and lie down, bobbing on the water. From there they would watch meteors: the Pereseid shower that always coincided with their visit. With the sky unpolluted by city lights it was the perfect tradition, passed down at least from her grandparents and maybe for more generations than that. At other times, Laurey and her brother used a glow-in-the-dark book about the night sky as a map for finding constellations. These days, they have an app on their smart phones that allows them to hold the device up towards the sky and be told the names of the stars.

The tradition of stargazing does go back pretty far. Observation of meteors and meteor showers can be traced at least as far back as 687 BC where they appear in the records of ancient Chinese astronomers. However, given everything we now know about meteors, it's probable that they have been observable by men as long as there have been men interested in observing them. I find myself wondering what the first men and women thought of the stars, and what they thought when they saw them appear to fall. How could they begin to understand such a strange sight, in the days before modern science?

To unaided observers, meteors appear to be stars streaking across the sky and burning out—shooting stars—but this is a trick of the eye. We see a meteor when bits of debris from space fall into the earth's atmosphere and burn up, creating a trail of light. During meteor showers, the quantity of meteors we can see increases because the earth is passing through a trail of debris, like a snail trail, left in the wake of a comet or asteroid as it travels along its orbit.

A meteor shower is named for its radiant, a constellation in the night sky from which all the points of light appear to emerge. The radiant of the Perseid meteor shower is the constellation Perseus, named for the character in Greek mythology who killed the snake-haired Medusa. Yet a meteor shower really bears no relation to its radiant. That the meteors appear to emerge from that point is a trick of the eye, a function of where the trail of comet debris causing the meteor shower crosses the earth's orbit. Constellations, for that matter, are made up of stars that only appear to be near each other to the observer on Earth. In space, they are hugely far apart and unrelated.

These are not the only tricks perspective plays on us. The meteors we see streaking the sky that look big enough and far enough away to be stars, are actually caused by bits of matter that are most commonly the size of a dust mote, and only rarely bigger than a pebble. That's all it takes to make a meteor visible to human observers lying on beaches on Earth, a bit like the pea that disturbed the sleep of the princess.

Stargazing in Chicago this year doesn't quite compare to Laurey's experiences in the north woods. For me though, even this polluted, dim little bit of the heavens is enchanting. As the night wears on, I am determined to get the full value of this experience. I lay on my back on a bumpy bed of sand, tuning out of the conversation and into the night sky. I see more planes headed for O'Hare than meteors, but my attentive watching pays off and I spot at least five meteors, each thin line of silent white light disappearing as soon as it is drawn across the sky.

When I later ask Laurey what the ancient stargazers might have thought of meteor showers, she thinks that a better question is what would they think of us if they could see us today, watching the same phenomenon with the Chicago skyline at our backs, the lights in the windows of skyscrapers shining in ever changing constellations? What would they think to see modern men holding cell phones up to the sky to stargaze? Could they accept how unimaginably different life would be? Yet on the cosmic scale of time, or perhaps to a far distant observer, we are closer to them then we might imagine.

To watch a meteor shower on a summer night is to be reminded that if we gather information only from one fixed point, one perspective, we'll miss a lot. Lying on my back on Montrose Beach I stretch out and absorb as much of the experience as possible. At midnight, park employees sweep the beach and tell us it is time to leave. We load up our cars and drive home under the night sky that is always there, and that tonight we have finally noticed.

DARK HEARTS FOR DARK MINDS
MARY MELLON
SCHOOL OF THE ART INSTITUTE OF CHICAGO

LOOK UP AT THE MOON as these private emotions riddle your thoughts. They disappear, then reappear, because they are no longer about her, but about you. Insidiously, they direct your actions, and when you speak, move, love and lust, watch them creep across your mind and settle down.

The man knows this. He knows this as he snorts a line of white powder and wipes briefly at his nose. He knows this as he stares at the glassy expression in her eyes.

She exhibits as much emotion as a doll. She has turned away, in both body and mind.

"Well, are you coming to bed then?" she asks the man.

WINDY CHILL
MARQUISE DAVION
COLUMBIA COLLEGE

At night
I too like the rain
I sometimes feel its pain
But when I see my reflection
I only see rejection
One that lingers with the city wind
Just to find its self
At the top of the Sears Tower
Alone

THE STAIRCASE
MEGAN SHATTUCK
COLUMBIA COLLEGE

I DON'T WANT TO GO TO WORK TOMORROW. *I don't want to go to work tomorrow. I don't want to go to work tomorrow.*

Her head bumped against the window with each small jolt of the train. It seemed to have stopped moving smoothly and chose to inch forward at small shaky increments instead. She sat up to check her phone. 12:20 a.m. That couldn't be right. The girl flipped the screen to black and then to life again in a desperate attempt to make the time change to something more reasonable, but she was only met with the tiny glow of 12:21 a.m. She let out an audible groan. There was only one other woman on the train, and she didn't even flinch when she heard a young woman making strange noises from the bench in front of her. She just continued to read her Kindle and occasionally scratched her head of frizzy hair seemingly only being held up by four mechanical pencils and a blue pen.

There was a certain time of night in Chicago. It was the time when people slowly began to recede into themselves. It was a result of being beaten up by the day. The price of the city being one of the most lovely and exciting places in the world is that it has a cruel and vicious side that appears without notice. Nothing worth anything comes without cost. One must pay for their rewards. In this city, one pays for their delights with uncertainty. The uncertainty of the weather, the trains, the parking, the people. One must enjoy every pleasant moment because the rain could come at any moment.

On those days, the days when the rain comes, the people of the city grit their teeth and stick up their chins and simply take it. It's the price, they think; the rain will clear soon. Unfortunately, when it rains, it pours. The cliche is all too true in this city. There will be a day, sometimes several days in a row, when it seems the city and its people have turned against you. Within those times, there is a line. That line divides you into two people. One of those people acts one way in public. They say thank you and excuse me, they make sure their hair is aligned and lipstick intact, they smile and wear crisp, clean clothes and they act civilized and polite on the train. Quite simply, they are the best version of themselves. The other person, the person who lies on the other side of that line, is someone who most try to keep behind locked doors and bolted windows. The city has been evil and twisted. It has beat upon you all day long, and it has finally succeeded in pushing you over that line. That person doesn't care that their hair came undone or that their lipstick is everywhere but on their lips. That person does not say thank you or excuse me, but instead pushes their way through everyone, cutting off the children and the elderly for that last seat on the train. Today was one of those days for young Rebecca Crane. It seemed as though it had been one of those days for her fellow passenger as well, which would explain why she didn't even look up when Rebecca growled at her phone moments ago.

The train shuddered to a stop. The other woman heaved herself out of her seat and slipped out of the doors into the rainy night. Rebecca was now alone. The lights cracked, then flickered. She sat up a little straighter and looked around. Empty train cars had a certain element of foreboding, and the malfunctioning lights certainly did not help. The train pushed forward, coming to another ungraceful stop with a screech and a hiss. The doors opened, letting some of the rain in, and then closed again. No one joined Rebecca on her abandoned car. She braced herself for the train's jerk forward, but it didn't come. A balloon of anticipation swelled in her stomach, and a deep voice echoed overhead. She couldn't make out everything the disembodied voice said, but she heard "equipment malfunction" and "delay," so she figured they wouldn't be moving for awhile. Perfect. The balloon in her stomach continued to grow as she waited for some sign that the train would move, but nothing came.

She leaned her head against the window, but her current state of exhaustion turned that lean into more of a fall. Her temple slammed into the window so hard that several droplets of rain quivered and slid down to the ledge. Letting out another audible groan and a few choice curse words, she rubbed her palm against her head as if it would help.

With the lights almost completely extinguished in the train car, Rebecca could see more clearly out the window. The outside world seemed to be as abandoned as her train. The only light came from the glass-enclosed stairwell attached to a nondescript building with no other windows to speak of. Rebecca had passed this building hundreds of times during her commute, and this stairwell always fascinated her. She could never figure out why a building would have floor to ceiling windows in a space that hardly anyone used, thanks to the invention of elevators. Perhaps there were no elevators. Maybe that was why someone took so much care in creating a well lit stairwell with a view, she thought.

Suddenly, on the top floor, there was a movement. A flash of yellow. Rebecca blinked a few times, and her eyes scurried around trying to catch it. Were they playing tricks on her? No, it was a girl. A young girl, perhaps Rebecca's age. Rebecca sat up a little straighter and pushed her face closer to the glass, trying to see through the rain.

The girl was blonde, and she was running down the stairs. As she twisted her body to reach the next flight of steps, Rebecca could see that her eyes were wide and her mouth was open as if she were screaming. Rebecca's face matched the girl's when she saw why she was running.

A man was chasing her.

Rebecca jumped up from her seat, and her hands flew to her mouth. The man, or what she assumed was a man, was wearing a long black cloak with a hood over his head like a phantom in some black-and-white film. The cloak billowed behind him as he descended the stairs, slowly, methodically. Another flash. Silver this time. A knife. Rebecca reached down and snatched her phone from the seat and frantically dialed 911. A woman answered, and Rebecca let out a stream of nearly incoherent phrases describing the scene before her. The woman on the other end was understandably confused, but simply asked for the address where the emergency was occurring. Rebecca stammered. She couldn't give an address, she was on a train looking out at a building. She was in the middle of explaining this when she saw the man was now only one staircase away from the girl.

The girl looked behind her, causing her to miss the last step. She crumbled onto the floor, a heap of blonde hair and tangled limbs. She scrambled to the window and pulled herself up from the floor. She began to pound on the glass, clearly screaming even though Rebecca couldn't hear it. The man was almost to her now, the knife brandished in front of him. It was over. The police would never get there in time.

Rebecca ran to the door and pulled the small red knob that opened the door manually. She burst out into the rain, down the platform, down the stairs, and across the abandoned street. She could see the girl and the man. They were on the third flight of stairs. A flash of red. *Please don't be blood. What do I do now?* She had never been to this building. She didn't even know what it housed, much less where the entrance was. She made the best guess she could and rounded to the side where the stairwell looked like it ended. A door. She yanked it as hard as she could, praying that it was unlocked. It opened with surprising ease, making her stumble backwards. When she regained her balance, she ran inside, her wet sneakers squeaking on the floor and announcing her entrance. She bounded up the stairs without thought, wiping away the hair streaked across her face. She rounded the second set of stairs when there he was: the man in the cloak. She froze, her shoes making a loud screech as she came to a sudden halt. Her breath caught in her chest. The balloon of anticipation returned. However, this time, it was a balloon of dread. He began to step down the stairs slowly, one by one. Rebecca still wasn't breathing. The only noise was the thump, thump, thump of his shoes and the light slither of his cloak on the ground.

Rebecca and the man were face-to-face. Well, hood to face. She couldn't make out any features through the black shadow his hood cast. He raised his arm slowly from his side, and Rebecca saw the knife. He drew it up, further and further. Every muscle in her body tensed, one by one, preparing for the penetration. Then, with his other hand, he reached forward. He gently clasped her hand and drew it to him before flipping it palm up. Then, he placed the knife in her hand, closing her fingers for her. He patted her hand, and before she knew it, he vanished. The balloon in her stomach popped.

She ran up to find the girl, drenched in her own blood. Rebecca slipped in it and fell to her knees. She slid forward, crying out for the girl to wake up, even though she knew she wouldn't get a response. The girl's blonde hair was now a deep burgundy. Rebecca's eyes scanned her body, hysterically trying to find where the wounds were. There was too much blood. Rebecca noticed her blouse. She hadn't noticed before because of all the stains, but now that she was so close she realized that she owned the same one. Rebecca put her hand to the girl's face. Please, please.

"Ma'am, please stand up and drop the knife."

Rebecca turned around. Three cops with guns drawn were now standing in front of her. She looked down. She was covered in blood, and she was still holding the knife. She dropped it, causing a small ripple in the pool of blood.

"No, you don't understand. It wasn't me. It was the hooded man! I swear, please!" Her eyes met each one of the cops, silently pleading. Each one of them met her gaze with expressions full of doubt and pity. They didn't believe her. Not even a little.

As they tightened the handcuffs around her bloody wrists, she had a thought. *At least I won't have to go to work tomorrow.*

WALTER: A REPORT
RACHEL ORMES
COLUMBIA COLLEGE

I WAS NEVER A DADDY'S GIRL, but he does have a way of boggling my mind. Often times with a cup of wine in his hand does he pause at the certainty of his own goodness, unsure. I too have wondered about this, but nonetheless he is a perfect example of a life that now has the opportunity to begin looking back at itself. I have spent time collecting memories, anything I can remember that might add up to something, and while I now find that to likely be impossible, I am left with the assurance that a life in speculation is not one to be judged but respected.

In my case here, there are just some people that we cannot help but sympathize with, and unfortunately one of those people is my father. Regardless of what my father does or says, he always wins back my affection and empathy whether he knows it or not.

1. My father, Walter, is not a stylish man. Born September 11, 1951, his current age has allowed him to hike his black work pants up to his

true hipbones, completing the look with his lucky scrub shirt, which is a classic blue containing a deep red seam just inside the collar.

2. He is a tall man, but his structure has lulled, and he stands with a physique that casts a tired shadow.

3. His hair is black and curly with a single white strip becoming more defined on the right hemisphere of his head. His nose has a bump in the bridge, and seeing it from a side angle, it is slightly hooked. His eyes are overcast, brown, and cloudy, but what is lacking in luster is redeemed in wisdom.

4. When I was a kid he worked in a maximum-security prison as the dentist. His workspace was marginally large and sterile. The room was loaded with needles for numbing and other shank-like tools that looked much like any piece of dentistry equipment would—thin, precise, made from titanium, that had an easy weight to them that made them perfect for assaulting, which I'm sure for the inmates made them all the more tempting. Nonetheless, he would always come home in a gentle mood. Presently, he works in a Veterans Clinic where one in three have emphysema and/or a stoma. If you ask him why he does what he does, he says that everyone deserves solace. I think that is stylish of him.

5. In my younger years, I took pride in eavesdropping on other lines of our phone while someone was having a conversation with whomever. I once overheard my father talking to a family friend of ours named Tony.

"I just don't know what to do, man. I've had it, my nigga."

"I know, I know, but you can't just leave your family like that. Lord knows I've thought about just gettin' up and disappearin', man, but I ain't gonna do that."

"I don't know, man."

6. My father would occasionally tell me bizarre stories from the prison. "Today a patient of mine confirmed that he was sure how to make a spaceship out of a lawn mower, and that's more than I can say about myself."

7. Walter was a fat kid. He used to steal Twinkies and other convenience-store items with his more athletic friends. It was the late '60s and once in the midst of making a run for it, my father fell way behind the others. He narrates that as he stopped for a breather, leaning on the edge of a building, he looked to his left and down an alley, he saw a man on his knees get shot in the back of the head by another man in black, heavy boots, wearing some kind of "French lookin' hat," in his words.

8. Regardless of the day he had, I'd always hear his brown leather shoes clop in through the back door, attached to the laundry room which had green linoleum flooring. A black lab and a golden retriever plodded behind keenly, greeting him. Sauntering into the kitchen, he would lay down his wire glasses. There was so little to them—just glass hung together with wire I might buy at a Hobby Lobby—and I was puzzled to learn later in life that they cost roughly in the area of $800. As he placed them on the calendar, which marked the days the dogs needed their heartworm pills, an uncle's birthday, post-cancer check ups, teacher's conferences, and other events, my father would immediately turn, opening the fridge to pull out a Vernors. Following was the pouring of pistachios into a dark blue glass cup no bigger than a side order of rice at a restaurant. If I happened to be doing homework in the kitchen, he would acknowledge me. "Hey Rachie."

9. Another after-work ritual was the donning of his sweatpants, while eating and lounging in his Laz-E-Boy in my parents' bedroom. He never saw the point in washing them, and they had large holes in the thighs and knees. Regardless of the season, he would wear them with a Champion hoodless sweatshirt, sometimes inside out. He never wanted a new one. He never wanted new things.

10. If the phone rang after he commenced sweatpants phase, one might hear him shout, "I'm not here!"

11. Often times we would have steak or chicken for dinner, and it was his job to season it. Rubbing the raw meat as one would with dough, it ran through his hands—tanned, blue-green veins expanded through the skin, flowing up to his dry knuckles. Once on a Memorial Day while I helped him, I remember him telling me, "Get into it. Use your hands—massage it deeply, just don't suffocate it. No one likes a flat steak." He had a way with flavor even after he lost his taste buds. His eyes would glaze over as he tended to the beef or pork or chicken, his face a content state. It was as if one were watching a symphony, the melody full of violin and piano, an act so beautiful I'd be unsure of its title, something like *Liebestraum No. 3 in A-Flat Major*.

12. With a tray of meat and tongs laid on top, wearing his slippers or "clod-hoppers" as we so often called them, he would step outside. If it rained he would still sit outside under the overhang of our roof, getting comfortable in a wicker chair, enjoying a bit of fresh unexhausted air. If the mood struck him as he waited for the meat, he would practice his golf swing, holding an imaginary club and looking off into the distance. I would watch from the kitchen window out into the yard, as he pictured the imaginary flying ball. I got the feeling he was very lonely, just from the voiceless sigh he would give as the ball disappeared altogether.

13. He gives odd pointers. While teaching me to cut a proportionate onion ringlet for burgers, maybe when I was ten or eleven, he encouraged me to finely slice the onion as if it were a human, applying the point first and making my way down until it was finished. I never figured out if that was a medical statement or a murderous one.

14. He is desensitized to death or maybe just overly realistic. My dog, a golden retriever, named Molly (Midge for short), developed intestinal cancer. I couldn't get her to take her throat medicine—it was becoming eroded from all the bile and acidy vomit she was producing. My father watched as I attempted to help her. "She is going to die," my father said, and continued to watch TV.

15. After my father had his first surgery regarding his cancer treatment, his neck was littered with a long orderly strip of stitches. They bled often and without warning. Days after the surgery, while my parents were lounging in the living room with me as we all watched *The Wire*, my mother asked if my father was ready to take out his stitches.

"Yeah, Rachel is taking them out," he said, informing me.

16. When I was in 7th grade, my father found a tumor in his neck the size of a golf ball. After driving home from the Ann Arbor Medical Center for his radiation and chemo, he would walk in the door and head to bed, not talking to anyone but my mother. I brought him a glass of water as he stared at the TV with a dead face. He grabbed my wrist. "What day is, Rach?"

"It's Friday, Dad," I said.

"Oh. Don't tell anyone I asked," he said, hardly moving his lips.

17. He considers himself "suave." While getting ready for my homecoming dance and dealing with the final touches—something that already turned me off—Walter suggested that I spray all areas of my body that have a pulse with perfume—wrists, both sides of the neck, carotid arteries, jugular veins, and my "hip area," as he put it. The advice was not useless, but surprising as I thought fathers would shy away from giving this kind of advice to their daughters.

18. Another time, while getting ready to have a drink with the other dentists from work, he came to me for advice. "Rach, can you come see what I should wear? I was thinking the black pants with the black shirt. Or should I do the red one with the khakis?"

"I don't know. I think both are fine."

"Well, fine doesn't really make friends."

"These people are already your friends, Dad," I explained.

"Do I have to go? Ya know, I'm not a social guy."

"Yeah, whatever, ya weirdo. You're going," I said, exiting.

19. I used to do my homework late at night after swim practice in my father's study, a small room at the end of our main hall. The wooden shelves supported one entire wall of books that I liked to pretend I had read: *Black in White America*, *Linear Systems*, *The Bible*, *Nutrition*, etc. On the far end of one bookshelf there was a human skull. My father never did tell me where he got it. Below the skull was a cold leather chair that no one ever sat in because it awkwardly creaked under the pressure of human weight. Beneath our feet was an oriental rug fraying at the edges; along the other sides of the room, a wall of degrees, a three-foot-tall filing cabinet. His desk overlooked the front yard; wooden blinds hung one-third of the way down the windows, a glass dog head resting in the corner of the desk, and a small lamp off to the side. My father never sleeps, and would always come in to turn on one more light.

"It's too dark in here. You'll hurt your eyes," he'd say, and leave in his robe.

20. My father returned home one evening when he was working at the correctional facility. "How was it?" I asked.

"Oh, another day from hell," my father said.

"Why's that?" I asked.

"Oh well, one of the inmates was all pissed 'cause when I went down to see if anyone was having any problems with their teeth, one guy start shoutin' at me, 'My jaw hurt.'"

"So his jaw just hurt."

"Naw, his jaw was hurting 'cause I socked him with my elbow when he try to get up and stab me with some little pick he made while I was workin' on him. I said it wouldn't have to hurt if you act right.'"

"Oh," I said.

21. He is a religious man. He once explained to me over a sandwich and beer that he had a pact with God—*his* God, apparently he has his own. He tells me every so often, and when he does he laughs to himself, looking lucky, "I asked God for a few things: to be the best dentist I could be, to help people, and well…you probably don't want to know the last thing." I figured it had something to do with my mother and "hip areas."

22. When I was ready to head off to college for the first time, at a certain point my father and I were waiting outside, next to my mother's grey Nissan Pathfinder, while she was inside using the restroom. He handed me a small Beretta knife, about as weightless as having a credit card in your pocket.

"Take this," he said. "You remember what I taught you."

"Yeah, I know."

"Okay, do what you have to."

"I will. Don't worry."

"Good," he said, rubbing the top of my head, creating static. "Oh, and also, swallow a little olive oil if you're going to be drinking. Evens and separates everything in there." He poked my belly, unaware of his force. My stomach throbbed for minutes afterwards, feeling like a ship blinking on someone's radar.

23. Our family has a cellar off of the finished basement. We tend to keep lawn chairs down there, air conditioners, skis from the '70s, dusty construction boots that would only fit a transitioning Neanderthal, and old *Life* magazines. Once while rummaging around down there, I came across a leather bundle. As I unrolled it, I expected antique dentistry tools or old cameras, but instead it was unusual hand knives—some with curves, others pencil straight. Their existence was a mystery to me until one day, while at a family cookout in Detroit, my brother Jake told me that our father had pulled him aside one Saturday as a young boy, and told him he used to be a spook (an undercover spy for the CIA, often times African-American). He insisted that Dad had shown him a knife that was shaped like a crescent moon and gotten involved through an ex-girlfriend's father. I never believed him until my escapades in the basement.

24. The basement of my parents' home has dark red carpet, leather couches, and a bar with a pool table that has three classic green shades over the lights, all of which hung in a row. My father is a good player but can have a temper. On one occasion as I was watching *SpongeBob Squarepants*, his irritability overtook him, missing just one shot too many. He turned around jamming the pool stick into the closet doors where we stored Christmas decorations and old encyclopedias.

25. My father has darker skin; perhaps one level above severely sunburned. I later learned that his great grandmother was a slave on Robert E. Lee's plantation. On days my father was feeling close to his roots, he would put his hand out to me, palm up, and say, "*You're black*," and with such principle, he would stare at me until he felt like I appreciated it. Maybe he was worried that East Grand Rapids, Michigan, the vast majority of which was white, had ruined my blood.

26. When I was a kid, my baby teeth never fell out on their own. Walter would call me to his side, poking his fingers at the loose teeth he noticed I'd been fiddling with. "Go get me a napkin," he'd say. He'd rise from his Laz-E-Boy chair, standing behind me, tall enough to hover over me like a fallen leaf above a passerby. Without actually counting to three, he would clutch the root of my tooth and yank; the sound of cracking in my gum's socket reminded me of an axe devouring the center of an inadequate door.

27. We put our dog Molly down once we knew she couldn't handle anymore—the cancer, the vomiting, the distress. I waited in the lobby of the vet while my father and Molly went into another room. I couldn't handle feeling the deflation of her ribs, my hand collapsing with her middle, witnessing her breath give out; but through the rectangular window, I saw my father, in his old age, lying down with her on the cold tile, kissing her ear, petting her side. I could hear him say, "I'll close my eyes with you." The nurse began to cry.

28. In first grade I broke my arm, and after my surgery my parents stood by my side as my mother was feeding me ice cubes. I swallowed roughly, and said my throat hurt. My father looked at me sternly and said, "Suck it up."

29. My father has reported that as a child he was not a bright apple. And in my times of distress, sitting over math homework, I could tell he sensed the disappointment I was feeling. "Ya know, Rachel," he'd say, "I used to have a Charlie Brown head. There was just not enough room for my brain to grow in there, and my mother would call me all kinds of stupid."

30. While cleaning out my closet, grabbing bunches of bent hangers and old leather purses from the bottom of the cramped closet, I bent down, my spine "C" shaped. I hit my head on a snowboard boot binding, and noticed a hole in the wall. I wiggled my pointer finger through it, and realized it was hollow on the other side. Using the rest of my hand's strength, I yanked the piece of wood open and it became a door that was hiding stacks of bonds from the '80s along with a rusty pistol, heavy and out of date. I kept it to myself.

31. On fall days if and when he is feeling artistic, Walter will cook seafood gumbo, making it an all-day event. He takes comfort in washing the lobster, crab, oysters, shrimp, and other vegetables. He brings out his arsenal of spices—cayenne, white pepper, paprika, black pepper, thyme—treating some with more care than others, but regardless manages to spread a fine soot of them all onto the counter. Finishing, he would pet the dogs on the heads as he exited the kitchen to check up on whatever football game was playing. "Noooo, none for you guys," he'd say innocently.

32. Our living room holds a large-scale framed painting in a gold rim. It is a watercolor—blues, greys, and purples, loosely forming a foggy thick hearted river, one that continues to flow after a harsh storm without complaining. The mist sets in on the river, and it's impossible to see where the river ends. My father's initials are in the corner.

33. One afternoon my father and I were watching TV while my mother was gone, taking groceries to my brother in East Lansing. We were watching *Have Gun Will Travel* when he interjected randomly, "Did you know I didn't even used have to drink when I could smoke weed? I used to smoke joints and drink a Coke all the time in dental school."

"Yeah?" I said.

"Oh yeah. The best part was that I started raisin' my hand in class, askin' all type of questions. Me and the professor was on the same page after that. Yup, that's when it all clicked for me, just had ta slow down."

34. The morning of the 2008 presidential election while all of us were getting ready for the day, I could hear my father shaving in my parents' bathroom, worried that the US wasn't ready for Obama. "What if we don't win?" he kept saying to himself. Then he would call to my mother, "Mary! What if we don't win?"

35. I was walking out the door, headed to a friend's house when my father, high from wine and golfing all day, stopped me in our hallway. "Ya know, Rach, when I grow up I want to be just like you."

I'm almost positive he heard that on *The Simpsons* before (not unlikely), but I guess it was the thought that counted.

TWO LIES AND A TRUTH
PHALLON PERRY
NORTHWESTERN UNIVERSITY

MAMA SAID THAT UNTIL WE TELL HER THE TRUTH about where we were last night, we are gonna stay punished. Our arms feel like pizza dough from all the housework she's making us do. We probably should've discussed it before we came home this morning. Maybe we should've devised a plan, or at least got our stories straight. Since only one of us told her the truth, she flipped her wig and has us doing chores until she figures out what really happened.

"Patricia, sweep the stoop and the sidewalk, I don't want to see any dirt around this building. Thomasina, walk over there to grocery on 35th and King and get dinner. It better be ready before I get home from work. Ramona, don't just stand around like you're cute. Get some work done!" She said we'll keep working until cows come home, and that will be a long time in Chicago.

RAMONA'S STORY

Okay, Mama, I'll tell you what happened, but can you try not to interrupt? Okay, yes ma'am. I'm sorry. So you know how Thomasina is the only one of us that has her license? Well, Patricia asked Thomasina to take her to see Aaron before he left for R.O.T.C. training. You know Aaron, Mama. He's that dude she's been going steady with, and since she *is* our little sister, I decided to tag along. I was just looking out for her, maybe being a little nosey, too. It's kinda strange that *she* would have someone to go steady with and *I* don't. Yes ma'am, I'll stay on track. So she said she would only need two hours with Aaron, so we dropped her off at his apartment building. She said his parents would be there. No, ma'am, we didn't check. He doesn't live too far from us; he's in the Robert Taylor homes.

Me and Thomasina needed something to do for two hours, so we went down to Vito and Nick's Pizzeria. Yes, ma'am, the one off 84th Street. We had the car, plus it was a Friday night, so everyone was there. We crammed ourselves into the 13 by 11 space. It was gross. It felt like we were on a crowded bus during rush hour, except the greasy pizza joint was actually less greasy than the bus. You don't believe me, Mama? Smell my hair, it still smells like a Pizza Supreme. No one wanted to leave and we were stuck for what seemed like hours. Me and Thomasina had to eat three or four slices of pizza just so it wouldn't be a total drag. Mama, you know how I am about my figure. I do too have a figure! I'm going to be the next Diana Ross.

Anyway, while we were at Vito and Nick's, some guy invited us to go to a concert at the Regal Theatre. I don't know, Mama, he said he worked there. He had three extra tickets and he gave them to us. The Gems were performing! I know we weren't supposed to be out too late but we thought it would be all right as long as we were home before you got up for work.

We went back to Aaron's to pick Patricia up for the concert, but she wasn't there. No one was there. We pressed almost every buzzer on the north building of the Robert Taylor homes before someone finally spoke over the intercom and said that the Lawrence family left a few days ago.

We left her in front of the building when we dropped her off. We didn't wait for her to go in. I know, Mama, we should've waited. I know that now, but we didn't. We drove around for about thirty minutes looking for her. We didn't want the concert tickets to go to waste, so we decided to go to the Regal Theatre. Mama, The Gems were so hip! I think they are going to be famous one day. The lead singer's name is Minnie Riperton, and she is bad with a capital B. I know you don't listen to that kind of music, but...yes ma'am, I'm sorry. The show was only an hour, so afterwards we came back to look for Patricia again. We parked outside of the Robert Taylor homes all night. Yes ma'am, we slept in the car. Hang loose, Mama, it wasn't that big of a deal. We're used to the sounds of sirens and women yelling for their husbands to come home. We were safe. We kept the doors locked. Patricia came back the next morning. She said she went to Celeste's house for the night. You always told us, "Don't come home without your sisters." So we didn't. We were just trying to do as we were told.

PATRICIA'S STORY

Mama, I bet they tried to throw me under the bus. I had absolutely nothing to do with it. It's four of us in a two-bedroom flat and since three of us share a room, you know how easy it is to wake someone up. They were scared that I would snitch, so they lied and told me that they were running an errand for you. So of course I wanted to help. You know how much I love you.

Mama, you were already asleep. I know because you had that blues record playing. You always play that record when you are about to go to sleep. Last night was just a regular night on the southside. I was actually watching the leaves fall from the trees, right before I went to bed last night. You know fall is my favorite season.

Remember that money that was missing from your pocket book? Well, I think Thomasina took it. She told me that she knew what really happened to it and that we had to go out to the Regal Theatre to get it back. We had to find it—thirty dollars is a lot of money to be losing. I got dressed and went with them. Mama, you should've seen what they were wearing. It was bad, real bad. And not the good kind of bad either. Their clothes were tight and showed off all of their goodies. Mama, I think Ramona was wearing a foam dome, you would've been so ashamed. No, I have no idea where they got those clothes from. What did I wear? Oh, just the regular clothes I wear to school. I've never been outside that late, but it wasn't bad. It was still a regular fall night in Bronzeville. You could hear the crunch of the dried leaves against the pavement under women's high-heeled shoes, and the angry voices of men frustrated with the cabbies that pass them by, and the jingle of change banging up and down and side to side in a homeless man's coffee cup. Oh, I'm sorry ma'am, I thought you wanted to know who all was outside with us.

Well, when we got to the theatre there was some guy standing outside. He wasn't even wearing a shirt, just a red velvet jacket and a gold chain. His name? Oh, I forget, I think it began with a C. As soon as we got out of the car, Thomasina ran up to him and demanded her money back. I think she gave that guy your money, Mama. It was some sort of bet I think, I don't know. She kept screaming to the guy, "I have to put that money back before Mama finds out." Thomasina and Ramona never tell me anything. All I know is that Thomasina and Ramona were hacked off with him, especially when he laughed in their faces. He told them if they wanted their money back, they had to go inside and work for it. The guy gave me a ticket to see The Gems, so I went into the auditorium. I don't know where he took them, but the show ran pretty late, so we met outside of the Regal Theatre at the end of the night. They were boiling hot mad and still didn't have all of the money to return to you. That's all I know, Mama.

THOMASINA'S STORY

Mama, I don't know what those two have been telling you, but I swear this is the truth. You know how everyone always says, "Ramona is so pretty, Ramona has good hair, Ramona should be a model." Ramona's head is getting bigger with each compliment. Ramona told me that a cool dude approached her and Patricia one day after school on that bus that goes up 31st Street. He said he owned a modeling agency and could make big things happen for both of them. Even Patricia, Mama, I saw his business card in our bedroom. His name was Clyde Something. He told Patricia that he could use her in a commercial. We all know that Ramona has always been the pretty one, so when someone took notice of Patricia too, you know aside from that Aaron boy she's going steady with, she got really excited. You've seen Aaron, Mama. He used to be real chubby, just like Patricia? He lives in the Robert Taylor homes. Yes ma'am, his parents are still together. Anyway, it made sense for the two of them to date when they were both chubby, but then Aaron started doing that R.O.T.C. stuff and lost all of that baby fat and they just didn't look right together anymore. It's the truth, Mama! They are still going steady, so who cares?

Anyway, Ramona told me that the guy invited them to a show at the Regal Theatre. The Gems were performing there last night, and he wanted to show Ramona and Patricia what it would be like to hang around famous people since they would be models someday. I told them no way! They were not going to meet up with that guy without me, and yes of course I wanted to see Minnie Riperton. I hear she may not be with The Gems for much longer. I told Ramona to check with you to make sure you were okay with everything. She said that she did. I was just tagging along as their chaperone since you had to go to bed early to rest up before your second job. I heard the blues music playing from your bedroom when I got home from detention. Oh nothing, it was silly. I'll tell you about that later, Mama.

I drove to the Regal Theatre where we met up with that Clyde guy. Mama, that guy was as cold as a pimp's heart and he had a chrome dome. No, no, I don't think he was really a pimp, Mama, he just dressed like one. He wore a two-inch gold-plated chain and his goatee was just a straight line of hair from the center of his bottom lip down to his chin. He had on sunglasses even though it was dark, and wore a red crushed velvet blazer with no shirt and black slacks with the crease ironed in them. His belly looked like he started drinking Double Diamond when he was an infant. Oh, and I didn't tell you the best part. Ramona and Patricia were dressed like something out of a hooker film: denim skirts, knee high leather boots, and red foam domes under a thin white shirt. No, I have no idea where they got those clothes from, Mama. I didn't even ask.

So the Clyde guy was waiting for us at the front door. Or should I say, waiting for Patricia and Ramona. He wasn't very interested in me because I didn't dress like I stepped out of a brothel. He asked me to wait in the car but I remembered what you always said, "Always stay together" and "Don't come home without your sisters." I told that guy, if I couldn't get in, my little sisters couldn't get in either. Ramona was desperately trying to ditch me once we got inside. The music was nice. Oooh Mama, when Minnie hit those high notes, I almost fainted to the floor. Yes, ma'am, I'm sorry.

So Clyde pulled Ramona through the crowd, and Ramona pulled Patricia, who pulled me. I don't know if you ever tried to move like a chain through a concert in Chicago, but it's almost impossible to stay linked. There were a few other people moving like chains, and their chains were bigger and stronger than ours and just like that I became the missing link. I searched that theatre forever before I found Patricia. She was in the john crying like a kid lost in the shopping center. They told her to lose thirty pounds before she ever tried to model again. I tried to comfort her as best as I could but we were still missing a link in our chain.

We continued to search the theatre until it closed and still no sign of Ramona. Most of the people there had cleared out and we finally saw Clyde and a few other men joshing and high-fiving each other when they came out of the men's room. Patricia was too embarrassed to face Clyde again so she stayed back. I ran up to him and asked what he did with Ramona. His buddy said, "What didn't we do with Ramona, right Clyde?" Then they laughed and walked right out of the Regal Theatre. Me and Patricia sat on the sofa near the men's bathroom, trying to figure out what to do next. That's when we heard the door to the men's room swing open again. It was Ramona. Her hair was disheveled and her shirt was buttoned wrong, and her legs were all scratched up. I asked her what happened, but all she said was something about it being okay because they told her that she had star quality.

CITY OF STEEL
ROBERT ERIC SHOEMAKER
UNIVERSITY OF CHICAGO

Fine steel slickens an orb, floating snow within
 shake-it, the snow flies—the grey city stands;
Soot bumps up borders and sloughs off,
 misdirected in the streets, shooting up free spaces;
The river bleeds life into the north, but someone here created it
 in a bloodless neo-lith.
Can we sit: Harold's Chicken Shack
 in a light vapidness?

THE SNUFF FILM
AMY KISNER
COLUMBIA COLLEGE

EVERYTHING BEGAN ON A NORMAL DAY in October, right when the city was letting go of summer and pulling out warmer clothes, on the northeast side of Chicago. Edgewater to be exact. It was not quite Halloween, but the holiday was everywhere, and in everything, she passed. The Jewel parking lot served as a pumpkin patch, advertising the ripe orange gourds. Each shop window was decorated with whimsical drawings of witches on brooms, black cats, and spooky ghosts. Pumpkin spice lattes, sprinkled with cinnamon, perfumed the air. The leaves were changing color and a chill clung to her rosy cheeks.

There was no mistaking it, autumn was here.

Maryann Meadows clutched her olive green military jacket closer to keep out the icy breeze, and flicked her wavy auburn hair out of her eyes. She was neither tall nor short, pretty nor ugly, fat nor skinny. She fell somewhere right in the middle of every adjective. Maryann was the type of person immediately swallowed up in a

159

crowd. Whenever her friends described her to someone who didn't know her, they simply said, "she has a great sense of humor." To this day, she wasn't quite sure what that *actually* meant.

Sampson's was littered with second-hand comics, records, movies, and musty old novels, and therefore was her favorite place in all of Illinois, possibly the world. As a self-described horror geek, Maryann was always looking for ways to freak out her friends; and occasionally, tucked between soft leather covers, she found a coveted morbid treasure. In Sampson's depths, she uncovered a book on covens, an illustrated history of torture, and an anthology of serial killer lore. Maryann rounded the corner to the old bookstore, intent on buying the scariest thing she could find. The windows were adorned with cotton ball cobwebs, but there was something creepy about the paper spiders with ripped off legs and sour expressions.

The musk of worn, yellowed pages greeted her fondly. The handle was adorned with a bell that rang out as the door swung shut behind her. The shop was dim and quiet, slightly claustrophobic due to the sheer number of books lining the shelves, books stacked as far back as Maryann could see, but cozy nonetheless. Tilda, Mr. Lawler's Cornish Rex, scratched at her tights. Her nails caught and a large run split along the length of Maryann's calf. She reached down, scratched behind the pointed ears and smiled when Tilda purred and nuzzled her face along the run.

"Hello, Maryann! No Joey today? I can't remember the last time I saw one without the other." Sherwood Lawler owned Sampson's and was the only employee. He always joked to friends that payroll was the hardest part. He was an ancient hippie and perpetually red-eyed and grinning. His favorite subject was philosophy, but he seldom got to talk about it. Any mention of the word "spiritual" in Mr. Lawler's shop led to a forty-five minute lecture about the meaning of life; Maryann found that one out the hard way.

Usually Joey was the one that conversed with Mr. Lawler, having a better grasp on socialism and Karl Marx, and the days in which Maryann came alone were filled with Mr. Lawler's awkward ice breakers. Neither one of them quite knew what to say to one another, so Mr. Lawler would usually mumble to himself until Maryann backed far enough away into the stacks that his voice sort of just drifted off.

"No sir, just me today," Maryann returned brightly, waving at him before she disappeared between the rows, headed straight for the horror section. Her gaze slid along the cracked spines, reading each title with increasing boredom. She yawned and turned her attention to the occult section, but then she saw it.

It looked typical enough: an everyday slender DVD case (packed between *Cannibal Holocaust* and *Demonology for Dummies*) but bound with black electrical tape. Bound so tightly, in fact, that the disc inside made no sound, even when she shook it with all her strength. Maybe it wasn't anything at all. Maryann squeezed the case between thumb and fingers, felt it spring back, and shook it once more.

Maybe it was nothing at all, just an empty case, wrapped around and around with black tape. But it could be something else entirely. Who would care enough to lock up a film? There had to be something good on here. Something embarrassing or gross or funny; hopefully all three. Maybe this would *make* Halloween weekend. Her friends usually gathered at Joey's house to watch horror movies and play with ouija boards. At the very least, this had to beat watching *The Texas Chainsaw Massacre* for the thousandth time, anyway.

Maryann bit her lip and looked to her left, then to her right, just once more, then behind her, before she shoved the case in the inside pocket of her jacket. She didn't usually steal, but this wasn't *stealing*, right? There wasn't even a price tag. Mr. Lawler wouldn't mind if she just borrowed it for a few days. Right?

She whistled her way to the door. "Nothing today? Well tell Joey hello for us, won't ya?" Mr. Lawler waved over the top of his aged copy of *Moby Dick*. Tilda jumped into his lap and curled in upon herself. His eyes never slipped from Melville's words, even as his deft fingers turned the page. "Be careful, girl. You don't know who is out there lurkin'—" Maryann didn't catch the rest, already dashing to the train.

Minutes later, Maryann walked up the garden path and paused to sniff her mother's orange cosmos. She lived on a corner lot just a few minutes' walk from the lake in a vintage Victorian brownstone. Ivy choked the home, wrapping around the front porch all the way up to the trim. Her bedroom was on the second floor and looked out onto the street, where she could peer out between the blinds every morning and make sure her forest green sedan was still parked, her back tire hopped up on the curb.

She walked through the front door and listened to the stillness. The house appeared utterly abandoned. Even her cocker spaniel was nowhere to be found. This was typical of the Meadows home, even at five o'clock on a Wednesday night. Her father worked as an orthodontist in the Loop and was hardly ever home before eight. Her mother was attending a conference in Milwaukee and would not return until Saturday morning.

Maryann headed up the stairs to her room, shutting the door behind her. She grabbed her pocketknife from the bedside table and cut away at the tape until she was able to wrench the case apart. Perched innocently against the dark background of the case, she saw a homemade disc with her name scrawled across the top in thick, shaky lettering.

A shiver licked along her spine. Everything suddenly felt cold, but Maryann had heat in her cheeks and palms. She pressed the knob at the center of the shell and let the disc drop onto her hot, open palm. Maryann gulped as she slid the disc into the DVD drive of her laptop.

The movie started up. Everything looked low budget. Shaky camerawork, dim lighting, guy in cliche pig mask, check, check, check. Maryann grinned, almost laughing out loud to herself. Obviously, it was nothing but a Halloween movie Joey made to scare her, then slipped into the store because he knew she would be unable to resist the mysterious packaging. He loved Halloween more than she did, and he was always fiddling around on his laptop making little horror movies. This one must have been made with added effort.

Nice try.

"Good one, Joey. You almost got me," she mumbled, watching as the pig-masked figure moved between a line of houses and appeared outside a brownstone with the lights off on the first floor. The camera panned upward. One light was on upstairs. There were curtains covering the window, but they were buttercream yellow transparent lace and provided little coverage.

The lens floated up effortlessly and peered in through the lace and gazed into the window. Maryann couldn't help but notice there were no trees in the front yard. The picture zoomed in, blurred, readjusted, zoomed out, and focused.

A young girl, about seventeen, with dirty blonde hair, long and pulled back, stood in front of a mirror removing makeup with a moist towel. Maryann had a sudden realization that left her swallowing hard, trying to fill the quicksand pit in her stomach. This was *her* house, but as it appeared years ago. She recognized the neighbor's weeping willow that spilled over the property line in the backyard, the wrap-around porch, the gravel path to the front door, even the ivy, although it was only an accent at this point.

That room, the one with the curtains, was her room! Maryann swallowed hard and looked over at the window. She didn't have curtains, but slanting venetian blinds. She moved toward them and lifted one panel, then another.

Everything was still. Not even a car drove by. She heard a dog barking off in the distance and looked out beyond the neighborhood. The sun was setting, a giant blood orange perched atop tangerine skies. She took a deep breath and smiled at her paranoia.

What a stupid thought. Maryann did laugh this time. Maybe Joey Davenport scared her a *little*.

When Maryann turned back to the screen, the same thin blonde girl from a few frames earlier was tied to her four-poster bed by electrical cords Pigmask had ripped out of the walls. Maryann's smile slid right off her mouth. The girl was crying pathetically as she tugged against the knots. A trail of tears mingled with the vermilion flood flowing freely from her nostrils.

Pigmask looked around the room for a moment. He appeared to be looking for something specific, but he didn't seem to know *what* that was yet. Then his eyes landed on her desk where a fat gray rat slept in its steel cage. The girl seemed to follow his line of sight and whimpered as she pulled against the cords until thin crimson cuffs decorated her ankles and wrists. Pigmask overturned the mason jar she kept her pens in and snatched up the rat.

The rat squealed and scurried across Pigmask's hands, trying not to be caught in the heavy leather gloves he wore. The girl's terrified blue eyes widened as Pigmask caged the rat in the jar, shoved her shirt up to her ribs, and then situated the glass rim against her stomach. The blonde wailed now, thrashed against her binds and begged for Pigmask not to hurt her. Maryann chewed on her nails subconsciously, a habit she had been working on for the last six months to break, wide eyes transfixed on the television screen.

From his pocket, Pigmask extracted a Zippo lighter with the American flag painted across the top, chipped and faded but apparent. He rubbed out a light and let the flames dance against the bottom of the mason jar. The rat started to squirm. Maryann had never heard a sound quite as unsettling as the squeal of that rat. It was like a baby crying and a rabbit being skinned and a dog's tail being stomped on all mixed together. The rat scratched at the glass, but Pigmask held it harder against her skin, ringing her pale flesh with a red coaster. She howled, yanking so hard on her restraints that the frame cracked audibly, but could not free herself. Pigmask did not seem bothered by the heat, nor the squeals of pain, as bits of flesh danced against the crystal wall of the rat's prison. Blood began to pool in the jar and leaked down her sides. It clung to the yellow fibers of her quilt, and spread like ink across a damp page.

The girl fought no more. The rat was drowned in a pool of blood. Pigmask stood with his hand wrapped around the jar for several minutes. The film cut out and static filled the room for a brief moment.

Stunned, Maryann reached for the trackpad in slow motion. Her stomach wriggled uncomfortably and she thought of the rat gnawing through her insides. She shivered and exhaled sharply, thinking of that rat, that *pet* rat. She wondered what being eaten by your own pet was like. Maryann pitched forward as a wave of nausea clawed along her throat at the thought of her own pet cocker spaniel, Barkley. She reached for the waste basket and retched up the ramen noodles she ate for lunch. At least Barkley preferred bones to meat.

Before Maryann pressed stop, a new scene formed on the screen. Still a girl tied to a bed, but a different girl. She had cardinal hair, dirty with mud and dried blood. She was naked and covered in yellow and green bruises, others black and brown, still more blue and purple. If she were a child, Maryann would have thought she could be covered in camouflage paint. Underneath her, the bed was stained sanguine and hay-yellow. The girl was gagged, her right eye swollen shut, her other green eye pointed at the ceiling. She breathed heavily as footsteps approached out of the camera's vantage point. At the bottom of the screen, Pigmask appeared and slid his bare hand along the girl's navel. Black fuzz spread across the length of his hand and his left thumb was nonexistent. She shuddered and whimpered against the rag clamped between her teeth and secured with black electrical tape. Salty rivers trenched her muddy cheeks.

The camera jerked into blackness and Maryann whimpered, feeling the goosebumps spread from the nape of her neck down across her legs. Who would make this for her? Who would go through all the trouble to stash it somewhere inconspicuous that *only she* would find? Maryann's breath froze in her throat. Maybe this wasn't Joey Davenport's stupid prank. *Maybe it was a warning*, she thought as another lumpy yellow splash of wet vomit decorated the garbage bin.

On the screen, her house came back into view; some years later, evidently, as the vines had climbed up past the windows of the first story. Trees were taller and the neighborhood grew larger and better manicured. Pigmask could be seen inside the house, reflected in the mirror on the second landing. He paused at the balcony looking into the living room, and headed for Maryann's bedroom. Except it wasn't Maryann's bedroom. Not yet.

The camera moved along the exterior of the house before a girl came into view. She was thin with long, black hair and brown almond eyes. Her back was turned to the door when he stepped into the room. She was already slumped over and unconscious by the time the door closed.

The scene jumped and Maryann squelched a scream when she saw the same girl, her feet bound together with black electrical tape and her hands nailed to the wall behind her. Pigmask hovered over her, a sharp little pocket knife in his right hand. Maryann looked for flaws in the makeup, gore, and production of the video, any clues that would indicate the film was fabricated.

But it looked authentic in the worst way.

Maryann chewed on hangnails until blood welled up in the folds of her fingertips.

The masked man circled his victim with heavy steps and Maryann inched closer to the screen. Her eyes were focused on the pocket knife, the green handle, the sharp thin blade, the gold *M* engraved in the butt. Maryann suddenly realized the horrible truth, her face paling as she raked a hand across her forehead, sweat tangling her hair across her face. She took a deep breath and looked down at her open palm, a pocketknife with a forest green handle and a golden engraved *M* into the butt. The same knife she used to open the fucking case that held this very movie, Pigmask had used to do something horrible to this girl. On screen the dark-haired girl shuddered awake, and started to scream and plead. She spoke another language, maybe Korean. But Maryann didn't need to know Korean to understand the words she howled.

Pigmask sliced at her with the blade. Once, twice, three times. Angry crimson ribbons decorated her tanned skin. Four, five, six times. Blood welled up along the raised flesh. Sanguine bubbles raised and burst. Seven, eight, nine times. The blade snaked silently along her flesh. Patterns formed in the slices. Droplets dripped down the curves of her body and rained down, soaking into the carpet. No wonder they had hardwood now.

Thirty, forty, fifty times. Maryann could hardly watch as blood stained the carpet, spread an outline of the bloody girl against the white wall. Maryann tried to understand why Pigmask sliced the skin rather than stabbed it, why he should waste so much time making such a mess. By the hundredth cut, Maryann realized, with a wave of revulsion, that Pigmask was going to let the girl bleed out. She heard about this once, in that illustrated guide to torture she had found in the stacks of Sampson's. Death by a thousand cuts: an ancient Chinese torture tactic intended to remove portions of the body after a long, meticulous process of choreographed cuts. Maryann pressed the fast-forward button and watched the cuts cascade across the skin until an arm fell off, an ear toppled to the ground, fingers rained down, thudding against the carpet.

Pieces were shed away until there was nothing but a slumped figure left, indistinguishable and mutilated, caked in blood both fresh and congealed.

The shot faded out and the screen was dark for several moments.

Maryann pressed the square button. The screen turned blue. She seriously considered yanking out the video. Was it real or not?

She took a few deep breaths and realized her hands were shaking like a Parkinson's patient. Maryann stood up and walked to the window. She hesitated there for a full minute before she peeked through the blinds down the suburban street. Leaves drifted from tree branches, people shuffled along the street, leashed dogs barked and sniffed, drivers lurched into tight spaces. Nothing out of the ordinary out there, especially not a man in a mask. The seventeen-year-old laughed to herself.

Of course this was just some stupid joke! And she had actually let Joey scare her. She felt a little ashamed. She had to admit the video was well-done, even for a gore-master wannabe. Maryann had watched all of Joey's ten-minute horror movies, put together on a nonexistent budget and usually with horrible, unrealistic dialogue, but this was better than all of them put together. Probably the lack of dialogue. Joey didn't really understand how to speak to anyone.

If Joey did make the video, and she struggled to convince herself he had, he deserved a goddamn medal.

Maryann pressed play, determined to finish it. At least to see Joey's stupid monologue at the end about how he had planned this elaborate prank for an entire year and how, haha, she stupidly fell for it. After all, that'd be the kind of time he would need for a movie like this. The blood seemed so real it made her squirm. Maryann wouldn't be bested, not by Joey fucking Davenport.

The redhaired girl was back on the screen, moisture dropping from her eyelids and muddying her cheeks. Pigmask stood over her, armed with needle-nose pliers. She scooted as far away from him as she could, whimpered against her gag, and yanked against her binds. Each tug cut more into her flesh but she couldn't stop. Pigmask lunged forward, clamped the pliers against her areola and yanked. A chunk of flesh came with him and the girl screamed out in anguish. The pliers jerked forward once more, seized at her left nipple, and wrenched it clean off.

Static rippled across the television screen. The scene was bathed in bright white light. Pigmask stood in the bathroom—Maryann's very bathroom, she could tell by the rippled glass behind the shower and the square pattern of solid white tiles framed around the opaque window. He bent over the sink and cleaned the blood from the pliers. He wiped them against the white hand towel and looked around the bathroom. He snatched up a charm bracelet and dropped it into his pocket. Pigmask lumbered out of the bathroom and switched off the light.

The bracelet jingled with every step.

A young girl appeared on screen, naked and being held by her hair. She clawed at the gloved hands that levitated her, cried out and thrashed her skinny body. Pigmask shoved her closer to the bathtub and she actually fought back. Her skinny arms reached out for every wall; her legs searched for potential ledges; her fingernails, long and sharp, swiped at him relentlessly until Pigmask suckerpunched her. The girl slumped forward like a little ragdoll. He shoved her closer to the tub. Her eyes opened wide and she dug her heels into the bathroom rug. She was screaming, but it sounded like a war cry.

There was something off about the hazy color of the water.

Maryann swallowed against the lump in her throat as she played "Name The Substance" all on her lonesome. Bleach? Acid? Piranhas? Snakes? Maybe some sort of poisonous creature? She didn't know what lurked under the murky surface, but she knew the girl wasn't fighting that hard for nothing. The camera panned over to the container of lye perched precariously on the toilet bowl, as if it sensed her curiosity. A shiver licked along the bumps of her spine.

This girl was the oldest Maryann had seen, probably nineteen or twenty, with full breasts and curvy hips. She was stronger than the other girls, with more fight in her, but Pigmask was stronger. Maryann admired her, rooted for her and even prayed for a change in the scene. In horror movies, there's always one who gets away.

Maybe there was hope for her yet!

She elbowed Pigmask in the nose. A sharp snap reverberated across the tile. If it hurt him, Pigmask never showed it. He wrestled the girl into the tub and held her by her hair under the water. So much for the-one-who-got-away.

A tear dripped onto her tights. Maryann instinctively reached a hand up to her cheek. She was crying and hadn't realized it, crying for this girl, crying for the Korean, crying for the redhead, crying for the blonde, crying for herself. Could something fake make her feel this terrified? Maryann stopped kidding herself that it could. She had seen every horror movie she could get her pudgy little hands on since she was ten. Seven years later, she had sat through several "snuff" films with Joey, and none of them looked like this. This was too vivid, too understated, too real. Where was this camera man? And how can he get so close to such an intimate execution without seemingly being seen? Maryann tasted blood on her tongue. She had been chewing the skin off her bottom lip.

The water bubbled and sizzled, turning from hazy yellow to pink as bits of flesh floated to the surface, her skin starting to rot away. The girl thrashed and screamed beneath the water, but when Pigmask let go of her three minutes later, distinguishable features eroded away: no nose, no mouth, no ears. Bile mauled her throat. Maryann swallowed over and over to keep it down. Whoever made this video—and she stopped believing it was Joey Davenport long ago—wanted to tell her something. Was it a warning or a promise?

The teenager shivered as the scene changed once more, but this time the subject was too familiar. The eyes: open, green, vacant, staring up at something beyond the scope of the lens. Her wavy auburn hair was splayed out behind her, spotted with droplets of water and blood. The nose was smashed in and blood pooled from both nostrils into the victim's mouth. Maryann gasped, staring into her own dead irises.

Maryann moved closer to the screen, gauged the authenticity of the shot. Each freckle was painted across the tip of her nose as they appeared in real life. Even the tiny mole at the corner of her philtrum was right where it should have been. She stared, open-mouthed, into the screen.

Static and white noise made her jump. Barkley, her cocker spaniel, lay on his stomach across the rug in front of her dresser, something locked between his front paws. He chewed, held it between his nails, gnawed the thing piece-by-piece. Pigmask appeared at the corner of the screen and Barkley stood up and growled. The dog backed further into the room and bared his teeth at the masked man. Pigmask dropped something that landed with a wet smack and Barkley approached it cautiously, sniffed it, and took it into his mouth. It was a finger, and Maryann gasped when she noticed the gold band it wore.

She looked at her right hand. The thin gold ring on her index finger with the ruby perched atop it was still there. She looked to the screen. The two were identical. Maryann inched closer, intent on spotting some sort of difference. There's no way this could be her ring, her finger. An ache made her feel like it was already missing.

Static and white noise. The screen was black again.

Her heart raced in her chest and she was certain she was having a heart attack. Her head spun. It was getting harder to breathe. Could you have a heart attack at seventeen? She wanted to throw up and shit herself all at the same time. Maryann swallowed the lump in her throat and focused her eyes on the screen, a squeak of panic escaping her lips.

The scene showed her Victorian brownstone, the ivy choking the house around the porch and all the way up to the trim, and the window in her room with the blinds drawn so that no one could see in. What startled her most, however, was her green sedan parked lopsided on the curb. Pigmask appeared in the center of the screen. His heavy steel-toed boots clapped against the sidewalk, passed her car, and then her mother's cosmos to her front door.

Maryann froze and placed her hands over her mouth to hold in her scream.

A knock at the front door echoed through the empty hallways.

TURN ME ON
KA'MIA MILLER
COLUMBIA COLLEGE

AND THERE SHE WAS RESTING peacefully on a sterile metal table. She looked exactly the same. Well, if you didn't include her pale cold skin and the large indent on the left side of her head still crusted over with dried blood. Jade hadn't been able to avoid the light post when her car slid and twisted through the blizzard snow. When her body projected from the window she was still breathing; it wasn't until her head cracked against the metal pole that death finally took her.

But even in death she was magnificent.

Pale hands twiddled with the colorful wires until he found them. He cut her brakes with a flick of his wrist. He stilled his shaking hands and took a deep breath. He had to do this. All of this was for her. His beautiful Jade.

Ian lost his breath. His eyes traced over her naked curves with reverence. He was completely in love with her and he wondered why he had never told her. Why it had to be something as drastic as dying to finally get a confession out of him. But he would tell her. Soon.

"Dude, can you do it or not?"

Ian sent an annoyed glance at Spike. The rebel was nervously pacing back and forth, the bright florescent lights of the morgue highlighting the worry lines on his forehead. Even his green Mohawk, pointed and towering like huge poisoned spikes, seemed to quiver under the overhead glare. A single silver hoop pierced the middle of his bottom lip and it twisted with the scowl he directed at Ian. He knew that Ian was different and now was the time to prove just how much.

"I told you I would. Be patient." Ian spoke like he would to a kindergartener. He wished he hadn't brought Spike, but Ian was no expert in late night B&E and Spike, in all his delinquent badass glory, had that area down pat. Plus Ian knew the rebel was curious to know if what he said was true. If he really did have the power to bring Spike's dead girlfriend back to life.

"You can bring her back to me?" The jagged edges of Spike's ripped jeans whispered across the floor. Spike's bad-boy persona was slipping and a scared little boy was peeking through the cracks. Ian rolled his eyes. He hated repeating himself.

"Yes, I can bring her back," Ian said. *To me*, he thought. *I'm bringing her back to me.* But Spike didn't need to know that. The fool could barely bring himself to look at his dead girlfriend. Ian mentally scoffed. Spike didn't love her half as much as Ian did.

Ian watched Jade walked through the halls, his eyes following her every movement. Her head and shoulders, slumped down; her feet dragged against the floor as she barely took the time to lift them. Her short dark hair hung limp at her shoulders, absent of its vibrant bounce. When she finally glanced up their eyes met.

For him it was a magical moment.

Her beautiful green eyes were dull and bloodshot and a thick black ring circled around her left eye-green standing out amongst a black and purple sea. She scowled at him before flipping him the bird. Ian bit back a smile. Jade was so tough and he admired her fire. He couldn't understand why Spike was trying to extinguish it.

Ian turned away from the nervous wreck and looked around the Chicago morgue. Everything was clean and bright. The cool temperature of the morgue cupped his overheated cheeks. A heavy stale dryness blanketed the air and every time he took a breath the toxic flavors of bleach and sterilization products would explode into his mouth, trailing achy streaks of numbness across his tongue. The overhead lights harshly reflected off the silver tables of the square metal drawers imbedded into the far right wall.

All those temporary coffins for the dead. Ian could practically hear their dead energy buzzing, could see and feel the wisps of grey matter lick at his fingertips, demanding him to bring them back to life. But he wouldn't. He was only here for one corpse.

He smiled when he finally found what he was looking for. He went over and wheeled the mini cart next to Jade's body, admiring how the many blades glinted off the light. The autopsy tools were already prepped and clean, ready to be used at his whim.

"Hey what are you doing?"

"Hey what are you doing?"

Spike had Jade backed into a corner under the bleachers. His hands were all over her. Ian saw her hands clutched tightly at Spike's shoulders, white knuckled and stiff. Her body was rigid and her eyes were empty. Ian glared at Spike and repeated his question.

"I said what are you doing?"

Spike turned to him, his green Mohawk wobbling dangerously. He sneered at Ian, eyes sparking with anger.

"What the fuck does it look like, loser? I'm spending time with my girl. Since you've never had one I know you can't understand that concept. Fuck off and give us some privacy."

Ian's eyes trailed back to Jade. She was staring off into the distance, quiet and still. Only the dead were that quiet. Ian casually rolled up his baggy sleeves and put his hands in his pockets. He tilted his head so that his pale blonde bangs fell over his eyes. His voice was calm and smooth.

"I suggest you two get back to class."

Spike laughed.

"Why would I do that, dweeb?"

Ian slowly lifted his head and smiled at Spike. His smile was cold. He knew his big blue eyes were glowing, pulsing with a blue glow that spilled onto Spike; a sinister cold kind've light.

"Because I said so." His voice deepened while his lips widened, the promise of death close behind them. The hairs on the nape of Spike's neck stood as he pushed Jade to the floor without thought. Just like when prey instinctively knew when predators were near, Spike just knew. He didn't ask questions nor explanations, he just sprinted off without looking back.

Ian calmly helped Jade up, dusting her off gently before walking her to her next class. The whole way there she was quiet, still staring off into the distance at something he couldn't see. But Ian still felt it. He felt death near, and it wasn't because he was seriously thinking about killing Spike. Death was here of its own volition, seeping into Jade's aura like an infection. All he could do was watch in sorrowed silence. Jade's spirit was dying, crushed under the weight of Spike's desire. But Ian couldn't let her die this way. He had to do something.

Ian ignored Spike's pathetic whimpering. He picked up the scalpel and tested its sharpness. The sweet sting as it pricked his finger satisfied him.

He brought the tip of the blade just under her collarbone, right between the valley of her small breasts, and pushed down. Dead skin resisted the scalpel at first, until Ian added more pressure, then it parted for him.

"What the fuck are you doing, man!"

Ian once again ignored his partner in crime. He had to focus. With one dragging stroke he made a clean incision down her center, only stopping once he hit her belly button. He gently placed the scalpel down and rolled up, his baggy sleeves. The edges of the skin he'd just sliced puckered up and without hesitation Ian grabbed each side of the cut and pulled it in opposite directions, successfully prying Jade open. With his sleeves still rolled up he plunged one hand inside of her, searching elbow deep for the one thing he knew was there.

Above the slosh and gurgle of his hand shifting through her body, the sound of splattering vomit exploded like bullets against the tiled floor. Brownish pink runny liquid continued to flow between the creases of Spike's fingers which were held desperately against his mouth. The pool of vomit looked lonely beneath Spike's black sneakers, a painfully bright island surrounded by polished white tiles. Ian scrunched his nose at the mixture of vomit and embalming chemicals but kept his eyes closed as his hand traveled through her insides. Searching.

Spike was moaning, groaning, and complaining and Ian wished he would just shut up so he could *concentrate*. Jade had been dead for less than 48 hours. The chemicals must have been recently added because her organs were still damp and squishy against his long probing fingers, which worked in his favor as he could easily maneuver his hand behind her heavy lungs to feel the internal smooth cage of her ribs. It was there that he found it.

A little round bump protruded out from the flesh, the size of a marble. He carefully fingered it, aware that if he didn't move it in just the right way Jade would come back as something *less*, something lacking, and he couldn't have that. With one graze of his finger he flipped the switch to the left and her body jerked. He stepped back and waited anxiously, absently leaving dark smears on his sweatpants as he roughly clenched the fabric. He worried his bottom lip between his teeth and shifted from foot to foot. It took no longer than 10 seconds before she came back.

When Ian was younger his kitten died and he had tried to bring it back. Not out of some silly sense of attachment, no, it was just a learning experience. He did it just to see if he could. But he messed up the first time. The thing he brought back was not his little Pepper Jack. What he brought back had six limbs that groaned and creaked with every movement, crouching near the floor like a frightened insect. Pepper Jack's black fur was replaced with scales and sharp ridges. It spit and hissed at him, snapping jagged rotting teeth with foul breath before Ian finally snapped its neck. He buried it in the back yard where it would rot and decompose for the bugs to eat.

Jade's twitching turned into violent spasms, shaking the table so hard that Ian was briefly concerned that she would fall off of it. His worry vanished when she abruptly sat up.

Her intestines spilled out onto her lap with a wet *plop*, tumbling and uncoiling like a snake, all pink and cherry red with speckles of grey. A kidney was awkwardly dangling halfway outside of her body, connected by strings of bloody ureters.

Spike let out a girly scream and Jade's head jerked in his direction, her short black hair falling across eyebrows that scrunched up in confusion. Ian softly called her name.

"Jade." It was the first time he had ever dared to speak to her so when she slowly turned towards him and opened her eyes, revealing unseeing pale milky irises, Ian couldn't move. She had never looked more beautiful than she did in that moment.

"Jade, I…I love you." Ian stuttered out. But Jade only cocked her head to the side in a dog-like fashion. Then she opened her mouth and screamed. Or at least she tried to, a weak slippery bubbling noise sliding past her lips.

"Ohmygodohmygodohmygod. What did you do? WHAT THE FUCK DID YOU DO!" Spike stumbled and fell, frantically trying to back away. Ian barely spared him a glance; he only had eyes for one.

"I turned her on," he casually replied. "Did you know that every living being has an on-and-off switch? It's the most curious thing really. Everyone thinks that once you die it's all over. End game. Finished. But it doesn't have to end, Spike. When your switch goes off life doesn't have to stop." Ian turned and looked directly into Spike's frightened gaze. Ian's eyes were large and unnaturally bright, shinning with tears of joy.

He sent Spike a soft quiet smile. "I simply turned her back on."

Jade was making moaning sounds now, deep and mournful, as her pale hands clawed at her neck. The rope of her intestines slipped from her lap and brushed against the floor, unraveling quicker with each frantic movement. Internal organs peaked against the surface of her incision, waiting to spill with just the right twist of the torso. Ian frowned; he'd have to hurry and sew her back up.

"W-What are you, man?" Spike finally crawled his way to the door, looking back once more at the gruesome sight before him. It was a frozen picture seared into his mind. Ian's bright blue eyes glared at him, an ugly scowl stretching across his face, as his girlfriend's corpse shook and trembled on the table, clawing away ribbons of skin from her neck.

"Stupid boy." Ian's voice was somehow deeper, carrying a rough undertone that seemed to resonate throughout the room. "Don't ask questions you don't want the answers to."

Ian turned back to his love as Spike's retreating footsteps faded away. Spike never loved Jade like he did. How could he when he could so easily abandon the object of his affections? No, Ian thought, shaking his head, Spike didn't love Jade at all.

But Ian did. Already he had plans to take care of her. There was a bed and shackles in his basement, right next to the furnace to keep her cold skin nice and warm. He already knew her clothing sizes by heart and had a wardrobe set up in the corner, filled with an array of black that Jade would like with a few articles of lingerie that he was sure to like. He didn't need to worry about food; Jade didn't need to eat. All she needed was him. And Ian would provide everything she ever wanted.

He would take care of her forever and every time she turned off, he would turn her back on.

JADE ELEPHANTS
ELIZABETH MAJOR
COLUMBIA COLLEGE

MY GRANDMOTHER HAS ALWAYS BEEN my sense of understanding. With our birthdays one day apart, she sees our connection through astrological signs. She tells me it's the Pisces in us that makes us so close. She also says, about my mother, that it's the Gemini in her that makes her touchier and more aggressive in nature. My mother was never fond of star readings. Similarly, my mother has her own coined phrase: "Luck would have it, I was raised by a Pisces, and now I have to raise a Pisces. God has a sick sense of humor."

My grandparents adopted my mother, Emma Crevier when she was just a few days old. They tried to conceive naturally for four years, but it never ended up working. They both were tested for infertility, and both came back with normal results, their egg and sperm count marked normal numbers, so my grandparents (being the Catholic followers they were) took it as a sign from their Lord. When my Grandma tells me the story of when she adopted my mother, she tells me, "It was just because there was already a little girl out there meant for us." And she was right, although the little girl wasn't born just yet.

My mother was born to a teenage girl who didn't have the help from the older, and married, father who couldn't afford a baby on the side. Two years later, my grandparents adopted my uncle as well, Robert Chonka Junior, from another teenage couple who had the tendency to drink and smoke, and saw no reason to quit since they weren't planning to keep the baby anyway.

Their family photographs looked synonymous. If you hadn't already known, you wouldn't assume that they weren't blood related. My mother took after my grandmother's Italian side. Her nose is curved, and her skin holds a tint of olive. Her hair is curly and reddish brown. My uncle took after my grandfather, with the round French face and the stark blue eyes and ivory skin.

My mother grew up in a small Chicago suburb, Naperville. She was involved in extra curriculars, played tennis, cheered for school football games, and had the body most girls wished they had. She was tall, slender, had thick hips and full cheeks; my mother resembled an Italian gelato-skinned dream.

Although my grandmother and I weren't matched in blood, we were in heart, which made our connection, although hundreds of miles apart, from Georgia to Chicago, swollen and translucent, like the stained glass hummingbirds she'd hang from her kitchen windows. She'd turn to me when my mother "just didn't understand."

When I was young, elephants fascinated me. They reminded me of Grandma's northern cottage. She lived as if out of a storybook. Her house was sunken in the middle of the woods, a western suburb that hadn't fully developed. The forests overtook the land around her and made her feel protected under the tall branches of trees. She was nestled between blankets of bark and the overgrown landscape she'd one day plow down to plant her basil and tomato plants.

My Grandma, Marie, collected elephant figurines, and other

small knick-knacks and trinkets, like most people collect shot glasses or colored stones. Some of the elephants were large, too large for me to move with tiny hands. There were three of them, with thick bodies made of jade. They rested at the back of her living room sofa, on the bottom shelf of a wooden chest. I'd gather the other elephants that were scattered around her house and bring them to the feet of the jade statues. My grandmother eventually moved all of the elephants to the first floor of her house, to make cleaning and putting the elephants back an easier thing to do.

They were all different sizes and textures, some smooth and glossy like my mom's new *Home and Garden* magazine pages, and others gritty like sand. Some came in a group, all posed and proper, their feet pulled high and ready to march. They all had one thing in common, though: Their trunks were raised high and twisted. Being a believer in magical aids in life, she told me that elephants seen in this pose were tokens of good luck and sturdy health, and that I'd never see an elephant with its trunk turned down unless they were in paintings or photographs, for artistic purposes only.

My grandmother never acted her age, which added to the tension between her and her daughter. At 87 years old, she resembled a twenty-something. At times, I could say that her rebellious tendencies were more flared than my own in my actual twenty-something body. It was as if our minds were switched. When other grandmothers were known for making their grandchildren expertly crafted baked goods, my grandma would sneak my friends and I alcohol on high school weekends when she was in town, even if we didn't pose the thought. She'd gather her favorite wines and beers and late night snacks in plastic shopping bags, tied tight in her best grandma kind of knot, and leave them on the top of my pillow. I never asked questions.

My grandmother also had a habit of hiding things from my mother. When Grandma hadn't answered her phone for a few weeks, there were only a handful of reasons that it could be. She was either dead—which we knew to not be the case, as my grandmother was the type of woman who would let us know before something tragic happened, so that we had her full attention when the time would eventually round the corner—or she was up to trouble.

When it hit day five of my grandmother's absence, it became my job to do the calling. She always answered for me. I called her up from my cell phone, so that her caller I.D. wouldn't register my family's home phone number, and lo and behold my grandmother was alive and guilty to the core.

"Hello?"

"Grandma." I nodded at my mother, her eyes rolled, and she unfolded her arms and walked into the living room to finish folding the laundry.

"Where have you been, grandma?"

"You can't tell your mom."

"I won't."

"Oh another car accident, Elizabeth. I'm telling you it wasn't my fault. Damn cops can't come sneaking up behind you like that. Out of all of us they should know better."

"You hit a cop, Grandma?"

"He came up behind me, and I hit him when I tried to turn right on red. But don't worry. I'm taking the son of a bitch to court, and there's no way he can get out of this one."

"Is your car okay?"

"I mean, I need a new one. Totaled the whole right hand side. Don't tell your mother."

When she was backpacking through Europe at the age of 72, she fell down a flight of stairs in an old English castle. After several surgeries and ankle braces, my grandmother's ankle had seemed to give into the temptation of old age. It sunk into her foot, making her hips uneven and her balance even shakier. To help, she needed to wear a brace at all times, a clunky boot that wrapped like a cast around her foot, ankle and mid calf. It measured three inches thick all the way around, making walking a difficult triumph.

My grandma was always preparing for death. After her husband passed away from a heart attack in 2001 in a Chicago hospital, she became fixated on the idea of one day joining him. I was eight at the time, which would have hopefully meant I could remember him well enough, but the only memories I had of him were his unkempt gray mustache, his love of authentic Italian cooking, and grandmother's stories of days long ago.

"I'D RATHER DIE than have you put me in a nursing home. God help yourself if you do, girl."

She and my mother would have the same conversation late at night over the phone. My mother would be in the kitchen, hunched over the counter, elbows down and her curls mangled as she pulled them nervously straight.

"Mom, I can't take care of you if you're all the way down there by yourself. How do I know you're okay?"

"Emma, you don't understand. I can't leave this house. Your father built it from the ground up. Each brick he helped place. I can't leave this house. He's still holding me here."

My mother would calm her down, insisting that it was just a thought, and hang up the phone as I sat with my brother in the family room, watching one of the last cartoons that played at night. Mom would walk over to my father, who also watched the late night cartoons, from a couch that rested opposite from my brother and me. She grabbed the remote that rested on the coffee table, next to my father's crossed feet, and turned up the volume, then turned her lips close to his red ear. "The whole time he was here all they did was bitch at each other, and now she can't stop thinking about being back up there with him. Heaven better get ready for a rock and a hard place."

During the spring break of sixth grade, my mother and I traveled up to the western Chicago suburbs to help my grandma around the house. She had forgotten to book her flight for March, the month of our birthdays, and wouldn't see us again for a few months, so my mother took it upon herself to change that, coached by my grandmother day in and day out on the phone. "I'm so lonely here, Emma. I sure could use some company."

We arrived on a Friday afternoon. Her stove was still burning, the house smelling of old gas. Piles of papers crowded the kitchen tables and counters, as my grandmother hobbled to the door, all open arms and lips freshly painted pink. My mother's nightmares were realized, and her face, melting from the heat and the smell, fell open and stayed that way, until my grandma wrapped her shaking arms around her waist. "I'm so glad you're here," she said.

After getting through two days of cleaning the bedrooms and throwing away old boxes of recipes and photo film, we had moved onto the crafting room, the room that rested upstairs at the end of the hall, too far for my grandmother to crawl to on a regular basis. It had now become a dumping ground for unwanted merchandise, a hoarder's delight that smelled of expired floral perfume and opened mints.

We had started at the front of the room. My mother picked through the cardboard boxes, performing open heart surgery, and my grandmother and I sat at the doorway, sifting through the piles my mother was creating on the floor. My grandmother's small knees would thwack as she shifted in her seat.

"What even is this, Mom?" My mother held the plastic wrapped parcel outward. It rested firmly in her grip as my grandmother leaned in for a better look.

"Oh let me see it." My grandma held her hand out, opening and closing her fist like a child grabbing at their mother's long hair. "Oh it's a No-No." It was a small plastic gadget used for hair removal, with several odd shaped heads for the different areas that need shaving.

"Why do you have it, Mom?" The plastic parcel was still wrapped tight, the corners still sharp and tacky. My Grandma was past her heavy shaving days. Her legs were soft and soggy and the hair already rubbed away from many years in tight pants. I sat by the window in the hall, the breeze coming through the small opening. My pale neck began to crisp and blister next to the warm Chicago July sun.

"Just give it here."

"But mom, what is it? Why do you need this stupid thing?"

"Because, Emma. I wanted to buy it. That's a good enough reason, I think. I have my own money."

"I don't know how you manage on your own, Mom. Please. One day you're going to keep not answering your phone and what will I have to think? I can't drop everything and just come whenever. This trip took two months to plan as it is."

"I'm sick of hearing this, Emma. I'm not coming down there. I don't need you to watch over me. Hell, it's hard enough to get you off my back with you living as far as you do."

I sat and watched as my mother's neck began to swelter, and not from the heat, as mine had done so well. We sat on the floor, sifting through a few more boxes before heading back downstairs for lunch. The crafting room door stayed ajar, and remained so for the rest of our stay. We didn't return for a few years. My grandmother would come down to visit us, the way my mother wanted it. My mother worried. "I can't go there, Elizabeth. I can't bear to see what she's getting herself into."

THE SUMMER AFTER EIGHTH GRADE I decided to head back to Chicago to visit my grandma while my parents headed upward to New York for another one of my brother's baseball tournaments. She would sit on her bed in the afternoons, the lavender sheets swirled around her flattened bottom, as she'd start to pick at the pearls she had once worn. Each Christmas, my grandfather would give her another strand, a new color or shape than the year before, including the year he hadn't the money to buy an engagement ring, and instead bought her a ring with a single rose pearl that rested as a halo on the top of a thin silver band.

She was her own garden, a dapple of pink and silver, lightly dipped in purple tones on the top of her queen-sized mattress, a bed too big that made her sink into its soil. Her dyed brown curls marked deep roots as she lay on her back, holding the pearls above her head so the light from the windows would dance on each small, curved body.

Her dresser had been stained a pulsating shade of deep red on a winter morning by my grandfather, who I pictured wearing a dirty white t-shirt at the time and balancing a cup of red paint at his knees, threatening to tip as he swore at the streaks in the grains. It was her favorite piece of furniture, and atop it sat her weekly pills, all packaged away by the days in which she needed to take them, and her magnetic bracelets that helped circulate her blood through her hands, making her arthritis less restricting.

She'd pick each piece up and place it back down, organizing the sections of her dusty jewelry box over and over again. "Elizabeth, come over here." I'd hop up next to her on the bed. I was fourteen at the time, too old to really care about the trinkets of an old woman, and too young to understand how ignorant that sentence always sounds. She always smelled like fresh linens and lemon juice. "Look at this one, isn't it beautiful?" Her arthritis bubbled on her knuckles and made holding on to small things more of a challenge. She tried to grab ahold of a pair of pearl tear earrings, the metal backings held on loosely. They jumped from her fingers like wet peas from a fork. She bit her thin lips and pinched tighter. When she managed to wrangle the pearls between her pointer and thumb fingers, she would let them roll into her spongy palms and rest in extra skin.

She took the pointer finger from her other hand and massaged each pearl's small body until they were warm. "Aren't they just beautiful, Elizabeth?" The windows were open, the way they always were in her house. The sun bled on the glass and leaked inside to stain the sheets bright.

"They are," I said back, starting to move my hand towards the pink marbles in her hands. I rolled them around with a soft finger, the backing getting caught on the mounds in her skin.

I picked up the engagement ring. It rested alone in its own felt trapping. I tried it on all my fingers, only fitting on my left pinky. Her fingers were so swollen now. It clung to my finger like a tight hug, the pink pearl surely leaving indents under my small knuckle.

"Oh, let me see."

I held my hand out, her thick fingers wrapping around, shaking as she turned my hand left and right, her head shifting like an owl in the opposite direction.

"Oh, oh…" was all she said. Her glossy eyes reflected like tiny puddles, shaking back and forth with our hands, shifting gears.

"Let's put them away, Elizabeth."

"Can I wear it a little longer?"

"No, I don't think that's a good idea." She shook the pearl earrings, still in her hand, off like a wet dog until they found their way back into their dusty compartment. The ring hung tight, swelling my skin underneath and rubbing it red and raw. It made its way over the hump and back into its lonely home. The red felt was starting to tear at the rightmost corner.

"I keep this in my closet. Top shelf." She scooted her bottom in slow circles until her feet met the carpet. "Can you put them back up there?"

I grabbed the small wooden chest and tucked it behind old magazines and boxes of collected fabrics. She followed behind.

"That isn't even the start of it all, Elizabeth. You need to know where everything is. I can't trust Rob. He'd pawn everything off before you would know what's missing. You have to know what's here."

I guided my grandmother's body, my hands held around her waist as she scooted to the closet. Grandma brushed my hands away, tapping when I wouldn't let her go. "I'm fine. How do you think I move without you here?" She had a good point, and I let go.

I sat outside of the closet, Indian style, giving her space to shift and move when she needed to. She'd stretch up tall, her small body reaching like a child to the highest shelf. She'd sink back inside herself, her muscles compressing on themselves and growing tired as she'd let out an "oomph," letting another box hit the floor.

"Aren't these pretty? God, I had good taste." She'd hold out a high heel from the nineties, the heel of the shoe trapped in her fist as she shook it at me. It had a soft blue suede body that she promised would hit your ankle in the perfect place, to make your calves tighten just right.

One thing you don't do to a woman is take away her ability to wear a good pair of shoes. It wasn't until my grandmother lost her ability to wear high-heeled shoes, wedges, and strappy sandals, that she felt her age. I sat in the white doorframe of her closet, watching her heels from the '90s and '80s frowning back at me. They sat in rows beneath her dresses and slacks on the same rack they hung on when they were first brought home. Their straps hung from loose buckles and their platforms didn't seem so high. I thought about asking if I could try them on, but took back the thought as she sighed and placed the satin heels back on the rack. She looked down at me. She was a Marilyn.

She took the dresses that lined the closet's exterior, hanger still attached at the collars, and began to lever her head between the two. She'd wriggle her ears past the plastic hanger until the dress rested against her lumpy form, the plastic hanger pushing indents into the back of her neck. "This is one of my favorites!" She swayed her hips, pinching the sides of the dress to her rocking midriff. It was satin and made her belly look smooth. "I'd still wear this if it weren't for this stupid thing." She threw her bad ankle up, making her balance uneasy. "Getting old is a bitch to do."

"But you look good doing it!" I sat in the white doorframe of the closet, watching my grandmother sway from side to side in front of the body-length mirror in the back corner. The cord that hung from the exposed light bulb swayed with her, just touching the top curls on her head with each swing it made.

"Help me get down."

"Grandma, we can go sit on your bed, come on."

She pulled the dress off, hanger still intact. "No, it's okay, just help me down here."

"Grandma, it isn't very safe in here."

"Oh shut up." She placed her hand on my shoulder and tried grabbing at the cloth with the other. Her balance started to tip, her hand shaking under the pressure.

"Okay, just wait a second." I stood up and helped her down to the closet floor, the warmth from her touch still kissing my shoulder. Her booted foot curled first under the weight, her other one to follow. She fixed her nightgown at the knees, making the frilled ends drape over. She never wanted to be seen indecent.

She threw her shoulders back and it took ten years off her face. Her cheeks sunk and mashed with her low-hung chin. Her heavy eyelids made her wide-eyed expression more of a squint.

"You have to promise me something, Elizabeth. Really promise me."

"What's that, Grandma?"

Her expression turned to froth as her thin lips started to curl under. "I need you to promise to pray for me, Elizabeth. When I die. I need you to promise to pray for me to get into heaven."

I found this thought strange, and not meaning to, I laughed. It seemed such a silly notion. If heaven and God were real, how would the prayers of an uncertain follower change the course of my grandmother's path? Yes, she didn't know my questioning of her faith, but still. To think I had such a power in a world I cared nothing for.

"I mean it, Elizabeth. I've made my mistakes in life. I'm not a woman cut out for purgatory." She grabbed my hand with both of her own, and they started to shake, more than they were already used to doing. Her veins were purple, like her week-old nail polish that she hadn't the time to fix up.

"I gotta see him again. I gotta see him again."

"I know, Grandma. I know. I'll pray, I promise I will."

"You have to really mean it. You can't forget, or I'll never make it."

"I promise I will."

She squeezed as hard as she could, which made the shaking grow.

Although my grandmother's fingers were bare of their wedding bands, her hallways and bedside tables were decorated with pictures of her past. Black and white framed photographs of my mother's second birthday and my grandfather riding Disneyland rides with my brother, no taller than my hip, at his side.

"I just miss the way he'd hold me. It just isn't fair." Her eyes, already heavy, couldn't hold the weight of tears, and they streamed down as she kept on. "I can't leave this house. It's the last thing I have of him, Elizabeth. It's like he can hold me here. It's the only place he can still do that."

"I know, Grandma."

"You have to promise to pray, Elizabeth, really promise."

"I promise I will."

Her hands softened and turned to froth like the expression on her face. She hung on her seat, her skin like tissue, too thin to hold it all together.

"Getting old is a bitch to do."

WHEN I WATCH MY GRANDMOTHER NOW, it's different than it had been before high school. She's shrunken and rolled up like a French croissant, her young eyes glassed over with grey and yellow filling. Her feisty heart has gotten dim, making it hard to fight back when we want to rough house. It still comes out from time to time, after she's rested a few days after traveling between Georgia and Chicago. Although she's debilitated after the long trek, she still refuses to move south with the rest of us, and I can't blame her. Her newest excuse is because of the dryness in the air. "You people talk slow down there. I can't understand a thing you say half the time. And the air is too dry. My skin can't handle that. I'd be a big potato chip!"

When you get old, people try and act as if you are a child again. You are now the one who needs to be raised and coddled and wiped up after. Your spills become their spills and accidents seem inevitable and expected as part of the job. You need nannies and family to watch over you, in case you need help. You need to tag along on family outings because you can't be home alone anymore. My grandmother once told me, while looking at herself in the mirror as she got ready for the day, "I did everything right, Elizabeth. I took care of my body, and old age still found its way in." She pulled at her cheeks, holding them back before letting them fall back down, a sack of potatoes. "I don't feel as old as I look, you know. I don't think I ever will."

Her last bit of independence is wrapped in the walls of a Chicago suburban home, too big to manage for any lonely soul. Maybe it's the Pisces in her and I that make us as stubborn as we are. I fight the signs of old age even in my twenties, dying my sparse gray hairs and making sure to coat moisturizers and serums into my face and neck to prevent sagging.

My mother, on the other hand, is more accepting of old age. The Gemini inside of her, the twins twirling around inside her mind, lets nature take its course, calling emotional ties to any earthly remnants a waste of time. She looks, instead, to the future, trying to grasp at things yet to be had. But the Pisces fish run constant through my Grandma's veins, churning the past through her, reminding her of who she was, who she is, and who she wants to be for the small amount of life she has left.

My grandmother says she sees herself in me. The way I talk, my thick Italian curls, and my love of blush wines. The connection she sees is ever present and scares me all the same with its constant reminders. Like a herding dog to its sheep, I'm lost and scared with and without her.

I fear death and old age more than public speaking, which seems to differ from the statistics of a typical fear blooded person, and I cope with this fear by not calling her. My mother reminds me of her old age often, asking me why I don't call her more often, or asking if I realize she's all alone. Yes, I know she's alone and she needs someone to shoot the shit with, and gossip with, and bitch about the weather with, but I'm scared. I'm scared of being her one day, alone in a house that echoes from the lack of things to fill it. It all feels too familiar, as if I've been allowed to watch my life play out in old photographs and family videotapes that aren't mine. It isn't a solid excuse though, because I know when I need to call her the most, when I need to hear her voice and smell the Chanel No. 5 on her neck and clothes, and hold her shaking hands, she'll be gone like a candle wick, burned all the way through. It scares me that I see her wick burning faster with each fall she takes or each doctor appointment she forgets, or when she repeats herself four times in an hour, telling me the same story of the trip she took to CVS for cough medicine.

I always thought that my mother was given to my grandma for me, although I wasn't sure why until recently. As if destiny can skip generations, I think back to when my grandmother told me to pray for her after death. The balance between the Gemini twins and the Pisces fish are ever flowing through me, reminding me that you have to have a balance in present and past, and that looking at the world through both realistic and fantastic vision is okay, when balanced in the best lights.

I called my grandmother a few nights back. She was drinking her Sutter House wine in individually wrapped plastic bottles, talking of the hummingbirds that passed by her bird feeder that morning. I asked her about the jade elephants, and where they were resting now. She laughed, her voice faded and thick with built up allergies and the sweet juice stains of cheap wine. "They are where they've always been. They're home."

NORTH OF GRACELAND CEMETERY
NICHOLAS SZCZEPANIK
SCHOOL OF THE ART INSTITUTE OF CHICAGO

Buried in the soil
I find myself again
treading over,
footprints smothered
by onslaught of summer.

Above the elm trees
wind upturns
vibrant leaves,
and broken beams
of light splinter
sodden dirt.

Am I any less lonely
here, surrounded
in the garden
by spirited birdsong
and blossoms
overburdened?

BILL
ZACK REITER
COLUMBIA COLLEGE

I WAS DRIVING DOWN LEHIGH, snow piling on my hood, the third blizzard of that frozen January. The striking blackness of the snowy night was broken up by tall streetlights, illuminating patches of the whitening earth every block or so. With every movement of the wheel, my hands clenched at ten and two, I momentarily lost control of the car, a dented and rusting 2007 Nissan Sentra. When I caught sight of myself in the rearview, I noticed that my hairline had receded another half-inch, an army of brown hairs marching backward, too early at thirty-four.

The skin flaps under my eyes were no longer a sign of sleeplessness, but a permanent indication of chronic fatigue with life. The failed luxury office supplies business and failing marriage manifested themselves physically in my posture, in my expressions. How clichéd I had become as I approached middle age: the lack of something to look forward to, the malaise of nine to five, the prescription for Lorazepam, not for a mental disorder, but rather just to keep pace with a soulless social landscape.

As flakes fell and built mountains and caverns in the road, they created a stark vision of nature in the most unnatural of settings: the meticulous construction of Chicago suburbia. Even the forest preserves, lined perfectly, well-maintained, held the stink of human hands. Audrey texted me when I was minutes from the house: *Plz bring milk. 2%.* I circled the neighborhood. Snow formed on the windshield, nearly blinding me before the wipers tossed it aside.

I couldn't bear to go home, couldn't bear Audrey turned away on her side, loveless, the cat refusing to acknowledge my existence, the bathroom masturbation that had become my nightly routine. So much coldness in such a warm house. I still loved her, and I thought she still loved me, but there was something else, perhaps a disappointment that we couldn't save each other from our natural plummets towards misery.

Almost every day when I came home, she was in bed, her curly blonde hair springing endlessly around her floral nightgown. The cat would play with toys on the floor beside her while she was texting or emailing on her cell, reading tabloid magazines, sometimes pretending to sleep. When I tried to connect, pulled my pants off and shaped my body around her, reaching over to hold her soft wrists in my palms, she would say "I'm not in the mood" even though I wasn't trying to fuck her, or "You're on my hair!", or she'd ask "How was your day?", but then scroll through her emails instead of listening to my answer.

So I had sunken into a pathetic desperation for affection. Just the barista at Starbucks being nice to me would make the hairs on my arm stand up. Maybe Audrey was fucking somebody, maybe we should get a divorce, but all of it, every option possible, ended in certain sadness on my part. Being alone didn't seem better than having her hate me in our bed which didn't seem better than her fucking somebody else in it. I needed to do something, which I've felt for probably the last year or so of our five-year marriage, but what?

As I pondered this, as I made plans to buy flowers and book hotel rooms and write mental love notes that would never be put to paper, I barely noticed the dog emerging from behind a nearby bush. It was a greyhound, thin and dark against the snow, and it took three pumps of my brakes not to run it down, sliding within feet of it.

The Sentra was turned sideways in the vacant suburban side-street. Without much consideration, I hopped from the side of the car, snow filling my shoes immediately.

"Hey doggy, you lost?"

The greyhound bounced around me excitedly, its snipped tail wagging. Its fur was brown and greasy, but the color became lighter around its snout and paws. I bent down, my worn knees popping in pain, and tried to lure the dog closer. It blew past me, my fingertips barely brushing the tip of its tail, and jumped into the open driver's side door and into the passenger seat, shivering.

"Hey, watch the seats. Uhh…"

I looked around, hoping the owner would appear and apologetically drag him from the car, but had no such luck. I hunched back into the driver's seat, and the dog was licking coffee from within the open cup I had from this morning.

"Jesus, buddy. I think you're energetic enough."

I pulled the cup from underneath his slurping tongue and poured it out the door before slamming it shut. The dog stared at me, eyes agape, licking his lips and nose for warmth. I reached over to his blue collar, a bone-shaped tag hanging from his neck with an address and his name, "Bill."

"Kind of a weak dog name, but it's nice to meet you, Bill."

He licked my hand as I pulled it away from his tag and headed towards his address a few blocks away. The house numbers were hard to read in the snow, so Bill and I drove slowly, squinting out of the small crack in the window, searching for numbers.

"You know, Bill, I was reading this self-help bullshit book once, and there was a whole chapter about acting like a dog. The point was that people only like dogs based on how much the dog likes them. If you're cheerful and loving, people are attracted to you regardless of any real merit."

Bill seemed genuinely interested in what I was saying, his panting breath stopping and his eyes broadening in curiosity.

"I dunno. Something about that idea is pretty nauseating, but whatever you guys do works. This is the longest conversation I've had with anyone in quite a long time, and you're a complete stranger."

Bill leaned over and nudged under the palm of my hand with his wet nose, begging to be petted. I obliged, stroking his nose, over his eyes to the back of his head, and then behind the ears. He seemed to love my behind-the-ears skills.

"Fuck, I wish I had a dog like you. My wife's cat won't let me go anywhere near it, just pisses and shits all over, scratches up my couches. Real prick. You'd hate him."

At the end of the block, outside of the corner house, was a small girl and her mother, the sort of woman you could tell had been attractive in college, but that children and labor had worn into a wrinkled shell.

They both held their hands in an O shape around their mouths and in the dead silence of the snow yelled, "BILL! BIIIIIILLLLLL! BILLY BILLY BILLY BILLY!" Behind them followed an overweight, bearded man, holding a beer, looking disinterested. He wore a grey t-shirt that looked to be cut with scissors to remove the sleeves, decade-old ripped jeans, and big black boots.

I pulled the car to the side of the road, barely making it over the snow pile made by plows, and rolled down the passenger side window.

"Hey there, I think I found your dog," I hollered.

Bill jumped from the window and hopped like a bunny through the snow to the excited little girl. The daughter laughed and smiled as Bill soaked her face with saliva. She was wearing a bright red jacket, a yellow backpack, and her wavy hair flowed like lava around her round face. I popped out from the car.

"Yeah, he was over on Lehigh. I nearly hit him. He seems like a great dog."

The mother approached me slowly while the daughter and Bill stayed behind, the father marching over in their direction.

"Thank you so much. We were so worried."

The woman walked with cautious glides on the ice, her full hips bouncing with each step. From behind her, a scream erupted from the little girl. The father, tossing his beer to the side, kicked Bill in his abdomen, the greyhound squealing and falling over. And then, the sound of the man's puffy palm meeting Bill's long jagged face, like a baseball meeting a catcher's mitt.

"Daddy, stop!"

"Little fucker. Don't you ever run again!"

Another *thwat* met the side of Bill's face. The dog squealed and tried to limp away, but the man grabbed him by his collar and dragged him toward the house, his legs kicking out but gaining no traction in the snow. The little girl ran behind him screaming stop, stop, stop, and the mother behind her screaming Larry, Larry, Larry, and before long, they had all stormed into the door at the side of the house, and I was left staring at the front steps, snow filling the passenger seat from my open window.

I stood like that for a few minutes, stomach sunken, before it hit me that nobody was coming out from the house. I wanted to go inside, fistfight the father, rescue the dog. But I'm what my friends might refer to as a pussy, so instead I got back into my car, and by the time I got home, Audrey was turned away from my side of the bed snoring, a note on my pillow: *Thanks for the milk...*

I didn't see Bill again for many months. Temperatures rose and Audrey moved back into her parents' house for a "trial separation." She filed for divorce three days later. So much for the trial. I was left alone in our unfinished home, all of her home improvement projects abandoned. Walls were left unpainted, there was a hole for a pond in the backyard that was now just a hole, and a room that was being designed for a child was gone, now fresh with new carpeting and rainforest wallpaper.

I often looked for Bill, taking the long route to get home, driving to where he lived and peeking into the yard from my car window. I hoped he was okay. I certainly wasn't.

But then, one day, driving down Lehigh, the sun beating off the hood, there he was, sitting calmly in the middle of the road. He looked gaunt and worn out, staring straight ahead at my car. I know it sounds stupid, but I could swear that there was a moment of recognition on his face when our eyes met. He immediately sprung from his seated position, his tail wagging as he limped to the driver's side door. I opened it, leaned out of the car, and combed the hairs on his head with my fingernails, his eyes squinting with pleasure.

"Hey, buddy. I've been looking for you."

And as if to reciprocate, he hopped onto my lap and climbed into the passenger seat, stepping on my groin unknowingly. He smelled of that sunbaked, unwashed stink of dog, which I breathed in gleefully. We drove around for a while, and I told him what happened with Audrey, how I had wanted to date but had forgotten how, how I had begun taking Ambien to fall asleep every night, more out of boredom than anything, the television echoing through an empty house. I told him how I had gotten an accounting job at a plumbing company, how I had dropped 30 pounds out of dread-induced anorexia. He sprawled on the seat, his head resting on the armrest, listening intently as I scratched behind his ears.

After about an hour, I figured it was time to take him home, so I headed in that direction. When we rolled up in front of his house, the grass tall and unkempt, empty cans of beer lined up on the front porch, Bill hopped back into my lap and licked my chin. When I opened the door to let him out, he let out a nearly inaudible cry, and stared back at me with worry. I looked at the front of the house again and back to Bill, my only friend.

I closed the door, and before I could second-guess myself, peeled out and hung a right onto Oak Park. Bill searched for leftover food under the car seats the whole way home, and when we got to the house, he followed me in through the garage. He sniffed around every room while I was in the kitchen, preparing a steak for us. After it was cooked, I cut it in half with a knife and put it on two separate paper plates. I sat on the couch and flipped on the television. Bill jumped up next to me, his nose in the air, his eyes wide in excitement, like it was the only decent meal he had ever seen.

"Here you go, buddy."

Bill lapped it up hurriedly, swallowing whole chunks. Dogs always eat as if they may never get the opportunity again. When he finished, he licked the plate clean. I had to pull the paper plate from his mouth when he tried eating that, too.

We sat on the couch for hours. He rolled on his back and breathed deeply as I rubbed his belly and contemplated the future, his hot steak-breath blowing up at my chin. When it was time for bed, I jumped in and Bill curled up around my feet, his face pressed into the sheets. I ignored the bottle of Ambien on the nightstand. And for the first time in what felt like many years, I fell asleep without feeling alone, Bill's snores erupting like music through the night.

SUGAR RAY IN THE ALLEYWAY
ERIC HOUGHTON
DEPAUL UNIVERSITY

WE LINGERED INSIDE THE BAR as long as we could after last call, chatting up the bartender and smoking one more cigarette. The temperature outside had dipped down into the single digits and I felt no urge to rush out into the cold. Another brutal night in Chicago. My friend Jason and I nursed our final shot, and tried to get Ian, the owner of Gold Star, to tell us one more story about ghosts he had seen in the bar, but he obviously wanted to go home. I would have stayed in the anesthetic warmth of booze and tobacco all night just to avoid the bare room and uncomfortable air mattress waiting for me at my friend Mike's apartment, my temporary home. I finally took the hint and geared up as best as I could to face the barren Chicago night.

Jason and I shivered through the empty streets of Ukrainian Village, making our way back to Mike's place. The city felt deserted, but then again, it was eight degrees in the middle of a Tuesday night, not exactly prime time for pedestrian traffic. The usual bustle of drunken hipsters and small time hustlers gave way to the crunch

204

of snow and ice under our feet. We talked about ghosts and passed a joint between us, both staggering a little as we went. We stuck to alleyways as much as we could, walking amongst the overflowing garbage cans that still somehow reeked of trash even in the sub-zero temperatures. My feet froze through my tennis shoes and I cursed my flimsy excuse for a jacket. I had fled Seattle only a few months earlier and in my haste to leave, I failed to consider the importance of good cold-weather clothes. Like a man fleeing a burning building, I grabbed what I could and left, only to stand shivering on the sidewalk wondering, "Now what?"

When I saw the car the first time, I thought nothing of it. Just another sports car with tinted windows driving slowly through a deserted alley, bass rattling the windows of the nearby houses. I knew Chicago had its rough parts, but I never considered Ukrainian Village one of them. My friend Mike had lived in this part of town for years and I had visited several times. Those visits usually consisted of one extended weeklong bar crawl, wandering at all hours through the streets and alleys of the neighborhood. The most danger we felt came from the crackheads who hung out in the alley behind Mike's apartment, yelling "Tom!" at all hours. In 2001, the gentrification of Ukrainian Village was well underway, but not complete. A long way from Nelson Algren's five corners, but not completely tamed either.

The car slowed to a crawl as it neared us. Jason and I wiggled between two trash cans to clear the way and let the driver pass. I tried not to let the loud hiphop thumping through the darkened windows intimidate or scare me. No reason to jump to conclusions, right? The car passed and we continued on our way, watching the brake lights flicker. Then it pulled into an open garage, reversed out, and headed back towards us.

FROM AN EARLY AGE I craved the excitement of the city. A trip into town was a thrill for me, never mind that the closest town to my rural home had just one stoplight, fewer than a thousand residents, and the most exciting attraction was the Galaga machine at the pizza place. I craved the sight of people, cars, activity. When my dad built our modest three-bedroom ranch, he chose an isolated, tree-lined plot smack in the middle of Montcalm County, Michigan. Equal parts farmland and forest, the main activities of the county were hunting, fishing, and farming. On any day, you could count on both hands the number of cars that passed by my house, hurtling along the dirt road, the billowing dust cloud lingering long after the roar of the car had passed. The city, even a tiny one, offered a counterpoint to the isolation and predictability of my parochial home. There were parts of being a country boy I loved. I wandered through the woods whenever I pleased. I climbed trees, built forts, and rode my bike wherever I wanted for hours on end. I just did all this alone. Just to be around others as they went about their day provided me with a sense of comfort. To be alone in a crowd was better than being alone.

My father, on the other hand, hates the city. The noise, the crowds, the traffic; it all adds up to a chaotic roar, turning his usual easy-going nature into a dark brooding. I witnessed this transformation whenever we would drive to a bigger city, like Grand Rapids or Lansing. Sitting in the back seat, I would watch his eyes in the rearview mirror, watch them grow darker the closer we got to the city, the more the traffic and noise increased. Normally easygoing, he would snap at my sister and me if we talked too loudly, or bark curt responses to my mother's simple questions. Any visitor to our home in the country would see a man holding court, jovial and assured, with the kind of self-confidence that made men silently jealous or long to be his friend. Take him out of his element and put him in the city and that confidence evaporated, replaced by frustration and fear.

I struggled to understand what scared him so. If your dad is afraid of something, chances are you had better be, too.

THE CAR SLOWED TO A CRAWL a few yards in front of us. The music stopped and the stillness of the night rushed back in to fill the vacated space. By the time I processed that something was off about the moment I was already in the middle of it. I had lived in cities for several years at this point in my life and thought of myself as an observant and wary urbanite. This, of course, is why I found myself staggering in an empty alley in Chicago at 3 a.m. But isn't that the way it goes? We operate normally right up to the moment when things become abnormal, and by then it's too late.

I contemplated turning around and heading back to the relative safety of Division Street, but before I could communicate this to Jason, the driver's side window of the car lowered. We stood no more than ten feet away from the car at this point. From out of the lowered window poked the head of a young man, somewhere in his mid-twenties. I wasn't sure, but he appeared to be alone.

"Hey, can I ask you guys something?"

He looked past us, down the alley, as if he were addressing someone besides the two of us.

"Yeah? What's up?"

"This is gonna sound crazy, but will one of you guys fight me?"

WHENEVER THE DANGERS OF CITY LIFE come up in conversation, my father likes to share his story about Saginaw, Michigan in the summer of '69. Fresh from Vietnam, he was finishing his tour stateside, burying dead soldiers across Michigan. He and his detail needed some laundry done, so while the rest of his men went to get lunch, my dad guarded their belongings in a public laundromat. In full military fatigues, he sat in the far back of what turned out to be a predominantly African-American facility. A group of seven or eight men came in, noticed the white Army boy, and directed a few comments his way. My father blames the racial tension of the time, he blames his own lack of situational awareness, but mostly he blames the city for incident. Before things got out of hand, the rest of the detail showed up and defused the situation. No one threw a punch and no one got hurt, but my father's negative opinion of the city as a dangerous place became cemented.

Upon completing his tour, my dad built a house in rural Montcalm County, Michigan, and settled there with my mother. My childhood home featured an abundance of flood lights. Growing up, I assumed that everyone had these high-power lights on every corner of their house. Not until much later did I realize the oddity of this setup. At any moment, with the flip of a few switches, my father could transform night into day around our home, just like one would do around a bivouac. Thousands of miles away from the jungle and the war, he still carried the fear of death with him, even in the sparsely inhabited woods of his home. Even in the countryside, where he felt safest, he never felt truly safe.

"WHAT DO YOU MEAN 'FIGHT YOU'?"

"Hang on a second."

The guy turned off the ignition and fumbled around with something for a moment before he stepped out of the car. Jason had begun to rock back and forth slowly in place. It occurred to me that I did not know Jason very well. In fact, until I had run into him a week earlier on the red-line platform at North and Clybourn, I hadn't seen him in about two years. Even when we both lived in

Grand Rapids, I had only hung out with him for a short time, six months at most. I looked at him and noticed his eyes were opened very wide, almost comically so, and I had no idea what that meant. Was he scared? Angry? Crazy? The driver closed the distance between us and shivered in the cold.

"Look, I know how crazy this sounds, okay? But I ain't crazy. I just got into this fight with my girlfriend and I feel like I'm just going to lose it, you know?"

I thought about why I was even in Chicago at that moment, how a few months earlier I had fled the scene of a toxic relationship in Seattle with just $150 to my name and a duffle bag full of clothes; how when I walked in on her in his bed I had truly contemplated murder; how I hated this cold, cold city and the toll the fruitless job search and nights sleeping on the floor had taken on me.

"Yeah, I know what you're saying."

"Good! Good. Well, you know, instead of just going and *stabbing* somebody, I thought, you know, I might find someone to box with me, blow off some steam."

When he said "stabbing," he had actually made a thrusting motion with his arm, like he imagined a blade in his hand. This idea unnerved me, this notion of him, this stranger, with a knife, cutting someone up. Until he mentioned the knife, I had not really processed the gravity of the situation. Conjuring the image of a knife gave more power to his rage than, say, the mention of a gun. He had my full attention.

"Yeah. I'll fight you."

MY FATHER OWNS MANY, MANY GUNS. As a hunter in the country, owning a few guns is normal. We had a weapon for every animal we hunted: .22 rifle and 20 gauge shotgun for rabbits, .270

Winchester for white-tails, a .410 bore for partridge, and a 12 gauge for geese. Nothing too crazy. At some point, his collection of firearms evolved from the few utilitarian rifles one would find in any rural hunter's gun cabinet to the impressive display of firepower he now stockpiles. I won't call it an obsession, probably because he's my dad and I love him, but many people would freely use that term in relation to his arsenal. The most conspicuous additions to this stockpile are the pistols.

I always wanted a pistol when I was a kid. Pistols looked cool in the movies and cop shows. I got my first gun when I was fourteen, a pump-action 410 shotgun, which I loved, but I felt incomplete without a bad-ass pistol. No matter how much I begged, my father always refused: "Son, the only thing a pistol is good for is killing another person." When I feel like stirring things up, I ask him if he remembers telling me this, now that he owns four or five pistols. He never provides me with an answer, and it feels cruel of me to press the issue.

Each time I visit, we will have the same conversation no matter what. He will ask me to bring a gun back with me to Chicago and I will refuse. On some trips we will fight about it; on others we will simply nod and continue playing euchre or drinking beer on his porch while the hummingbirds buzz around us. I know it drives him crazy when I refuse to arm myself. I can see the concern for his one and only son alone in the big city with nothing to protect him. I know it scares him.

My father has a joke he loves to tell. An old woman gets pulled over by a state trooper. When the officer gets to the lady's car, he asks her if she has any firearms in the car.

"Yes officer, I have a 9mm in the glove box, a .45 under my seat, a cute little .32 in my purse, and a sawed off 12 gauge in the trunk."

The officer stares back in amazement at this little old lady and says, "Ma'am, that's an awful lot of firepower you're packing. May I ask you what it is you're so afraid of?"

The little old lady looks him dead in the eye and says, "Not a goddamn thing."

"YOU EVER FIGHT BEFORE?"

I knew if I said anything but the truth, which was no, this guy would be able to tell. The way he began bouncing on his feet, jabbing at the air, rolling his head around on his shoulders; he knew how to box. He reminded me a bit of a young Sugar Ray Leonard, especially once he took off his jacket, revealing dark, sinewy arms. I was about to get my ass kicked.

I walked over to Jason, whose eyes were somehow opened even wider than before and said, "Watch my back, okay? If things get weird, the police station is two blocks that way."

I said this more to reassure myself. I knew that if things got out of hand there would be no time to save me. Jason nodded and lit up a cigarette. I took off my coat and tried to stretch out and warm up, throwing some weak punches at the air, mimicking the moves my opponent made. At one point we shook hands and exchanged names, but I've long forgotten his. Sugar Ray seems fitting.

"Okay, you ready?"

"I guess so. Go easy on me, okay?"

"Let's just spar a little first, okay? Take a few swings. No face shots to start."

I danced and bobbed around the icy alley for a minute or two waiting to get the nerve up to punch Sugar Ray. I had no malice towards him, so I couldn't swing out of anger. Part of me feared he was just waiting for me to hit him once so he could pummel me into the pavement. I stood a good six inches taller than him, even taller when he crouched down into his stance. The whole thing seemed absurd. I thought about backing out, just running as fast as I could back to Mike's apartment. I swung at him instead.

WHENEVER THE GUN QUESTION ARISES between me and my dad, I employ a number of strategies to decline his offer of free armaments. Usually, I hide behind my wife, who has her own complicated feelings towards gun ownership. Raised in a family that never owned guns, her first time ever holding a weapon, let alone firing one, was at my dad's house. I will never forget the day she aimed my dad's Ruger 9mm at the paper plate target behind his house and squeezed off all ten rounds. But she still fears guns, as any sane person should. Going to the country to shoot up targets is one thing, bringing a gun into our home is another. So if I'm not feeling like fighting, I just tell my dad that she still doesn't feel comfortable with a gun in the house and he usually leaves it at that. I take the cowardly way out.

On days when I feel like fighting, when I get tired of hearing about how the government wants to disarm the people, when I have heard enough about the perils of an unarmed populace against a militarized police force, when I can't stand to listen to one more paranoid theory about the imminent economic collapse of America and the fallout forthcoming, I let him have it. I ask him, what will one shotgun in my hands do to help me survive the city? How will storing a gun in my Chicago apartment save me from this world of fear? If things get as bad as you imagine, will I really be able to shoot my way out of the city and back to the safety of home?

The reason I don't accept his offer to bring a gun home, the reason I live in a city where the possibility of danger exists, the reason I do the things I do is I don't want to live in fear.

AFTER A FEW MINUTES OF SPARRING, landing a few meager punches, receiving a few in return, I was ready to call it quits. I breathed a sigh of relief when Sugar Ray backed down and caught his breath. I felt as though the roller coaster I had stupidly agreed to ride had broken down before climbing the first hill and I could safely return to solid ground.

"Good fight, man. Thanks."

"You serious? We ain't done, man. We just warming up. Catch your breath, then let's go for real."

"Look, I don't know. I think you…"

Before I could finish, Sugar Ray came at me full force. I barely had time to get my arms up before he attacked. The guy knew how to punch and he had speed. The punches that hurt before now made me see stars. I heard Jason shout something. Fear took over and I flailed back, windmilling my arms as hard as I could. We went on like this for what seemed liked minutes, but probably lasted no more than thirty seconds, until Sugar Ray landed a punch directly in the center of my chest. An audible *crack* echoed through the alley and I sat down, hard.

"Shit! Dude, you okay? Hey, look here, you okay?"

I blinked, shook my head, and squeezed back tears. I felt my neck to assure myself my heart was still beating. I looked up at Sugar Ray and saw genuine concern on his face. He held his hand out to me and helped me to my feet. "Yeah," I said, "I'm okay."

Before I met Sugar Ray, I always imagined what it would be like if I had to fight someone. I still catch myself fantasizing about the damage I could do to another person if pushed to fight. Having your ass kicked tends to put those thoughts in check. I know that Sugar Ray took it easy on me. Had he wanted to, he could have seriously hurt me. But he didn't. After the fight, the three of us sat in the alley and talked. Sugar Ray criticized me for smoking, telling me it made me weak and winded too easily, and recommended I hit the gym and put on a few pounds. I tried to tell him I never planned to fight again.

"Yeah. Bet you didn't plan to fight tonight, either."

With that, he got back in his car and drove off, hopefully not to stab his girlfriend. Jason and I went back to Mike's and tried to cool off the adrenaline rush by killing a pint of whiskey. I never saw Jason again after that night. A few weeks later I moved back to Seattle to give it another shot and lost touch with him.

I DRIVE DOWN CROWDED BROADWAY AVENUE. Beside me sits my father. Somehow, I managed to coax him to visit me here in Chicago, to witness the life I have built here. We roll slowly through the mess of traffic, the jaywalking pedestrians, and the shadow of the El tracks by Wilson Avenue. I see him fidgeting in his seat, nervously eyeing the guy walking towards us.

"What's this guy doing?"

"Just crossing the road I guess."

"Well, he's awfully close to the car."

He shifts nervously in his seat and looks for the door's lock. The guy passes behind us and continues dodging and weaving his way to the other side of the street.

"See? Nothing to worry about."

I have never told my father about that night in the alley. I don't know how I could. I consider it a victory to have him here in the city, to have him see things from my perspective, even if just for a day or two. He'll return to the country soon enough. One weekend in Chicago won't change his opinion of the city right or wrong, but at least now he will have seen it. He will have an image in his head when he starts to fret about his son wandering through the city. I take him to my favorite Mexican place for dinner and he laughs when all the waiters recognize and greet me. After, we drive to the lake and walk along the path, watching the city sky give way to dusk.

"It's almost beautiful if you look at it just right," he says. "Still can't beat the country, but it's nice."

He gives me a little jab in the ribs to let me know he's joking. We walk back to the car and I drive us both home.

TAKE THE BULLET
MELISSA HUEDEM
COLUMBIA COLLEGE

IT WASN'T WHERE I WANTED TO BE. We were just doing the same old shit. Tonight the boys went to the park to shoot some hoops. That really meant tagging the whole place with words I wouldn't want my nieces reading. Jamal told me, "This is the last time, promise." But he said that last time.

"J, I don't want to be doin' shit like this."

"Whatcha mean?"

"I want out."

"Kewane, don't be sayin' shit like that. You want 'em to be after us? Cuz you know that them being after you means they after our whole fucking family. You know that, right?"

He'd say this especially when his kids were in the room with us, playing with their scratched-up Lego blocks in the living room slash dining room slash my bedroom. The two wide-eyed four-year-olds would laugh loudly not knowing what we was talking about and still believing the world was a good place. Jamal would pet their heads like they were his prized possessions.

I would stare at them, knowing that their tomorrow wasn't guaranteed. "Yeah, J. I know."

I had been part of The Reds since I could understand what gangs were. I got in easy because of my cousins. They're all in the same no-fucking-good gang. My cousins tol' me that I wouldn't survive out there if I didn't join 'em. We're not into any hardcore shit. Them guys smoke dope. I don't. The rest of the guys say I'm all high and mighty, but I just don't like what it does to me. Ain't got nothing to do with right and wrong. I really don't do much of the shit they get themselves into. They call me dere "Eyes and Ears" because I don't say much. Just lissen and watch. I'm good at it though. I ain't one of 'em. I'm just along for the goddamn ride.

Tonight was different than all those other sleepless nights because I was the one who pulled the trigger.

We were out at Cornell Square Park. Just last September thirteen people were shot here, includin' a three-year-old boy. News like this should make me feel sad, but I hear stories like this every day, new ones, old ones, and some about to happen. These are the stories that make people stay away from me and my boys.

"The longer you hang around with trash, the more you start to stink." That's what my momma used to say when she was still around. From her rocking chair she'd yell at us to stay in the house because it was normal for bullets to fall from the sky like it was hail or some shit like that.

Now The Reds is the only family I got. So the longer I stay with 'em the more I start to smell like shit. I'm a straight-A student. I'm in the tenth grade like my fifteen-year-old ass should be. But everyone still thinks I'm some scum thug who ain't gonna go nowhere in life. They look at me like I'm gonna kill 'em. The gang's never killed anybody, but we look like the people that could. They hear that you in a gang and that automatically means you have a body count.

We usually met up when it hit 11:11 p.m. Darnell was real superstitious about everything. He'd be the one to call his momma after he stepped on a crack in the sidewalk to make sure he didn't break her back or nothing. To him, 11:11 was a lucky number. Not one of us would be shot at or killed if we met at 11:11. This superstitious thing seemed to be working, but tonight Jamal and I were late.

"God fucking damn. There you bitches are! Do you know what the fucking time is, J? Fuck." Darnell had a can of blue and red spray paint, one of each, in his sweating palms. He slapped Jamal on the back with one. Jamal pushed him off, and snatched one of the cans out of Darnell's grasp.

"So we're a minute late. Calm the fuck down, Darnell. It ain't like you doin' anything important. Just standin' around in the dark lookin' like some punk ass who don't know how to dress yoself."

Jamal plucked at Darnell's dusty black hoodie and scoffed even though he was wearing the exact same one. Darnell ignored him and shoved the other aerosol can into my chest. "Here, K. You better not say no to this. I paid seven bones for this can. Montana gold. Could've been feedin' my girl with that money."

"What girl?" Cleary yelled from across the court. "You ain't go no chick ridin' that dick!"

Jamal started laughing and I tried hard to stop the smile from running across my face. Darnell stuck a long finger out at Cleary.

"You one big ass idiot."

"Yeah and you one stupid—"

"Shut up!" Jamal screamed, standing between the two. Cleary knew what buttons to push when it came to anyone, but especially Darnell. He was smiling about it like he always did. Life was one big game to him. Cleary was a small guy, but he could jump high, swing hard, and run his mouth off fast.

Darnell turned his back to him. His face was leathery and older than its eighteen years. It was seeing all that death that made him look like the crypt keeper. From the age of five he saw his momma beaten to death by his pops, his older brother shot by a rival gang member, and his best friend stabbed over a sherm stick. I was surprised Darnell hadn't picked up the gun himself and turned it loose on everybody else, but he always said he'd rather be tagging than shooting. The only red on his hands was gonna be paint.

"So you in, Kewane?" He narrowed his black eyes at me.

"Nah." I pushed the can back at him.

He shook his head and turned to the rest of the guys.

Jamal cupped his mouth and let out, "If you put a gun in this skinny ass kid's hand he ain't gonna shoot. He just gonna stare at it because he don't do that type of shit."

Darnell laughed long and hard. Cleary joined in. It was funny because it was true.

When they finally stopped clutching their bellies and throwing their heads back, Darnell faced me. "You just gonna watch us, then? Be our 'Eyes and Ears'?" He smirked at me, knowing my answer.

I just nodded and scanned the park. Cleary began walking up to me, limping. Since he was always climbing shit he was bound to get hurt. He's been limping since he fell out of a tree in this same park. "Kewane, whatcha wanna be when you grow up?" Cleary always asked me this whenever I hung out with them.

I always said, "President of the United States," but tonight I said, "I wanna be God."

I just said it because it sounded good. I didn't know what I wanted to be when I grew up. I just knew I wanted to get out of this shithole: The Chicago that you don't see on postcards or t-shirts, but on local news channels with some white woman with pearly teeth and a jacked-up bob, saying things like, "Death toll rising. Another young life lost."

Darnell began backing away, moving closer to the big white building behind him. It had just gotten a new coat of paint a week ago, but you could still see cracks and where old tags used to be. Cleary was hanging off the rim of one the nets, looking like a well-trained monkey. His grin was wide and he began laughing for no reason. Jamal was already on the highest step near the wall.

"So who's this girl you talkin' about, bro?" Jamal nudged Darnell with his elbow as the two popped the caps off the cans.

Darnell looked to the ground, "She.... She.... I dawno, dawg."

"What, boy? You fucking whipped? Dis girl has got you hyp-no-tized?" Jamal said it like it was three different words.

"Shit. I can't explain it. I ain't fucking whipped 'doe."

"Aw yeah right!" Jamal pushed off Darnell's back and jumped around. "I see dat look in your eyes. Dis girl's got you ball an' chained!"

"What the fuck are you talking about?"

Before Jamal could answer, Darnell's cell phone began ringing. Darnell looked down at the shining screen and he smiled, showing all his chipped teeth. That grin only lasted a half-second before Jamal began ragging on him.

"IT'S YO' GIRL? Goddamn boy! Answer the phone!"

Darnell shook his head. "Not with your punk ass around me!" Bounding down the steps of the white building, Darnell gripped the cell phone he lifted off some cocky college goon on the train.

Jamal slapped him on the back. "I'm just playin'!"

Darnell slipped behind the side of the building, phone to ear.

I was standing, staring out past the swaying tree branches, illuminated by the bright orange lights above the basketball courts.

Darnell and Jamal were the closest out of the four of us boys. We were in a gang, but most of the time it was just the four of us, and most of those times it was just the two of them, bullshitting each other and talking about shit eighteen-year-olds talk about.

Cornell Square Park closed at 11 p.m. The court was clear except for a few empty Cheetos bags and plastic bottles of Sprite and Diet Coke. There was a giant black fence surrounding the side with the oak trees. For being in the Back of the Yards neighborhood this park was tight.

There was a purple playground nearby. Slides and swings and even a seesaw. Most of the equipment was faded, broken, or busted, but like with everything else, we made do. Jamal would bring his little girls, Courtney and Camia, here when their mama was out working in the salon.

We would've probably made our way over to the playground so the three boys could smoke their dope, but we were all halted by the echo of gunshots.

Cleary dropped his spray cans, letting them roll around by his feet. Jamal hurriedly ran down the steps toward me.

"The fuck was that? You see anything, K?"

I bulged my eyes out at him. Jamal turned around. Darnell was barely standing and hobbling toward Jamal. Before he could say a word, Darnell dropped to the floor, face first. Blood seeped out from under him, gushing from the wound—a single shot to the chest.

Cleary and Jamal ran toward Darnell. His body was still heaving up and down.

"Who did this?" Cleary tried rolling Darnell over, but he was too heavy for him. I stayed back, my head twisting from side to side. It felt like someone was behind me. I peered into the darkness, past the trees, past the playground and saw two guys in hoods running along the fence.

"They're over there!" I immediately regretted saying that. Jamal's ears perked up and he began to bolt in the direction my finger was pointed in.

Jamal shot a guy three years ago. It was some rat who used to bully me over shit like my lunch money and my five foot one stance. Jamal just wanted to scare the kid, but the gun went off in the parking lot of my school, hitting the asshole in the leg. He cried and whimpered in front of everyone as he bled. Jamal served his time, got out, and started a family. That was another accident, but one he considered a blessing.

"Family first," he'd always say. That was something he took seriously.

And that was what I had running through my mind when I left Cleary with Darnell on the basketball court.

"J! Stop!"

Jamal didn't even flinch at the sound of his name. He kept running even as he panted and wheezed. The heavy, hot breaths of J and the thugs he was running after made me tired.

We found out later on from some loud mouths in the neighborhood that when Darnell went to answer his girl's phone call, a group of Kings were waiting for him. Darnell was set up. They'd been planning it. His girl was a rat that used him. Her boy was the one that shot D. They wanted him dead because of some petty gang shit. Drug money or something like that.

At that time we didn't know why this coward shot Darnell, but it didn't matter to Jamal. Darnell was family. Family first.

My second-hand Nikes snapped necks of twigs and branches. That sound made the hair on my neck stand up. No matter how many times I've heard gunshots, it's the sound of breaking bones that really gets me scared.

The heavy air settled in my throat. I breathed through my mouth so my tongue was dry and I could taste the sour stench of pollution our neighborhood was known for.

"Yo, J! Leave 'em alone! We'll get 'em later!"

Jamal grunted. I thought he was gonna topple to the ground, his legs giving way, but he just bolted even faster. He wasn't gonna listen to anyone, not even his own body. Darnell was the godfather to his little girl Courtney. He was his best friend. There was no way Jamal was going to let this go.

We had run past the chain link fence. Everything looked black. After hitting my knee on metal I realized we were in some trashed playground with yellow "Do Not Cross" tape wrapped around it. The piss yellow slides and rusty swings were supposed to be torn down months ago, but the mayor or whoever is in charge of coming up with these decisions forgot about it. This playground closed after some fucking asswipe taped blades on the monkey bars and kids sliced their little fingers open. It should've been taped off way before that, after a little girl was pushed from the top of the high part of the slide and broke her neck.

I was gonna stop in the middle of the park and lean against something to catch my breath, but just as I stopped in my tracks, so did everybody else.

They stopped because one of the guys tripped and fell on his face. He was bleeding from the nose. The guy's so-called bro left him, his shoes stomping on wood chips.

It was the sound of bones breaking that made me jump. I felt chills dance along my spine. Jamal stood stoic in front of the motherfucker.

The guy with a big ol' face was bleeding from the nose. He smashed his whole fucking head against the metal slide. I'm surprised his red eyeballs didn't get pushed into the back of his head. The way he was wailing sounded like his body was cut in half.

The asshole was trying to talk through all the blood dripping down his face. He kept licking it off his lips like it was honey, and smeared the rest of it on his cheeks with shaking fingers. This skinny guy had on a black hoodie, black jeans, and a black skullcap. He looked like a skeleton. His bony index finger was still clutching the trigger of the gun, warm at his side.

Jamal didn't say anything. When he got mad he looked like a gentle person. That was the scariest thing about him. He didn't get a hint of anger in his eye or a rage building from the inside of his stomach. There was always a calm look on his face like this was his natural way of being.

Tonight his lips were a thin line across his face, like someone's lifeline gone code blue. His glassy eyes were black marbles that only gazed down at the shiny, silver gun pointed at his chest. My body lurched forward toward Jamal. I held my breath waiting for the pop of the gun to go off. The familiar POW that made my teeth ache and my nerves rattle.

Silence. Just the heavy wheezing and coughing come from the guy with the jacked-up nose. He started choking on the metallic taste of blood lodged in his throat. That's when Jamal reached down and pried the gun out of his fingers. It was a swift movement. No struggle between the two.

It was like I was living this moment in flashes. Somehow my feet guided me so I was standing next to my cousin. He smelled like spray paint and sweat. His face was blank.

I had an image playing in my head of the last time I saw Jamal with a gun in his hand. He pointed it at the kid who stole my lunch money. I was twelve then, Jamal was fifteen—my age now. That was only three years ago, but everything was different. My cousin was a father now. I wasn't going to let him be a killer. I took a deep breath.

Family first.

I placed my hand over Jamal's, pulled the gun out, and let it fall into mine. It was heavy, like a weight. I wanted to drop it on the floor, but I let my arm extend down at the bleeding kid. He was probably eighteen, just like Darnell and Jamal. I could've left him there to die. He was losing a lot of blood.

I looked over at Jamal. His teeth gritted. I knew that if I didn't do this now, Jamal would find him and do it himself.

I couldn't look at the motherfucker as I did it. The moment I pulled the trigger I felt my breath go with the bullet, like someone kicked me in the gut. I thought I was the one lying on the ground, bleeding to death. POW. My whole body hurt as I let go of the gun. It dropped to the floor as I opened my eyes.

The kid slumped. His blood seeped into all the wood chips underneath his now death-heavy body.

"Kewane! The fuck did you do?"

It was as if the sound of the bullet woke Jamal up. He stood tall over me, his finger pushing me down. His voice bounced all around us.

I couldn't answer him. I couldn't even look at him so I turned around and began my walk back to the basketball court. I pulled my hood up over my head. The air suddenly felt chilly and it settled in my throat. I felt ice running in my blood. I kept my eyes focused on the blackness ahead. By taking the bullet, I became God and his fallen son all in one night, and there was no use in looking back.

ABOUT THE CONTRIBUTORS

Virginia Ilda Baker ("Because of Daniel") is a 2014 BFA graduate from Columbia College Chicago's Fiction Writing Department. Her writing has appeared in *Hair Trigger 36, Ms.Fit Magazine, Hypertext* and *Word Riot.* She is an educator and enthusiast of books, writing and the environment. She currently resides in New Orleans, Louisiana and can be reached by email at virginia.ilda@gmail.com.

Hal Baum ("Insomnia") is a fiction writing major at Columbia College Chicago. When he's not writing dramatic short stories about murder-suicide he can be found at various theaters around the city performing with his sketch group Warm Welcome, or as a part of the improv team Droppin' $cience. He also recently joined the cast of the pH comedy theater. For other things Hal has written check out his blog at halbaumwrites.blogspot.com. Very professional.

My name is **Marquise Davion** ("Windy Chill"). I was born in Virginia but raised on the south side of Chicago. I currently will be attending Columbia College Chicago where I will be majoring in Cinema Science for film. During my free time I like to write poetry, take pictures, watch films and explore music artist. This is my first time publishing my work and I am really excited to be included in this all-star student anthology.

Don De Grazia (Introduction) is the author of the novel *American Skin* and other writings. His work has appeared in *TriQuarterly*, *The Chicago Quarterly Review*, *The Great Lakes Review*, *The Chicago Tribune*, *The Chicago Reader*, *New City*, *Rumpus*, *The Prague Review*, *The Italian American Reader*, and other publications. He teaches full-time in the Creative Writing Department at Columbia College Chicago, and is a screenwriter in the WGA (east).

Cam Enos ("Shikaakwa"), also known as Cameron Sidhe, is a fifth-year English Major at University of Illinois-Chicago, minoring in Classics and Gender and Women's Studies. Enos has authored two books of poetry, *Bitter Grapes* and *Riot Act*. Enos is also active in the social justice community, working for Porchlight Counseling Services, a non-profit which provides free counseling for college students who have been sexually assaulted during their studies in order to help them remain in school and complete their degrees. Enos enjoys kayaking, knitting, and reading about Neolithic Scotland and criminology.

Austin Eskeberg ("Quiet Deaths") is currently a Junior at Columbia College Chicago, where he is studying Fiction Writing. Originally from Kansas, he turned to writing because the thought of doing math for the rest of his life gives him panic attacks. So for the good of his health, he decided to become a writer. In the future, he'd like to solve world hunger, write more short stories, and possibly finish the novel languishing on his hard drive. This is his first publication.

Francisco Espinal ("Chicago After Dark") received an Associate's Degree in Arts from Wilbur Wright College. Currently he is a junior at UIC and also a writing student at the Second City Writing Center. His goal is to graduate with a Bachelor's in English and pursue a writing career. He was born in Michoacán, Mexico. He was three years old when his Mom brought him and his two sisters to the United States. As the youngest child, he would always be relegated to the sidelines, where he would create fables and short stories to get attention and to create a more colorful world for others. Now Francisco observes life in two languages and writes in three: comedic, absurd, and defiant. He is grateful that his Mom got him safely to this point in his life where he has a chance at success.

Angie Flores ("Your Everyday Lie") is a sophomore at Dominican University. She is double majoring in Theatre Arts and Corporate Communications. Besides acting, her second passion is writing, especially poetry. She published her first poem at the age of 8, just like her favorite poet Sylvia Plath. She hopes to continue writing poetry and to someday publish a poetry book, along with working with the Theatre world.

Alyssa Fuerholzer ("Bus #146") is a Chicagoland native and a third year MFA candidate in Fiction Writing at Columbia College Chicago.

Kendra Hadnott ("Sparrow's Nightcap") is a graduate student in National Louis University's Written Communication program. She's been published in National Louis University's literary magazine, *Mosaic*, and in 2012, was the university's sole recipient of the Friends of American Writers scholarship. When she isn't writing mystery, humorous, or horror stories, you can find her in her local library—or any random well-lit place with a seat—entrenched in the latest YA novel. Her short-term goal is to become a well-recognized name and face in the literary world. Find out more information about Kendra and her forthcoming projects at kendrahadnott.com.

Charlie Harmon ("On the Hunt") has spent most of his life in and around Chicago. After lengthy stints as a barista, receptionist, camp counselor, children's bookstore manager, and barcode salesman, he decided to return to college, and is now an MFA student in Columbia College Chicago's Department of Creative Writing and grateful recipient of the Follett Graduate Merit Award. His work has most recently been published in *The Jersey Devil Press* and Columbia's *Story Week Reader 2014*, and he is the graduate production editor on the forthcoming *Hair Trigger 37*. He works as a writing tutor at the College of Lake County and lives with his parents, because MFAs don't grow on trees.

Alicia Ann Hauge ("Graffiti Evangelism") is a Creative Writing MFA candidate at Columbia College Chicago. She is an arts writer at *The LoganSquarist* and has performed with 2nd Story – Chicago's premier storytelling series. Her work appeared in the 10th anniversary edition of the *Story Week Reader* in 2014. When she isn't in her usual cycle of writing and coffee, she is honing her cirque skills as an aerialist. Alicia is happily married to her husband, Chad – a real live clown and damn good bartender. They live in Logan Square with their bunny that looks like a cow, Masala.

Eric Houghton ("Sugar Ray in the Alleyway") is a junior at DePaul where he is pursuing his BA in English with a concentration on Creative Writing. He writes creative nonfiction mostly, with the occasional short story thrown in as well. Originally from rural Michigan, he followed a mysterious childhood urge and moved to Seattle, where he lived for ten years, before returning to the Midwest. He currently lives in Chicago. He intends to pursue an MFA in writing once he graduates from DePaul and would like to teach creative writing in a quaint liberal arts college in the mountains.

Melissa Huedem ("Take the Bullet") is currently a senior at Columbia College Chicago, earning her BFA in creative writing. Her work has been published in *Word Riot*, *The Columbia Chronicle*, Columbia's First-Year Writing Anthology, and CCC's Publishing Lab Website. You can find more of her work and musings at melissahuedemwriting. virb.com or on Twitter at @mehuestories.

Libby Kalmbach ("Points of Light") is a nonfiction writer and a student in the Master of Arts in Writing and Publishing at DePaul University. She holds a bachelor's in international studies from the University of Illinois at Urbana-Champaign and is returning to writing after years working in non-profit organizations in a variety of capacities. She loves Chicago's beaches in any weather and at any time of day.

Amy Kisner ("The Snuff Film") is a Las Vegas native pursuing fiction writing at Columbia College Chicago. Her work can be found in *Paper and Ink*, as well as at litliterature.com, the online literary magazine she's started, along with fellow Columbia and DePaul students, *Lit Lit*, a place for highbrow inebriation literature.

Thom Kudla ("Innocence and Experience in the City at Night") is a graduate of Indiana University, Bloomington. With the help of his tailored degree from the Individualized Major Program at IUB and a grant from the Indiana University Hutton Honors College, he was able to write his first novel, *Confessions of an American*. His book *What My Brain Told Me* was selected as a finalist in the short story non-fiction category of the 2009 National Indie Excellence Awards. To learn more about Thom's writing, visit thomkudla.com. Currently, he runs his own manuscript editing business and is finishing his last year of graduate school in the Master of Arts in Writing and Publishing program from DePaul University.

Elizabeth Major ("Jade Elephants") currently attends Columbia College Chicago, where she studies both Fiction Writing and Marketing. She is excited to say that this is her first publication. After her final year at Columbia, she plans to attend law school to specialize in Child and Family law. She currently resides in the western Chicago suburbs with her family, who continually inspire her stories of the human experience, and remind her that there will always be a place to call home.

Maggie McGovern ("Violet in the Night Sky") is a senior at Columbia College Chicago studying Fiction Writing and Theater. Although born and raised in Naperville, IL, she has spent the last three years in Chicago, the city life inspiring her work and influencing her passion for not only literature, but acting and film as well. "Violet in the Night Sky" is her first published piece although she spends most of her time writing short stories, screenplays, and she even has a novel in the works.

Mary Mellon ("Dark Hearts for Dark Minds") was a merit scholarship recipient at The School of the Art Institute of Chicago, where she studied fine arts and creative writing. She graduated with a Bachelor of Fine Arts with an Emphasis in Writing in May 2014.

Ka'Mia Miller ("Turn Me On") is a senior at Columbia College Chicago, after transferring from Waubonsee Community College. Born and raised in Aurora, Illinois, Miller has been writing since the age of six, and plans on continuing to do so after graduation.

Nicole Montavlo ("Wake Me Up When It's Green"), a native of Chicago's south suburbs, is a creative nonfiction major / cultural studies minor at Columbia College Chicago. Hybrid forms, lyrical essays, flash, and new journalism are her favorite writing forms and her subjects are nearly endless. She has previously been published in *Blotterature Literary Magazine*, *The Stereo Studio*, *Entropy Threads*, and *The Columbia Chronicle*.

Matthew Morley ("Metacognition") is a senior of History of Creative Writing a DePaul University, where he works at the John T. Richardson Library in the Special Collection and Archives department.

Born in East Grand Rapids, Michigan and graduating from East Grand Rapids High School in 2011, **Rachel Lee Ormes** ("Walter: A Report") is now a senior at Columbia College Chicago where she studies creative nonfiction with a minor in marketing. While interning at the career coaching facility, Bright Livelihoods, she worked as a content creator for their website. Most recently, she has been employed by Suit Social Media, where she handles online content for Chicago businesses. She is a Seinfeld aficionado—"Boy, these pretzels are makin' me thirsty." —Cosmo Kramer

Aaron Osborne ("Free Zombie Dust") graduated from DePaul University in August 2014 with an MA in English. Originally from East Tennessee, he now lives in Chicago.

Phallon Perry ("Two Lies and a Truth") is a 2014 graduate from Northwestern University's Master of Fine Arts in Creative Writing Fiction program. She was raised in the Art District of Baltimore, MD and because of that, many of her stories are inspired by visual or performing art pieces. Since graduating, Phallon is toying with the idea of getting an Interior Design degree so that she may create a public sanctuary just for writers.

Zack Reiter ("Bill") lives in Morton Grove, a suburb of Chicago, with his fiancé. He is a recent graduate of Columbia College Chicago's Fiction Writing Program and manages a comic book and collectibles shop. This is his first publication.

Megan Shattuck ("The Staircase") is one of Chicago's sassiest residents. She spends her time writing, reading, watching *Gilmore Girls*, and generally trying to be an awesome human being. She also enjoys having strong opinions about things that don't matter much. Megan graduated from Columbia College Chicago with a degree in Fiction Writing and Journalism as well as a minor in Theatre. She currently lives on the North Side of Chicago where she is working on her novel and trying to figure out post-grad life.

Robert Eric Shoemaker ("City of Steel") is a Chicago based poet-playwright, theatre artist, and journalist. He is also published in *Newcity Stage, Artisans Magazine*, Persistent Editions, and the Pulitzer

Center on Crisis Reporting. Eric's plays have been staged or read at City Lit Theatre, American Theater Company, Horizon Theater Company, 3 Brothers Theater, and Mary-Arrchie Theatre Company; he was awarded the 2014 Olga and Paul Menn Foundation Prize for his musical *PLATH/HUGHES.* Eric is a graduate with honors from the University of Chicago, where he was Artistic Director of the Classical Entertainment Society.

Lauren T. Silverman ("A Little Light Looks Through") is a Chicago native and a graduate student at DePaul University's Writing and Publishing program.

Kendall Steinle ("Dissertation Outline") hails from Akron, Ohio. She recently received her MA in Writing and Publishing from DePaul University and is currently a freelance editor in Chicago. She is available for hire and for beer consumption.

Nicholas Szczepanik ("North of Graceland Cemetery") grew up on a farm in Maryland and now lives in Chicago, where he is finishing up his last semester as an undergraduate at the School of the Art Institute of Chicago. He goes for frequent walks and pays just as much attention to the trash on the ground as the people passing. He sees his current poetry as a series of reflections on selfhood made manifest through an empathy with the ordinary.

Want to participate in next year's student anthology? Drop CCLaP a line at **cclapcenter@gmail.com** to be placed on the mailing list for future announcements concerning next year's theme and submission dates, coming April 2015.

CPSIA information can be obtained at www.ICGtesting.com
Printed in the USA
LVOW07s1025050515

437134LV00005B/130/P